CRANDOLIN

CRANDOLIN

Anna Tambour

蝶
夢

Chòmu
Press

CRANDOLIN

Published by Chômu Press, MMXII

Crandolin text and illustrations copyright © Anna Tambour 2012

Published in November 2012 by Chômu Press.
by arrangement with the author.

ISBN: 978-1-907681-19-6

First Edition

This is a work of fiction for readers who can also enjoy surreality. Names, characters, places and incidents are either products of the author's imagination, or not.

Design and layout by:

Bigeyebrow, Chômu Press, Carr Graphics and Anna Tambour

Cover artwork: Christopher Conn Askew
Cartoon "Borscht!" © Kathleen Jennings 2012

Set in Literaturnaya

E-mail: info@chomupress.com
Internet: chomupress.com

to Alistair Rennie

Chapters

The crandolin wakes

THE LUMINOUS STAIN ON PAGE 67 contained traces of quince, rose, grains of paradise, ambergris, pearl, cinnamon, and what could only be surmised. Kippax surmised, all right. Blood. The colour of the stain (livid pink) confirmed what he had read, though no test could. This cookbook was indeed, as the frontispiece said, *For the Adwentoursomme.*

It had once been common knowledge that drinking crandolin blood cursed the drinker to a long life of madness, and the recipes on the two pages driving Kippax mad were for *Crammed Amphisbaena,* and *A Pudding Mayde of Crandolin.* The recipe for amphisbaena added only butter, no spyce, and said *serve with no sauce but onely salte.*

This morning Kippax fed a miserly scrape of the stain, smuggled out under his fingernail, to his portable electronic tongue. The gas chromatograph, as sensitive and stupid as a bloodhound, tasted spyce compounds aplenty but no butter, and then ran just to look like it was doing something. It was clueless.

The sauce had to be crandolin.

Amphisbaena was a daring catch, this serpent with a head at each end. But crandolin cost at least one life. It was once-upon-common-knowledge that crandolins were light pink as the dawn they imitated as they probed cracks in the shutters protecting pink virgins in their beds. They could only be caught when *Crikey! This blood is also ancient virgin blood.*

He felt an attack of dizziness coming on, but a quick double punch made his ears ring—that problem solved, the better to tackle the big one.

The temptation to taste the crandolin had been terrible before (he was confident that his palate could sieve the spices from the meat). But the temptation was too much now, for any mortal. And in some moods, Nick Kippax did tell himself that he was indeed, a mortal.

He wet his finger and touched the stain—almost.

At the last millimillimetre, he drew his finger back into his meaty palm.

He felt his blood rushing around his body. It moved with as much purpose as a crowd of people released by a crosswalk light. Fascinating? No.

He picked up the open book and sucked the parchment.

A honey-lake in suspension

WHITE HONEY was the only honey that would do. The honey delivered was brown as wet leather, and smelled like a stables. Burhanettin the confectioner showed the merchant the whites of his eyes. "Drown him," Burhanettin implored. "In a honey lake."

The donkey snorted, eager for its load to be removed, yet the sweetmaker hadn't finished his wish. "Drown him in a lake of honey from the flowers that grow around the cesspit!"

The fat little honey merchant squirmed like a newborn maggot. "The season for white honey has end—"

"As your life will, if you say another word."

The merchant showed the confectioner an obsequious mouthful of rotten teeth. "I'll try—"

"By my Will, you'll do more than try!"

No mortal soul in the town had the confidence of Burhanettin. The sheer blasphemy would have stolen most men's breaths.

Not Ekmel the honey merchant. "This afternoon," he smiled. "Go feed your nightingale and settle your nerves with its song, dear friend."

Burhanettin leaned over and shook his fist in the man's face. His forearm was thick and gnarled as the trunk of an old carob tree. "Move," he said.

The honey merchant stepped to the side, and the confectioner reached into a bag suspended from his belt.

Out came a long stick of nougat.

The donkey's lips opened like a flower at sunrise.

Moans of the bladder-pipe

THE BLADDER-PIPE PLAYER'S eyelids flutter like a virgin's heart upon awakening. The sheep's bladder crackles faintly, but the voice of the pipe is all that the guests will hear, if they listen over the din of their own lips. Faldarolo doesn't care if they listen or no; only that they will pay him enough to eat, or toss him a scrap of something before they are too drunk to know he exists—a few piastres would be nice. A small gold necklace shouldn't be too much to expect—but a gnawed bone would be luckier than some nights.

In the meantime, the music keeps him fed. The bladder-pipe has a will of her own. Sometimes she sounds like a great swarm of bees, sometimes a goose, a magnificent goose; and sometimes she's a woman with a voice that could skin a man with one long sigh.

She has ruled the poor musician from the first moment that he, having grasped her sides, put his mouth to the pipe that leads at right angles but as straight as beauty to grief—to the bladder, and then down, following the line of his torso to his lap where her moans emerge, mingled with his hot, wet breath.

His eyelids are the colour of bruised violets. Above them, great black eyebrows dance, left, right ... left, left, left, right. He had never trained them to do this, but over the years they developed an incapacity to sit still. Smitten with song, they leap to its command, arching, flattening and stretching, sinuating. Now, when the bladder-pipe sings with the speed of a flow of honey, the eyebrow dance is strange but dignified, with the hauteur of a great moustache soaking up fat.

But wait.

The poor musician's eyelids now dance as if they walk on fire. And his eyebrows! The muscles around his eyes are slaves to their command, but his eyebrows are slaves to the bladder-pipe.

How ridiculous Faldarolo looks. But even the deaf man doesn't notice, his feet soaking up the sound of spoons, hands, wooden bowls hitting the table; wooden clogs pounding the dirt.

The evening progresses...

And now is the time for the songs to those guests who aren't dead to the world from drink. They waited for this—the time of magnificent torture. They sit, the old men, lips slack as a donkey's whose ears are being stroked. The music grips their memories, and shakes.

The young hunger for something not on the table, but under it. By ones and twos, they follow the suggestions of the wordless song, and slip away. O heartless bladder-pipe! Even as Faldarolo fills her to repletion, she cares nothing for his insides.

The stream above the rails

THE SPUTNIKS stamped into the steel glass-holder were black, as if the steel were old silver. Savva finished his tea and sighed. Work must be done. He swung his legs out from under the window table and left his train compartment. He refilled the samovar at the end of the passage and looked down the length of the carriage. Six hours'-worth of sunflower-seed shells decorated the rug. Although the day was not yet born, and most of the passengers were sleeping, lulled by the regular thudding of wheels on rail ties, a faint crackling betrayed jaws that were busy. *There!* A spray of spit flew out of a compartment halfway along. He bent to the carpet's end, picked up its sides, and twitched his right hand. His technique was so good that he didn't need to take another step. The carpet flipped quickly as a woman's mind.

Time for a cup of tea? He looked at his watch, and dithered. Would Galina have any new supplies of caviar? Might be worth a walk.

The restaurant car (where the only menu item was borscht) was three carriages down, so he locked his compartment, walked straight down the swaying carriage, opened the door and was immediately arrested by an uncommonly fine smell. He'd expected the usual crowd of smokers: infrequent travellers puffing fast and looking anywhere but down, regulars hunched, drawing deep. The sound was deafening, so words between the cars was rare, but this was no time for small-talk.

"You look like you need a bar of chocolate, sir," he said to the only person there, a person of such width but such admirable self-knowledge that he played a drum roll on his stomach with his left hand.

"You have such a thing as a bar of chocolate?"

The passenger held his right hand out at arm's length and gazed at it. Held between forefinger and thumb was a long, white cigarette out of whose end wastefully poured a stream of smoke as delicious as caviar should taste.

Savva did not, if the truth must be told, have even a lost dried fish, but Valentin ... Valentin probably had a bag of lost dried fish. Valentin probably had a lost bar of chocolate—no, a case of lost chocolate. And only yesterday, Savva had earned himself a fortune when he accidentally came upon Valentin pulling a knife the size of a sabre on a passenger who looked to be the sort who has cases of anything you can imagine—but was very alone. Savva left quickly at that point.

At this point, the fortune begged to be spent. Valentin would most likely laugh at the blackmail. He should. Valentin was a regular depot of lost goods. And I can't help it if I don't have his skill. I was raised with standards.

The passenger hadn't taken another puff. He seemed to be acting like a sculptor's model, holding his hand out with that almost unsmoked cigarette—a long white beacon in the between-car gloom.

The smoke stream stretched, and it now reached Savva's nose, where it slid down the short length, flipped at the upturned end and plunged down into the space between the cars.

"So, chocolate?" Savva smiled, finally catching the passenger's eye.

"Don't care for it."

And he flicked the cigarette out, onto the steppes.

A psychic tempts the omniscient

LIKE SO MANY BEFORE HIM (and likely, many more to the end of Time) the Omniscient's scepticism fell before his overwhelming need for certainty. He disguised himself as a voice and hovered over the telephone, desperately yearning to ring the $2.95 per minute "Live psychics answer your call".

Paying was ponderously difficult.

Yet I must do something.

Again, he went to the mysterious Web and read:

The Channeling Threshold

Each guide and each connection is different, special, and unique. Some guides are poetic, some are inspirational, and some are instructive. Some of you may find yourselves able to channel books or write with such ease that books just seem to "get written" for you, for channeling seems ideally suited to writing. Channeling helps you connect to a constant, steady source of inspiration and information. Some of you will channel art, music, and other forms besides writing.

Art, music and other forms didn't interest him, but writing! Who was being channelled, and how? It surely wasn't him. He could barely get into the Web, and the only channelling he knew about was story #ζλξβ-897Ɖ89#7ƉƖD, and, in that, the channellers were a thousand naked slaves and ten thousand donkeys. And in that story, there certainly weren't any guides, just drivers.

This channelling was something as airy and unreal as the Web itself, and the guides—were they as real as stories or as rubbery as people? People, in all their frustrating glory—people for whom he existed, rubbery beings, not characters—and who, as beings, hadn't changed their stock personalities one trait, from millennium to millennia.

The whole idea of channelling made him ill. "I know I haven't been my best lately," he said to no one but himself. The rubbery didn't even credit him, though they used his work, took it for granted, without a thought of acknowledging his role in the writing. Why, if it weren't for him, story-tellers would be dry as that well in story #ξ6ƀƕ6455-3ƉꭶΩ/ϓ77. Drier!

As he hovered over their shoulders, *But for me*, he had often chuckled, *you'd be crawling, seeking stories in the dust.* He looked down upon them, watching their so-called pain, but he had enjoyed his powers. He, the giver of stories, the magic ink that flowed from the writer's pen.

Not now. Now, curiously, he felt a bond to the rubbery ones that he had never expected. His problem was common to the rubbery, and from them, he might find the cure.

The beloved at home

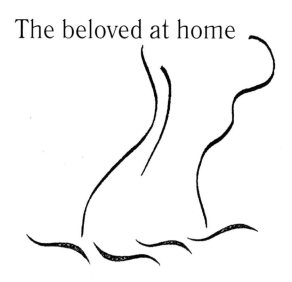

SHE TOSSED A CLUMP OF HAIR out of her eyes, jerking a tower of ash off her cigarette into the pot. The butt was too short to smoke, so she dropped it into an emptyish bottle and rolled another cigarette from the papers and leaf-litter in the pocket of her once-flowered apron.

The stuff in the pot—animal, vegetable or otherwise—smelt burnt. She huffed off the flame and reached for a full bottle, twisted its cork out, stuck her lips to the rim and pulled glugs till she had to unlock for air.

"Falleydo-hooh ... ugchhh!" Her burp—racy, sweaty and pungent on the nose—resonated with almonds and flint to the fore, perhaps an unreasonable amount of broccoli coming through on the finish, but redeemed itself on the afterscent with a lingering note of something indescribable.

She tilted the bottle to her full lips and sucked again, and again till its contents were only a sludge unreachable to her long, experienced tongue. She murmured the judges' comments on that winning Sauvignon Blanc in the latest Sydney International: "Quite a cat's pee ... a lovely wine. Sweaty armpit character." Those were the sacred words of Nick Kippax himself, who also declared the winner "a great combination".

"Ayee! This combination's greater."

The earth groaned with the egos of 'artists', staked out like graveposts from Vietnam to Antarctica probably, covering the ground in great vats and supercenters and little brick and wattle and daub and roadside tin and bubblewrap bistros, and glittering glass dumping grounds, and bottles bobbing in the—

"Gorgonna!" She pulled herself out of that spiral of complaint, something new she had picked up lately, from *them*. Never before had she realised that they could affect *her*. But all their exhibitionism, their competitiveness, *had*.

What do I care what they think?

"Ruump! Quit your whinging, yar boofa sister." She planted her hands on her hips and pushed herself up straight.

"Yow-ay o! You love to be loved," she reminded herself.

"Yor-mah o," she argued back. "But they don't love *me*."

"Enough!" It was best not to think of that, or she might as well carry an axe to work.

To work.

She shrugged, and tossed her apron.

Time to put her face on.

They expect that of the Muse.

12

The cinnamologus' treasure

THE CINNAMOLOGUS had plucked the wad of fluff from a thorntree. Pickings were rare out in the desert, and this fluff, glossy as fresh blood, was a nest decoration that outdid all his rivals'. While they had to spend their time killing to refresh all the red decoration that attracted females, this wad of fluff glowed with a red that never darkened, even when night fell.

The cinnamologus had never seen its like, but he was not the contemplative sort at this time of year when there was dancing, mating, and nest-guarding to be done.

At this moment he stood on the edge of his great nest of cinnamon bark frilled with red fluff, beaking his scented body oils through his iridescent feathers in a post-coital preen. The female of the moment was arranging her drab little self in his nest. She had just tucked without complaint, the eggs of three other females under her breast.

And watching without eyes, feeling without skin, screaming without sound: Nick Kippax, or to be exact, the chimera that Kippax had become after sucking the parchment with that crandolin blood.

Nick (for lack of a better name) screamed irrationally, but as he was only red fluff in the eyes of the cinnamologuses, he was unable to communicate anything other than colour—an extremely attractive hue, to be sure, requiring eternal vigilance if it were not to be plucked by an indifferent wind or a rival beak.

The worst part of his new state could have been that his mind was still the same as it had ever been, and that he was trapped in this bit of fluff till the effect wore off.

But that was not the worst part of his new state.

Kirand-luhun

EKMEL THE HONEY MERCHANT waited outside Burhanettin's sweet shop, cursing himself. "Why didn't I fill my stomach with pilaf before I came? Why didn't I fill my nose with cotton?" The donkey's eyes were black curved mirrors reflecting Ekmel, enlarging his considerable nose. But the donkey's ears were pointed toward its Mecca.

Great invisible clouds floated from Burhanettin's kitchen, out into the nostrils of Ekmel and his ass. Roses, sesame, hot butter, toasted flour, pistachio, cinnamon, mastic, ambergris—mere wisps compared to the great bulk of the clouds as same and yet individual as all clouds are: the scents of those expertly made confections of the honeybees.

Ekmel rang his bell again and sang his peculiar song. The donkey's sides heaved, the sign for a heartfelt bray—

And pointed yellow hat first, Burhanettin emerged, his striped outer-robe flapping with the sound of a tent in a storm. "I've missed you, dear friend," he said, throwing an arm round the neck of the donkey, who answered with a happy crunch, its nose in Burhanettin's hand.

"And you, scoundrel,"—Burhanettin didn't even glance at Ekmel—"who smiles as he cheats me as if I've got the sense of an almond!"

The honey merchant's eyes answered Burhanettin by

15

producing two tears big as Tīmūrsaçi's pearls, wasted on the confectioner.

"Is the sun to set before your master speaks?" Burhanettin asked, his nose beside the donkey's, who had taken one sweet-smelling horn of the man's moustache into its mouth and was gently tugging.

"For you, Effendi," Ekmel said, bending till his face was close, "I have brought something so special that, that..." He straightened, and reaching to the rump of the donkey, patted with his left hand, the hand that wore a ring with a little pin.

"Oh!" The animal jerked its head up and glared at Ekmel, who was sorry to see that there was not even one hair hanging from the beast's lips.

"But for you, Effendi," Ekmel continued, seeing that Burhanettin had finally decided to stand and look at him, "I thought of going to Özdem in Gaziantep, and would have, but for the friendship you show this bag of bones."

Burhanettin had never worked for a Sultan, so he was no Effendi. He was a guild member of the shop *helvassis*, specifically, the *helvassian-i-dukkan*, specialists in honey-based confections. But his shop was far from the halls of power, his town more celebrated for its storks than its populace. Ekmel's flattery would have annoyed him if the honey merchant hadn't supplied him for years with honeys of quality and variety so outstanding that Burhanettin could never allow his admiration to show. The honeys that Ekmel found were what Effendi Celebi, the Great Tīmūrsaçi's own *helvassia-i-dukka* would have bribed anyone to find. And Burhanettin's sweetmeats were so good that he was a secret in the town, as no one wanted him to be lured to the Sultan's palace, to their loss.

He twirled his moustache into shape again, but if he were a bull at that moment, you would have called him 'crooked horn'.

"Well, out with it, you fox that has never been caught."

Ekmel reached into one of the donkey's baskets and pulled

out a little glass, shaking it free of straw and polishing it with a cloth. Then he reached in again and pulled out one of his one-occa-weight sample jars. He handed the glass to Burhanettin and with a magician's flourish, uncorked the plain glazed jar. Now he held a stick of olivewood, which he stuck into the jar and pulled up, carrying with it a rope. He caught the rope on his stick and reached to the glass, where he held the stick just *so* high—you could see the rope slip off the stick and coil happily into the glass. Then he handed Burhanettin the stick.

Making ropes of honey was something Burhanettin had been born to do, so this could not impress him, nor was it meant to.

Ekmel busied himself sealing the jar and bedding it in straw again in the basket, his eyes turned away from Burhanettin, who poked the stick into the glass, pulled it out, sniffed the glass, held the glass up so that the sun peered through it.

Finally, "What is this preposterance?"

"What does it seem?" Ekmel countered, leaning an arm on the basket as if it were an embroidered cushion and he were at home, enjoying his hubble-bubble.

"But it couldn't be," Burhanettin said, talking to the glass.

"Not so loud," Ekmel shushed.

"Enough with your theatrics."

Burhanettin's eyes burned. "I've work to do and you mock me with your Effendi and your ... your fakes. You and your orchid honey, your primula honey from the forests around Xo Man."

He thrust the glass toward the honey merchant, but somehow whirled away toward his shop. "This is too much, Ekmel. For all I know, you've bled her to play this trick on me." He lifted the glass to the donkey, and walked the two steps to his doorway.

His back was bent now in the motion of entering, but time seemed to have stopped.

"May your children treat you as you have treated me," Ekmel said, though he must have known that Burhanettin had never married.

Then Ekmel cried, "To Gaziantep, beast!"

Burhanettin emerged so fast, the lintel shoved his hat off. He didn't stop to pick it up in his rush to clutch Ekmel's wrist.

Burhanettin was the strongest man in town. He had to be, to make his *helva-i-sabuni* (the nougat so favoured by Ekmel's donkey), stirring bubbling pastes of honey and butter and starch and sesame and ... never varying the direction—till if you were in his place, your arm would grow a throat to scream with, and the sweet cement would *still* laze in its pot, not ready to be poured. He made striped taffy by pulling great ropes of boiled honey till a golden rope turned pale as a woman's throat. He twisted that rope with another he had coloured *blush* with violets and hearts of— but enough already of his secrets, for it is said *All precious things obtained free come with a complimentary curse.*

Ekmel's fingers were swelling to fat blue plums, choked by Burhanettin's grip on his wrist. But Ekmel's eyes were locked steadfast on Burhanettin's eyes which from narrow slits, grew wider and wider ... till the helvassi mouthed without daring to expose the word to sound:

"Kirand-luhun?"

"The very." Ekmel's smile was broad. "Or you may twist my arm off."

"How much?" Burhanettin whispered.

Before the nightingale awoke

AT THIS HOUR, the nightingale's head is tucked under her wing, the baker is kneading, the sun is sleeping, and Faldarolo's eyebrows hang by their roots, exhausted by a night of dance.

Faldarolo is trudging home, heavier than the day earlier by a few piastres, but lighter by ten occas of his own flesh, melted in the fever of his music: the commands, not of the wedding party nor the guests. No, they are only thoughtless. His commands come from the bladder-pipe herself.

Faldarolo's flesh demands flesh, his head and limbs and those eyebrows and eyelids demand sleep, but the bladder-pipe must first be satisfied.

His slippered feet slop faintly against stone and dew-laden dust, and soon one can hear other slipper talk. In the musicians' quarter now, they in their weary ones and threes are coming home to eat their odd-time meal, and when the sun awakes, to sleep.

As soon as Faldarolo enters the room that is his home, he closes his eyes. It is a measure of sleep, and he knows where everything is, for everything is so close to nothing that his toes have nought to fear.

He sits on his scrap of rug, takes the velvet cloak off the bladder-pipe and lays her in his lap. On a wooden shelf jutting from the rough stone wall, an earthenware pot sits in a glazed dish of water. The cloth covering the pot is damp, its ends in the water. He lifts the cloth with his left hand and with his right, scoops a wad of something.

Faldarolo massages the pale yellow stuff into the bladder-pipe, all over the skin of the bladder and into the wood of the pipes. Though (or possibly *because*) her bladder once lived in a sheep, sheep fat she will not consider, nor olive or shea oil. She demands butter—and only the sweetest will do—butter from ass's milk, no less.

Faldarolo covers the holes in the bladder pipe and blows silently, the better to puff out every last wrinkle so that he can massage the butter into her skin.

The air in the room is cold, but the measured friction of his patient fingers melts the butter till the bladder-pipe is glossy and fragranced and resilient to look at and feel, making a healthy faint crackle every time she draws breath.

And finally, when she is satisfied but not a moment sooner, Faldarolo places her cloak around her and lays her on her soft, padded shelf.

Sleep takes pity on him, and wraps herself around him.

And when the nightingale wakes and the streets of the musicians' quarter resound with snores, when Faldarolo would normally be fast asleep, fed in his dreams by the scent of ass's butter mixed with the voice of the bladder-pipe—just when this would normally be the case—on this morning, he woke with a start.

"Quiet, stomach," he growled.

But it wasn't his stomach, who was quiet as a thief.

Something was wrong.

He jumped up from his pallet and picked up the bladder-pipe. His stomach panicked, stumbling against his bones like a blind beast in a race.

With a lack of respect that showed his urgency, Faldarolo tore off the bladder-pipe's cloak.

And not a moment too soon! *There*, on the swell of the bladder—the cream-pale skin—a blotch glowed like a slap on her face.

Virgin in the restaurant carriage

SAVVA, VALENTIN, AND GALINA huddled over the book in the only place on the train that was secure from prying eyes: the restaurant car. Galina had locked it at both ends, her wont when the restaurant ran out of food, and when she had a delivery of something special from Valentin.

Large CLOSED signs on fore and aft windows and a long stretch of featureless land unbroken by settlements ensured privacy. Cosiness came from the feast (just polished off, to the last smear) of juicy smoked salmon and thick, rich smetena, compliments of Valentin (the salmon) and Galina (smetena liberated from the restaurant's supply).

Valentin had been unusually nice to Savva, inviting him (with Galina's reluctant permission). *The more, the smaller*, and Galina's appetite was growing, as was her belly. Was it Valentin's or Savva's? She shuddered at it being the product of that snub-nosed worm, but when Valentin wasn't around and the cars were unheated, and she'd had enough to drink... Well, what is one to do in this job, when the rocking of the cars, ever and ever and ever makes one long for... Better not to think of what one longs for. *Romance is for nightingales. People have only each other.*

And Savva, thought Galina, smiling at him regally behind the cold but gorgeous Valentin's back—*Savva would jump off a carriage to show his love*.

The book, though.

21

Savva had been unusually brave. At the passengers' breakfast hour when he folded the bedding in 3H, he found it: a book in English. He could see that. He knew some English. It was useful, after all. The passengers were in the restaurant car at the time—foreign tourists. He shoved the book inside his jacket and left the compartment quickly. They would expect other things to be stolen. Maybe they wanted to complain about these Russians. So many tourists did. A walkman of theirs tantalised from where it lay on their window table. Savva smiled as he filled the samovar. He wouldn't give them the satisfaction.

Now, his pirated prize on a wiped-down restaurant table, he could hardly stop from gloating. He had not only spelled out the letters to Galina and Valentin of that word on the cover, but had translated what it meant. VIRGIN. And the picture on the cover. What a woman! Those nipples—sharp enough to draw blood, but what a way to die.

Valentin picked up the book. "The Impossible Virgin," he read out in English, his accent not only not bad, but disgustingly good.

"Is there anything you can't do?" Savva burst out, embarrassing only himself.

"Make a bed."

Valentin leafed through the book, Galina leaning over so that her hair must have tickled Valentin's nose.

"You don't know an S from a samovar, Galina, so give him room," Savva said.

"What means 'impossible'?" Galina asked.

"You too?" Savva couldn't believe his ears. Galina could talk English as well as him.

Valentin shut the book. "Impossible is what Savva finds, whenever he tries to do something he can't, which is all the time. This book included. It's a novel. Just a trick cover, you fool."

Savva didn't believe him. Valentin was probably pretending it was worthless, trying to sweep the book into his clutches, like sunflower seedshells into a dustpan. But maybe Valentin was right, and the thing was really garbage, so he asked, "No scenes of you know what?"

Valentin rolled his eyes. "He can't even say the word, let alone find it."

Galina puffed out her chest, a little miffed. After all, if she was carrying Savva's child, and it was likely she was, Valentin being almost always too busy for love, then Valentin's slurs against Savva were both an insult to her offspring and an insult to her taste.

"It was a good try," she said to Savva. "Of course you couldn't have read the book out there." She turned to Valentin and poked him in the chest. "He couldn't have, working as hard as he does."

Valentin picked up the book and opened it to a random page.

"You know what? Here's your 'you know what'. From the top of page sixty-two: Uncle Volodya looked out across the wide field, its golden richness cut down in the prime of life by the army of tractors that he commanded. His broad smile showed strong white tee—"

Savva stalked out of the car, leaving the door open for air and who knows who else to rush in.

Galina sighed. "Leave us our dreams, Valushka. Even I thought that Westerners wrote books worth reading. That's as decadent as a Department Directive."

Valentin laughed: two elegant coughs. "The world is a boring meal, Galina, and all the players are leftovers in it. You're lucky that you're sheltered from reality here." He put a hand to her plump cheek, and as a leg kicks when hit by a hammer, Galina puckered her lips.

"That lipstick is wrong for you," he said.

"What?"

"You should wear something more delicate. And you must look in a mirror. You do have one, my little *golubetz*? Half of it has missed your lips."

The wind from the door that Savva had left irresponsibly open caught Galina's carefully built haystack of hair, and gave it a vicious twist. "Some of us must work, Valentin."

She grabbed the door and held it open just enough for him squeeze out. "And take that book. I don't want to be caught with it."

Valentin bowed and clicked his heels, something he did for women, as he did look pre-Revolutionary in the most delicious way.

The book against his chest burned. He couldn't read English very well at all, but what he'd read had steamed up his imagination enough that he was desperate for a sit on the toilet. He'd use the one in Savva's carriage, as maybe Savva had filled the hook there with fresh newspaper scraps.

Galina's face burned. The shame of it—that Valentin! *Golubetz* indeed. Even pregnant, she had a figure that could satisfy two men at once.

"I am *not* a cabbage roll. And *what* lipstick?" With all her food needs these days, her pay didn't stretch to lipstick, and no lover had been thoughtful enough to give her cosmetics. She locked the door and stuck her hand in her pocket for her mirror.

Two thousand a session

THE MAN GAZED up into the woman's eyes as if he wanted to throw himself into their depths. But then his eyes wandered down her long throat, to the mountains—

"Before the time of Gwandurf," she said.

Her belly, so close to his head, was flat as—

"of Gwandurf" she said with even crisper enunciation, though that voice, musical as—

"Don't sit there like flat beer."

tap tap tap...

His fingers finished what she'd dictated, so he looked into her eyes again.

"You get more beautiful every—"

"Type or I'll leave."

"Okay, okay," he said, placing his hands over the keyboard. "Shoot."

"when the little people of Bungendore..."

The man was obedient for the rest of the session, and when the dictation ended at the 2,000th word, he dropped to his knees and clasped her legs (their shape peekabooing through the flow of her neo-classic robe).

"I can't live without you. Stay," he said, for the nth time. "Melissa can't—"

"Melissa can't what?" His wife's head appeared in the doorway, like an apple on a stick. "D'you want dinner or should I give it to the dog?"

"Melissa can't hear me when I say I'm coming," he said.

"And get up from the floor, Rick."

The man left his study backside first, kissing his open hand and extending it like a tray, mouthing as he backed out, "To you, my lady."

He squared his shoulders going down the stairs.

"I hope, I really hope," he loudly announced without actually speaking, "that someday, Melissa, you *will* see. And I hope that moment reveals to you: your husband, Richard K. Stubbs, in *flagrante delicto* with the only woman who *does* things for me, who does things *to* me: the Elusive One, the Supportive One, the Adorable One: The Muse Herself."

Lucky for him that Melissa Rowe-Stubbs didn't hear him. Nor did the Muse who'd already left to get herself ready for her next call: an as-yet-unknown author, a librarian.

The virgin crop

THE GREAT TĪMŪRSAÇI (Tīmūr the Hirsute) was so named, not
because he was a Great Tīmūr with strength-giving hair in
abundance, but because in truth, he had none, thus the need to
appel him with this distinguishing characteristic so that he would
never be thought Otherwise.

This Tīmūr was not only lacking hair on the top of his head. He
was smooth-cheeked as a cherry and his lips were soft and wet.

Thus, since the day his father the previous Great and two
older brothers were strangled and he was released from the Prison
of Princes and Old Wives, he wore a moustache that rivalled the
greatest bulls of all Time.

Each horn was so long that any man could stretch his arms out
and the Great Tīmūrsaçi's visage exceeded that man's grasp.

The moustache was held on by a fragrant gum collected, it was
said, from the droppings of the cinnamologus. This is probably a lie.

The truth is that since he ascended many years ago, a new
moustache has been made annually for the Great Tīmūrsaçi, and
this moustache has required the hair of every virgin in a village so
secret it must pretend to move every year, and is only visited by a
man known to the villagers as 'him with the basket, who finds us'.

* * *

The basket descends from the hole in the wall, its load weighed down by a rock the size of a theoretical loaf. When it reaches the peak of Munifer's reach, he grabs it, his jerk on the rope making great show of the value of his time and its waste here amongst these peasants. His eyes, hidden from above under his long lashes, shine like wet coals. He'd climbed up steep terraces to get here, to this cluster of piles of stones. In each rough tower, people and beasts (in good years) live all in a closeness. The village-of-no-name's great disguise is that this village looks exactly like so many others, with as little to show for itself.

And what had he seen on the way up to this teetering village? Terrace after terrace with not a soul to protect them. Not only that. Last autumn's crop was here for all to see and take. Bunches of what looked like small stones hung inside a casketry of vines — stones coated in sooty black. And instead of wide green leaves, the vines had flourished, ingrowing mostly, with a few dry grey tendrils grotesquely reaching out. The weavings were too tight to reach in and steal a grape, but who would want to? It would be bitter as burnt bread. *A widows' vintage, eh?*

Crush bitter widows to make the Evil One's wine.

As for the jug of wine that is his due after his exertions to reach this place, it would be an hour's walk once he got down the mountain again, till he could have a drink.

So that is this year's play on me? he chuckled. *What better time to arrive?*

Even on good years, spring was a long wait for a full belly. But their killing of their sustenance to foil him this time is their boldest deception yet, and will be their undoing.

After such a strenuous morning, this game of theirs put him in a splendid mood. To have done this — this year's virgin crop must be the best yet. He had never questioned why the virgins of this village gave the right hair, but they always had. Perhaps it was the hardness of the life. The hair was strong, and black, to be sure, but there were virgins in every town with strong black hair. Why here? *What does it prosper me to wonder?*

"I'll be generous," he sang. "I'll hand out another ribbon, for amusement." He felt in his pocket to see if he had an extra ribbon, but he always travelled light.

That was moments ago. He is thirsty and winded after the long climb up, and impatient to get back down the mountain and on his way.

He lifts the stone from the basket, but instead of the long thick tails of hair that he expects, shiny and midnight black and fragrant with virginity—what is under the stone but the sour rats'nest combings of a grandmother—a thin pad of hair, the colour of peed-on cotton.

"What's this?"—as if he didn't know.

A crone leans out of the hole in the wall that the basket had been dropped from. You could not call it a window any more than you could picture her plump and fresh. Yet her breasts swing above him in a manner that would have been coquettish half a century ago. "You liked my hair well once," she giggles.

"Where have you hidden them, old fool?" Munifer's tongue sticks, and he is suddenly fed-up with this annual runaround.

"Ayeee!" she laughs delightedly. "Who's the fool? They've died."

"That's a new one. Let's have it."

"Starved, I tell you."

He shakes his walking stick at her. "I'm not playing."

"You'll have to dye it," she says airily. "That is all I have." She pulls herself back into her decrepit tower as if she were a tortoise and could walk away, her home on her back. He can hear her laughing, as if he were just *anyone*.

Munifer jumps up and down, enraged beyond need. After all, she's only an old woman. "You don't care for your life!"

"Why should I?"

"I'll give you a reason."

Half of him says, "Just go to the next house up," and the other half of him says that he so badly needs to beat this woman, he can already hear the sounds of her fruitless begging.

He looks around him on the stony ground, and finds something that will do, though his better half hates having to put himself to such measures. *I'm an artist. That I must be the collector as well is quite insufferable.* But the need for secrecy had loaded him with this burden, for his status.

An old beam. Possibly from a cart, or a woman's yoke.

He picks it up and swings it like a ram—*knock, knock, knock ... crack.* But the wood is hard. "Open this door," he yells, as the beam is heavy. "Open this door or I'll—"

"Come in, come in, wherever you are!"

"Hiyahh!"

In fury, he backs off, kicks up dust, repositions himself, and runs at that door, the heavy beam jutting out from under his arm like some giant's head readied to butt any opposition into the heavens, or hell. The timbers burst through, and he falls upon splinters and rubble. One of his knees must have hit a pointed stone. Sharp pains shoot up to his groin, and he screams.

Above, laughter tinkles.

The darkness here is broken only by the opening he's made but he faces away from it, so his eyes need time to see. Tenderly, he feels under his robe. Yes, the skin is broken and wet, but his bones are there, strong as staves and stones. He puts his hands out to steady himself, swearing to give this old hag to Providence. His leg isn't working quite right yet, and he is unbalanced, the fingers of his right hand flail out in the murk, and stop, tangled in a mass of hair—the last straw of his good feelings about this village.

He yells so loud, his ears hurt in this close stinking space: "So now you're so poor you have sheep, do you?" He is so angry now that his voice squeaks. Worse, his weeping, swelling, burning, stiff and silently screaming knee will not let him climb the ladder and choke the hag into telling him where his virgins are (and everyone else, for that matter, not that he cares) for some time.

He closes his eyes and tenderly touches, then clutches his

knee, trying to deaden for a moment, the pounding pain. Soft sounds come from above—wet, old-womanish burbles. He wonders if she is too crazy to be made to tell.

He must have dozed, for he wakes with a start. The moon is awake, lighting things in here with a peculiar glow. He turns his head to the sheepskin, and sees that it is not. It is, must have been, a virgin. And lying beside it is another. And another.

His screams meet laughter from above.

"I'm too old to die," she says, maybe to herself, not that it makes a difference. He is halfway down the slope already, running and rolling, hands to his sides so that he can't touch anything here again, not the stones nor the bones nor the rotted hair nor the naked, reaching vines.

Tantrumic wrecks

"Not that way," the Omniscient pointed out. "When the satellite tumbled, it flashed the *moon's* reflection, not the sun's."

The author by-lined as O.P. Mantz kicked a library book across the room and yelled incoherently at a dumb machine. Then he turned his face back to the screen. The mistake glared, but he did not correct it. Instead, his fingers pecked faster than a flock of chickens, and as indiscriminately.

The Omniscient sighed, but only privately, in the professional manner of any doctor faced with a condition that bores him. The Omniscient's eons of experience had made him rather proud of himself as a behaviour expert. His diagnosis? Tantrumic self-destructiveness—a fit that would blow itself out. Today Mantz's tantrum was mild. Yelling at his computer was a piffle compared to the mess he'd made once with that .44 next to the thesaurus.

The Omniscient waited, his nerves fraying—but as he was born to be and was destined to be forever, he was the soul of patience. This session had been trying, *but that is the nature of rubberies.*

The END came very soon. Mantz SAVEd in his workmanlike manner and scrolled to the top of page 1. He read faster than the Omniscient, or possibly didn't finish what was shriekingly so untrue that it *isn't worth finishing*, not that the Omniscient had shrieked or been anything other than a model of forbearance.

The author swivelled in his chair, cursed to a pattern that

made the Omniscient wonder yet again, *Why do modern rubberies use such a poor and simple stock of curses? No wonder they need physical violence,* and treated another book like a football. (The Omniscient would have said *he raged,* which just shows another of the Omniscient's multiplying problems.)

Then finally, Mantz performed what the Omniscient recognised as the man's calming routine. He grabbed a squeaky toy and poked a pencil up its bum, said "Fuuuuuuck," put a hand to the back of his neck, gave it a vicious tug, and exhaled "Heh!"—bad air out. He squared his shoulders and poised his fingers over the keyboard. Tantrum over.

Truth will always out in the END. The Omniscient felt such a warmth of happiness, of empathy, that he wished he could "Heh" too. Instead, he only emanated: *I forgive you.*

But the author pressed no DELETE key, began no fresh anything, corrected nothing, nought, absolutely zot. Instead, he turned his music (*music!*) on, sprawled back in his chair, stretched out his arms and smiled; and tripping down those paragraphs, he played with *words.* He laughed in delight at one insertion (*why?*) and took his hands off the keys. He must have liked this part in the music because he out-shouted the shouter and hit his desk violently with both hands, to a rhythm. The song ended (*at last*) and he turned off the noise and read the story again.

His brow creased. Then he picked up an open book on his desk and looked up something, then flicked pages to some section in it, and began to read. It couldn't have been a thesaurus, because this was taking too long.

The Omniscient wafted but it was a few moments till Mantz held the book up sufficiently so that the Omniscient could see its spine. **THE SEVEN BASIC PLOTS**.

Plots. Seven. Basic. "And which are you?" he zzinged.

"Yeow! Whadthe?"

"Your life." *Stake, cesspit, garrotte, lightning strike. I've been pushed too far.* The Omniscient yearned to be something other than a reporter. As it was, he'd only caused a power surge.

The model author millions looked up to as "ineffably cool" picked up a paper cup and drank deeply of its one drop of coffee. His hand shook.

The Omniscient was shaken, too. He was angry at himself for losing his temper. And worried. After all, he had broken at least one rule: Non-interference.

That didn't mean he wasn't mightily peeved, and hurt. *What non-observer wrote that trash, with its predictable seven?* he asked himself but he couldn't ask anyone else. And now he couldn't see, either. The book was lying in a disordered state between the chair's feet.

The Omniscient left the room as unnoticed as he had been unheralded. *Mustn't I observe? Don't they want new stories? They always did. Who will watch if not myself?*

Those thoughts should, logically, have reassured him.

I should write The Seven Basic Rubberies. Fancy being ignored when I'm kind enough to correct. And to think I etc. etc.

There had always been stupid storytellers, and those who babbled like babies in love with the sound of their own blubbering language imitations. But the Omniscient had *never* before put O.P. Mantz in those categories. After all, Mantz had—for his first six books—taken dictation almost always as faithfully as a secretary.

If they no longer seek to know anything, what about me?

Q. Do you remember to have lost a blue coat?

A. Yes, it was taken out of my wardrobe; two volumes of Smollett's works, and a silk handkerchief.

—Proceedings of the Old Bailey

Poached capercaillie

Watching without eyes, feeling without skin, smelling without nose, tasting without tongue and nose and throat; dry as the wind yet sparkling with bubbles of drool as undeniably appearing out of nowhere as the water that flows from a rock when struck by a magic rod—Nick (for lack of a better name) did all these things from his perch as a frill around the cinnamon-stick nest of the cinnamologus.

He had never been so well cared for. Not even his mother had tucked him into bed as well as the male cinnamologus tucked the wind-loosed wisps of Nick (or more properly, in the cinnamologus' eyes: the glossy red fluff).

And what of the crandolin? That crandolin blood with Type Female Human Virgin blood, a part of the mysterious whole wakened in its every 'cell'. That blood had sat for centuries— ever since the cook dropped a splotch of crandolin pudding in-the-making upon the parchment page. The splotch had aged and dried (trapping the blood in frustrated suspended animation). And the book was tossed, lost, found, and finally treasured by some. But the stain was viewed as a blemish that hurt the value of the illumination—till Nick, back in the library in his other life (how many days ago?) gazed at that ugly ancient dessicated splotch. And he saw, not a stain, but the ultimate romance: the most dangerous, delicious, *adwentoursomme* tasting of his life. And though the offering was frustratingly small—an *amuse bouche*—this was one amusement that could kill, or worse. So of course, he fell upon the stain and ravished it.

And what *of* that crandolin? It was now a part of Nick as surely as he was the crandolin, *flesh of my flesh, soul of my soul, a part of me as surely as I am a part of you, a part of myself—but what the hell* are *you?*

In this scrap of himself, as this *flesh*, if you could call it that, he sensed now as he had never sensed before. Smell and taste were tuned to such extremes that he would have wept if he could, from the joy of it, and the tragedy. The cinnamologuses would taste insane, inexpressibly divine, even though he hadn't plucked their feathers, spitted them, torn their flesh with the traditional two forks in preparation for making a giant bastila, the pigeon pie redolent with rose petals, toasted almonds, cinnamon, black pepper, ginger, and orange flower water, the mess nestled in pastry so thin that when you take it from the oven and pour the clarified butter on it, the crispy, golden layers of pastry glow. He memory gorged; fingers ripping into pastry; fragrant, buttery pigeon juice running down to his elbow. The meat had been tender as an unborn, but needed all the extras. These cinnamologuses needed nothing but themselves. They would make roses pucker in jealous rage. As for other exotics, the macaw had tasted surprisingly domestic. The Madagascan hoopoe was a characterless fop. And the bird of paradise downright medicinal from the berries it had been gorging on, or possibly the poisoned arrow.

The cinnamologus—all these years he'd thought that the nest was the reason for its name. Sure enough, the sticks were fresh, real cinnamon and not cassia. "Who knows the difference these days?" Nick asked himself, which brought on a wave of culinarist's disgust until he veered into the question: *What is these days?*

Nick salivated over the cinnamologuses in the only way he could. Their skin was thin as a raspberry's, and the colour of the male's: periwinkle blue.

When Nick had had fingers, he had never touched anything

so sublime. As a chef, he yearned to have them, pluck them, spit them; ah, forget the spit. He wanted to sink his teeth into them raw. Nick lusted after their reek. They rubbed their beaks on the cinnamon sticks and gave the cinnamon its scent. No flesh had ever invigorated Nick before, nor humbled him. Certainly, none had ever tortured *him*. He watched them, and every tick that climbed up onto their skin. He *hated* those ticks, who drank till they were sated and then unstuck their lips from their birds-as-bottles, falling onto ever-ready sofas of cinnamologus down where they slept off their stupor. What could they appreciate?

Nick (for lack of a better name) was maddened with want and literally stuck—watching, smelling, tasting in the only way he could at the moment, for however long that moment was.

Late for an appointment

"YOR-*MAY*-OH," (They don't love *me*), the Muse exploded, as if she'd said "Eureka!"

"A plague on your aspirations."

She'd yelled that many times, too, but at each fresh outburst she was the sole audience, so no one pointed out, *You repeat yourself ad nauseam.*

She readied herself with many a moue in the mirror, and furious jerks of limbs, though expertly as ever.

"Why me?" she demanded of the mirror.

It reflected silently.

She opened the lid of what she'd recently begun calling My Glory Box, and began tossing ribbons, corsets, sandals, jewels, veils and petticoats into the air.

"Жæzox oowa bbrrr ..." (*To each, according to his need*) she sang tunelessly as she chose ... *the red red dress. And the red rubber, thigh-high boots.*

Dressed and ready to go out, she pumped a fist in the air. "Sod them all!"

Nick Kippax's column in *Oenologist's Digest* just had to be read again. She uncorked a bottle with her little white teeth. The librarian could wait. After all, he'd been calling for three days. She'd never serviced him before, but already she hated his whine.

The third daughter

MULLIANA ALWAYS SINGS while she works. Her father has three daughters, one more beautiful than she is good, one more good than she is beautiful, and Mulliana, the youngest, whose voice is so lovely that before she lost her milk teeth, her father shut her in a tower so that he could enjoy her voice without being disappointed by either her goodness or her beauty.

She kneels beside a grass mat, placing pieces of coloured felt down to make poppies and roses and a cinnamologus—a design she learned from her mother. Her back is warmed by a fire but her hands are cold. When the cinnamologus is finished to the last claw, she obscures it with layer after gossamer layer of wool that she has carded, tili the mat is covered with a great white cloud.

Over a fire hangs a cauldron of water. She unhooks it and tips it in dribbles all over the mat till the pot is empty and the white cloud flattened and grey as any waterlogged cloud. She kneels again and rolls the mat tightly, binding it with cords that she has also made, this of her own strong hair.

And now she steps on the steaming roll, and stamps on it in a rhythm that she first felt in her mother's womb.

The water runs into a drain and escapes laughing into the face of the sky.

Steam escapes the tower through filigreed windows cut in stone. Her voice flies through the openings; rises, and falls down upon a field of sunflowers, boys netting larks, women kneading dough in distant houses; and her ancient father dozing beside a pomegranate tree.

The stone nightingale cage on the threshold of her father's house has been empty for many years. Who needs a nightingale, when they only sing for their supper, while Mulliana works for hers. Her father is as celebrated for her rugs as he is for her voice.

He wandered lonely, as a cloud

THE OMNISCIENT DISGUISED HIMSELF as mustiness, and used-bookstore crawled till he was so filled with stories that had gone right with their authors that he forgot his own life.

He woke in *The Call of the Wild*. That author had been a good scribe, damn fine.

The Call (story #UY9* * *) was a favourite of the Omniscient's—a more complex job than some. With *Call*, not only had the Omniscient given the writer the story, but he'd given the writer (an old clerk who had never lived anywhere other than his mother's house) *a life*.

Oren H. Entsminger is a terrible name for an author, the Omniscient had subtly made known. So the clerk took the Omniscient's advice and assumed the name and history of a man the Omniscient had watched and admired—a man who had actually *done* things, been a man as the Omniscient would have liked to be, if he could ever settle down.

What a damn fine time the Omniscient remembered—though Oren was duller than a pencil stub. He was a damn fine author: conscientious, always getting the message right, always checking with the Omniscient, "Is this the truth?"

Damn fine.

Truth was so easy then, only a speck of time ago. The Omniscient, in Oren's day, had no problem seeing everything, recollecting perfectly, retelling with the accuracy of that

43

reliable court witness whom he celebrated in story #G/84* * * (unfortunately, every time he gave that story to an author, the author failed to sell it).

"Damn fine. Oren. Or did I call him Jack?"

The Omniscient roused himself enough to examine where he was. Nestled right in the beginning of *The Call*, the ditty that has the line "chafing at custom's call".

Chafed was a good word for how he felt, and *why come to custom's call if I'm not appreciated?* He began to feel mighty depressed again, and was thinking about wandering out for another almighty jag—maybe to end up in a *Decameron*, when his senses awoke enough to allow him to feel the rawsome pain of his grief.

His recent attempts to learn from people made him dose himself with self-analysis.

The stress of work is making you want to escape into books. And that leads to more stress, and more escape. These bookstore-crawling jags will only end in disaster.

"Love yourself," he said. "And accept yourself as you are."

Easy for some to say.

But then he thought of the shame of his last encounter, and he wanted to sink into pages again—never to come out. He could, in this bookstore. There were many comforting books that he could lose himself in, never to be disturbed.

Never to be used again.

"Damn them all!"

Is cursing the world the answer? And would Buck and D'artagnon and Scaramouche and Parker and Modesty curse the world? or run away, let alone choose suicide? They had no time for cowards.

But the pain of it, the shame:

Another best-selling author, *my best scribe...*

* * *

Everything had been going swimmingly, till page 487, when the Omniscient forgot. He could not, for the life of him remember what came next. "What did you see?" he asked himself overandover again. He had always remembered everything he'd ever seen and told it in every detail. *It made me who I am today*, he kept telling himself ... *or who I was.* The great bulk of that story (a long one, the Omniscient remembered that) wandered like a cloud in the Omniscient's memory. The closer he looked into the cloud, the more misty his memory became, till the cloud that was a story became an angry grey opacity, and his memory of what he had formerly seen became its own unfathomable cloud, and his memory of what he had reported of the story in times past became... O! He felt that he could not move, as all around him was turmoiled. He might as well have been the eye of a storm, so calm looking, yet...

The author was patient for a time. Then he was furious. Then he was frantic. The book was expected by the author's publisher. The story was expected by the author. And, though the Omniscient turned his memory inside out and shook it, not one word fell from him into the mind of the author, whose face purpled as he began to fulminate at volcanic blast.

In a panic, the Omniscient told the author the ending of quite a different story—just to have an end, *or because I thought it was the correct ending?* Either way, the shame was unbearable.

But if that were the only shame, the Omniscient would only suffer unbearable shame, a common enough sight in his observation of people.

But the false ending that he'd given the best-selling author wasn't his only source of shame.

The author, after having sat, raged, and swallowed lots of pills, didn't take the false ending the Omniscient gave him. He had known that it was false. The author *lost faith in him*... And shame of shame, horror of horrors, called upon the Muse.

"I've med up many a new tale," she said, "when I hadn't nobody to talk to, and was feeling a bit down, but I never think nothing more about 'em, and if you was to ask me to tell you one I couldn't for the life o' me; they're all clean gone out'n my head."

—Eva Gray *

* * *

* quoted by Thomas William Thompson in his "The Gypsy Grays as Storytellers", *Journal of the Gypsy Lore Society*, 3rd series, vol. I, 1922; excavated from library stacks, displayed and discussed by Neil Philip (self-confessed "precious apothegmaticall Pedant" **) in his *The Penguin Book of English Folktales* (pp xviii, xix), Penguin Books, London, 1992.

** *Dear Mr Philip,*
We should form a Society.
Yrs in solidarity,
the O.

The relativity of pillows

WHILE SHE SAT ON THE NEST and he stood beside her, waiting for her eggs to hatch, a stork couple shared their time of luxury, watching the street below. They saw the normal clump of little boys clustered around the sweet shop. They saw the honey merchant's donkey, standing half hidden in the doorway, blocking the entrance not by its bulk but by the promise of its swift back hooves. The stork couple saw the usual bustle of people, but they saw no Burhanettin nor Ekmel, for Burhanettin had practically wrenched Ekmel's arm off in the rush to pull him into the privacy of Burhanettin's kitchen in the back, where Burhanettin, the *helvassi*, made his secret-reciped honeyed sweets.

On the way, Burhanettin reached into his robe and pulled out a leather sack. He counted five coins into the hand of an old man behind the counter. "Go, uncle," he said. "My toe is aflame again, so take this to Marwalitep with my respects."

The old man bowed, but remained where he was.

"The storks miss your presence," Burhanettin said, "and the shop needs a bit of quiet, so don't come back today."

Like a cedar in a storm, the top of the man moved slightly.

"The sweets will wait for you like your wife did when she was alive," Burhanettin assured him.

So the old man bowed, not to Burhanettin but to the counter where the sweets sat under their veils of silk, protected from the flies that craved them, and the bees that always came, confused by this hive that was not a hive. Then he grunted some concurrence to Burhanettin and squeezed past the donkey, leaving Burhanettin and Ekmel alone.

Burhanettin pushed Ekmel into the back room and pulled shut the thick wooden door.

Ekmel trembled. Burhanettin's secrets lived here, and in his head. Each *helvassi* had his own—the specialities that made them masters far above tradesmen; and in the case of Burhanettin, Ekmel knew as well as the whole town: Burhanettin was the master above masters. Burhanettin could teach the bees about honey, could teach the Heavenly One himself about Heaven (Holy be His Name, He who says *Keep the Truth for it is holy*).

But now to Ekmel, whose teeth ached always from Burhanettin's sweets—*the sharper the pain, the sharper the pleasure*—Ekmel's teeth ached now from the mere suggestion of their presence. His saliva flowed, pricked by the rich scents and sights of nougats, jellies, helvas, pastes, syrups, piles of pistachios and almonds and candied honey shards.

But Ekmel's teeth always ached. And Ekmel always trembled in Burhanettin's presence. He noticed now, neither his trembling nor the complicated feelings of his teeth. Burhanettin was all—or rather, Burhanettin's attention to the glass in Burhanettin's hand.

The helvassi's face had turned the deep red of a baked quince. The veins on his forehead stood out and pulsed. He poked the olivewood stick up and down in the glass, pulling up a shiny red rope each time that slipped smoothly from the stick into the glass. He sniffed it, stuck his tongue out and almost touched it, and pulled his tongue back each time at the critical moment.

"Kirand-luhun?" Burhanettin said—out loud for the first time.

"Kirand-luhun." A shiver ran down Ekmel's back as he said the word.

"How much?"

Ekmel, an expert himself in the gauging of desire, saw with a sense of joy that surpassed everything on earth except his joy in eating Burhanettin's helvas, that Burhanettin would pay anything he asked. Anything.

He forced his feet to move, his head to turn. He forced himself to stroke his little moustache, to stretch out his joy, the flow of pleasure from Burhanettin's attention wholly centred upon him in a most delightful, newly *respectful* way.

"I haven't decided," he said.

"Who did you get this from?" Burhanettin blurted, silly as a foreigner.

Ekmel's trembling stopped, he was so surprised—Burhanettin was smitten, crazed with desire.

Ekmel smiled, drawing out his pleasure. His eyes closed like a cat's, and he opened his mouth and yaw—

"Aaaaaggh!"

Burhanettin's hand gripped Ekmel's throat. The sweet maker's eyes peered into Ekmel's.

"Who?" Burhanettin thundered. "Before I peel your eyes like grapes."

Ekmel's hands flapped. His slippers fell off his waggling feet. His throat made noises but Burhanettin's grip was too tight for words. "I tell," was what he was trying to say, and finally Burhanettin dropped him, carefully, in a corner where the honey merchant's body wouldn't get in his way.

"Who did you get this from?" Burhanettin demanded. Ekmel knelt on the floor, trying to suck air at first, then pretending for precious seconds.

The question was outrageous. Ekmel's commercial contacts were as much his trade as Burhanettin's recipes were his. Burhanettin's desire had driven the man insane, dangerously so. The mighty Burhanettin had flown into tempers before, had always frightened and excited Ekmel, but all cooks have their moods— and helvassis are the moodiest of master cooks. *May he spend eternity with another as sweet as himself*, Ekmel had prayed on other occasions. But Burhanettin had never done anything this

51

surprising.

Now Ekmel was alarmed. Burhanettin's eyes were mad as a thirst-crazed horse. But the theft of Ekmel's livelihood—the demand to know who sold him the Kirand-luhun was nothing less—this outrage gave Ekmel strength. He stood up and dusted himself off, and a fine mist of powdered sugar fell from his clothes.

"I gathered it myself," he said. "In my distant travels."

And with that announcement, his knees began to shake. Somehow, he made his way to the door and opened it, and in the shop the old man was behind the counter as usual, and the sweets beckoned as always, and the donkey brayed from the doorway, and somehow Ekmel made his way to the counter where he purchased a three-occa bag of assorted sweets, including a long stick of nougat.

He bent his head to leave the shop, and still stooping at the threshold, broke off a piece of the nougat stick, handing it to the donkey who was blocking the way to the street. Then he slipped by.

The donkey turned around, following the rest of the piece and, incidentally, Ekmel the honey merchant.

* * *

If Burhanettin had wanted to stop Ekmel's escape, he could have done so, easily as cracking an egg. He shut the door instead.

In his room of secrets, the master *helvassi* blew out the oil lamps. Now the only way he could tell night from day was the light that came from a high window with a stone-filigree screen, and the voice of the hour-keeper.

Burhanettin sat on a stool, his back against the windowed wall. His right arm held out the little glass, hung from the tips of his fingers.

The hours passed till the lace that mantled benches and the far wall dissolved. By the time the hour-keeper's voice changed, Burhanettin was in no doubt. The glass held honey that possessed an undistinguished smell, but its colour! Not of honey, nor bled from alkanet root, nor sandalwood, nor even crushed kirmiz bugs, brilliant though their reds all shone in Burhanettin's many helvas.

The stuff in the glass changed reds as the light dimmed without, and each red was more terrifyingly beautiful. Kirand-luhun. *Take too little, and madness seizes you. Take too much, and Death swoops you up. Take just the right amount* (which must be as expertly judged as the amount of powdered pearl to stir into a batch of *helva-i-golub*) *and the Kirand-luhun gives the unearthly sweetness that is love* (mocking the stuff that rots the teeth). Burhanettin had never married, never dallied with a woman, because none had ever rivalled the ones in his dreams.

As a master helvassi, Burhanettin pondered the stuff in the glass. No recipe had ever eluded him, but he always tasted to find his way. The Kirand-luhun was not to be tasted.

"Be temperate in your taking, or..." Burhanettin murmured the legend and strictures till they melded into a song.

"A man must know exactly how much Kirand-luhun to take," to leap over the chasm of madness, defy Death's grasp, and reach the place where the Kirand-luhun would give him Love—love that Burhanettin had yearned for and never sought. Why the Kirand-luhun had chosen to come to him, and why suspended in honey, Burhanettin studiously avoided considering.

"Never question the inexplicable." He had no choice but to treat this as a Personal Order to be obeyed with more alacrity than a Decree from the Sultan himself.

The glow in the glass beckoned, commanded, tantalised and shamed. Burhanettin massaged his toes in the pre-dawn chill while his mind ran over the names for his most popular helvas. *Pillows of delight. Lips of love. Pshaw! The higher the pile of pillows of delight, the lonelier the lover of my sweets. The hotter the tongue that melts my helva, the icier the bed.*

When the hour-keeper's nightstick tapped two hours past midnight, Burhanettin pushed himself away from the wall and stood, with much cracking of knee-joints. Normally he would have sighed at the pain, but he didn't notice now, there was so much work to be done.

The librarian wore gloves

THE LIBRARIAN WORE GLOVES, common enough when handling precious works, but these gloves were fingerless and lined with sheepskin. He put down his pencil and blew on his blue-tipped fingers.

He had spent his day like most days, writing, or to be exact in today's case, *trying to*. Today the plot had frustrated him so much that he spent much of the day staring at faint-ruled lines. A migraine trifled with him as he agonised over whether adhering to the story he was converting to present day was the ripper he'd once thought, or a bloated bore, and if a bore, *where can I find inspiration*, the pains of rising panic exacerbated by the pangs of guilt over Unproductive Time (he did try to reach 2,000 WPD). The migraine stabbed his right eye playfully with a shard of broken-glass light till he raised his hand to rub his face and noticed that time had, for once in his life, flown. *Hah! Too late to worry today.* "He smiled ruefully," he said. The migraine withdrew, miffed.

He changed his spectacles and stood, uncricking his back. There was only one client left in the library.

"Check out a book today. And take his Chequers away," he chanted in the dimly lit room. The sound cheered him. He'd yelled that ditty with two thousand others on that glorious Sunday in May when librarians from McMurdoo Blight in the north of North to Ill of Tinks in the money-dripping South converged in London for the only demo in which he'd ever participated, in all his twenty-nine years.

"Will we have to burn wee books to keep warm?" fiery Fiona something-or-other (University of Edinburgh Special Collections) had asked the admiring throng, to the exciting heckle of "Don't give 'em big ideas!" and the throng-swell in reply of "Librarians ... unheated ... will never be defeated!"

That was some day ... and the next morning, at that flat (he never caught whose), there must have been fifty librarians sleeping it off. *Whoever thinks of librarians as staid would have blushed to have seen the pictorial tumble of limbs in the lounge.*

He smiled at the memory. "Pictorial tumble's good," he said, toward the woman whom-you-would-know-by-her-picture-on-the-back-of-scads-of-books-and-the-top-of-many-Books-pages sitting at one of the two precious-volume-examination tables.

"Pictorial tumble's good," he repeated, louder.

Louder yet, she tore a page from her yellow pad.

He walked over to her. "Shall I be keeping this for you?" he said, closing the book and picking it up.

She gave him one of her looks.

"Her eyes smouldered," he said.

"Worm, thou'rt." She rearranged her black and mirror-things shawl so that it covered half her grinning face.

As she pushed open the priceless door, she tossed back, "Quit while you're nowhere."

Giles Moneyfeather grinned to himself. He liked her, the batface. And she *could* write a damn good historical thingamy. Actually, many. She was like a queen bee, popping them out with a regularity that kept many workers in work. She was one of Giles' constant 'clients', as the library called them these days.

A bit soppy for his taste, her books. And for anyone he cared to write for. That's why, he supposed, she hadn't felt threatened when he'd shown her his efforts. *Paltry*, he'd called them.

Not so, she'd corrected.

So kind, he'd said, but what is one to say?

He'd only shown her the once. After all, he didn't want to give her ideas. And he'd never shown her where he'd got his from. A little perk, a human weakness, it could be called, entirely innocent, and common as grass on a lawn, yes it is. That glorious, debouched evening of love and truth had taught him that.

"My flat is safer than that termite-eaten igloo," he'd said to Simon International-Conflict-Resolution-Museum-Archives.

"Heathens, all of them these days," Simon had said. "You want to see some good stuff, ask me."

And the whole evening had been like that. The really special collections were, these days, in the loving hands of specialists.

The murder mystery that Giles was writing was something he found in ... but he's got the book, the only copy in the world.

Giles Moneyfeather had the idea to bring it into the present day so that no one could accuse him of plagiarism if anyone had *ever* noticed the small, handwritten volume. He'd removed it from the catalogue, easier than stealing candy from a baby. Thinking of that, he was sure it had been *much* easier than that. A computer system can't scream.

He carried the book she'd been examining to his Special Collection Reserved shelf behind his desk.

Then, with a jolt, he remembered that he wasn't finished for the day. He walked around to the other precious-manuscript-examination table where a typical self-important foodie, this one with an Australian accent, had been looking for the past few days at items from the Ardeith Bequest. Rude bugger, he'd left without even stopping by to say "Thank you, Mr Moneyfeather" for having granted him permission.

And the book!

Moneyfeather's heart beat. Kerflump. and again. Whah-hoo. His forehead pulsed. The book was lying skewiff on the table, and in the centre of the right-hand page, *a pucker!* Mauled and twisted as a piece of pie-dough.

"The lout!"

It wouldn't matter with most books, but cookbooks are perversely popular; even the most obscure ones are *known*.

"Bloody Australians. No wonder we sent them there."

Moneyfeather changed his spectacles so feverishly that he dropped his reading glasses down his bare chest instead of under his jersey and into his shirt pocket. *Why should I need to watch? Skin a brick! I'll be—*

"Calm down," he said.

That helped. *Always so quick to jump to conclusions.* "Just plonk some weights on it."

Of course!

If there was a chuckle emitted from the hovering migraine, Moneyfeather didn't hear it over the noise of his own ragged breath.

Trembling, he closed hypercarefully, the medieval cookbook that was *hideously, pervertedly, too bloody known, dammit* for him to delete it from the library's files. *O!* how he wished that safely before his time, it had been souvenired by some collector.

His lips were a clenched rictus as he picked up the damned thing. With all that parchment or vellum or whatsit, it was heavy as a sheep—oversized yet slippery, covered by acres of ancient leather smoothed by time to the texture of suede. He clutched the book to his chest. One of its great hanging buckles caught the cableknit of his mother's handknitted jersey (damn her and her knitting), but no matter. He would extricate the buckle at his desk. With his bum, he pushed the chair toward the table, but something sounded wrong.

Bending down, he saw: sprawled from chair seat to floor, a jacket, shirt, pants ... and shoes, with the sockfeet still in them.

A bladder-pipe in arms

HERE! Take, for your pleasure, this rotten egg and throw it at the fool who first said: Time heals all wounds.

It has been already four whole sleepless nights and sleepless days since Faldarolo woke to find the red blotch on the bladder-pipe's beloved skin.

Despite Faldarolo's frantic, and then exhaustive and methodical efforts, the mark not only remains, but seems to Faldarolo, and more importantly, to the bladder-pipe herself, to have spread its hideous blush.

* * *

A pink sugared almond hits Faldarolo on his right eyelid. A green one thuds against the bladder-pipe's skin. Faldarolo's eyes are closed in a concentration new to him. His eyebrows don't dance, and his body doesn't sway to the commands of the songs that the bladder-pipe makes him play. Now his body is rigid, his brows flat and heavy as an iron bar laid across his head. The joints of his fingers are white, and he could almost be made of wood, he moves with such mechanical particularity.

Auy! That was a sheep's head with the cushioning meat chewed off.

He plays on, till a well-thrown wooden clog hits his skull just so, and with a screech from the bladder-pipe, he makes his final contribution to the hilarity of the party by falling onto his side, insensible as a plate of pilaf—but holding his instrument in his hands. One of the guests compares him to a dead cockroach, arms stiffened around a piece of cake.

* * *

He wakes in the street, when he feels the bladder-pipe being tugged from his hands.

"Ugah," he cries, more of a whimper than a manly curse, but he could attract unwelcome attention. The little boy drops the bladder-pipe and runs with his friends. They disappear around the corner, faster than a scurry of rats. Who wants that ugly thing anyway?

Faldarolo is so weak from hunger that for a moment, he hates the bladder-pipe. "Drunkard," he hears as he staggers to his feet. Dizzy, he falls.

A policeman makes his way like a cedar walking, through the crowd. He perches his giant hands on his hips, and stands over Faldarolo's ragged form.

"In the name of public decency," someone says.

The policeman picks up the bladder-pipe in his left hand and with his right, picks up the back of Faldarolo's shirt, raising Faldarolo with it.

The policeman says, "Faldarolo, where is your robe?"

Faldarolo jerks as if he were a puppet and his behind was pricked by a puppetry sword. The crowd laughs. He cranes his neck to view the ground all round, but the crowd is too thick. His robe is missing, his only robe good enough to be worn to work. And his feet are bare. Faldarolo blushes, wondering how long the soles of his feet had stared out for all to see.

The policeman steadies him and hands him the bladder-pipe. "If I find any of the scamps with them..." He glances at the richly carved door that had opened the night before, for an unconscious Faldarolo to be kicked out into the dust.

The policeman makes a cluck in the back of his throat. He reaches into his waist wrapping, pulls out a five-piastre piece, and pulls Faldarolo's right hand free of its clutch on the bladder-pipe.

"Eat, Faldarolo," the policeman says, earning the indignation

59

of some prominent members of the crowd, and an official complaint (but his woes are another story).

* * *

That was days ago, and four piastres of the five went to the bladder-pipe. Lemons, white wine, salt, spirits of lead, mercury salve, the very finest ass's butter massaged hourly into her skin; tincture of pearl-ash and moonstone made by the fakir in Akshehir Lane—each and all as effective as a wish.

In her rage, she paid Faldarolo dear. At each engagement after the appearance of the Stain, she sang like an angel, lulling the crowd into a mood of generosity and admiration—and then—blurt, squeak, fart, sniff, screech, peel, scream. No matter how much concentration Faldarolo put into blowing and controlling every note, no matter how much he showed her he loved her, no matter how much he starved himself for her—she made others listen, so that when their ears were most open to the flow, they could be most hurt.

Thus, she drew patrons to Faldarolo, and repelled them at the critical moment. Each night, Faldarolo blew into her with fear. He touched her with an even higher respect than normal, the respect he would pay to an angry asp. And at each engagement, she bit him again and again, till the night he was thrown out onto the street.

* * *

And now there were no further engagements, nowhere that he could take her to sing. Even before the Stain, she would no more tolerate singing in the street than he would expose her. Now, to the taunts of the crowd at the lurid blemish on her body, her cries were those of a madthing. But her demand to Faldarolo was not that of a madthing. *Rid me of this mark! Or, as I feel, so shall...*

Oh, she was logickful. Pain for pain for pain for pain...

The mirror that didn't change its mind

GALINA EXAMINED HERSELF in her mirror, which was remarkably like Valentin—heartless and shallow. It showed her what had disgusted Valentin—a lipstick smear, he thought. Tears trembled on her eyelashes as she gazed at her mouth. The shame of it, the irony! Valentin must have thought that she had made herself up while she was drunk, or while she danced while her potatoes boiled and she imagined being kissed by him. Lipstick! None of her lovers had ever given her something for her femininity, not so much as a tiny bottle of scent. Her salary had never stretched to cosmetics—and certainly not now, not with her growing food needs. And the worst part of the shame is that Galina had always been so proud of not needing enhancement—all that white white skin and red red lips. Her mother had called her Gvozdika, little carnation.

But Valentin, that snake in the form of a charming prince. I should put him out of my mind.

Fancy that wind pulling her coif to pieces in front of his eyes. Horrors, that she had put her face to his, awaiting his kiss, only to be rebuffed with not only, "That lipstick is wrong for you," but "Half of it has missed your lips."

Alone in the restaurant car, doors locked fore and aft, her hand-written CLOSED signs blocking prying eyes, Galina examined her face.

She spat on the little mirror and wiped it on her apron, but when she looked again, the mirror's mind was quite made up. It showed her the same horror, with a spiteful little bonus of viscous snot flowing onto her upper lip. She blew her nose and wiped away her tears.

What Valentin saw (and how many others?) reminded her of her father. It sprawled anyhow like her father used to when he staggered home.

Galina touched herself on the skin between her lip and nose. A rash? She had eaten rather a lot of radishes this morning. But there was no blistering, no itch. No reason on her previously unblemished skin, for that splash of revolting colour.

"I look like a clown."

Worse.

"Clown lips are symmetrical."

A knock on the door reminded Galina that she had work to do. It was almost noon. She had to open the restaurant carriage for lunch. She had to find something to make the borscht with ... something she hadn't eaten. Two hours ago, she had finished the remains of the breakfast borscht, and all the meat.

A frowsy cabbage, two hairy carrots...

Galina grizzled as she chopped them to the sound of people pounding the doors. It was too much to ask of a woman: to invade her privacy when she needs it most. As she poured salt into bubbling water, she took a handful and rubbed it on her mark.

Madly, she scrubbed.

She looked into her mirror, and the mark was not only there, but surrounded by angry skin.

Furiously, the soup bubbled.

Ignominiously the windows fore and aft whimpered at the beating they were taking.

The door knobs fore and aft jiggled uncertainly ... till ... one door popped open, the traitor.

Lunchtime had come to the restaurant car—Galina was powerless to stop it. What could she do? Pour more water into the pot and dish out the contents.

There was only enough for nine bowls.

She served the soup.

Nine tourists.

She turned away quickly, not just because she was embarrassed to be seen. She always washed pots during the meal service, as the banging helped to drown out the complaints.

* * *

Three carriages away, in the car that Savva thought of as home, Valentin left the toilet with a smile on his face. Under his jacket, warm against his skin, the solid block of The Impossible Virgin sheltered, certain page edges neatly folded back.

At the other end of the carriage, in the compartment nearest the samovar, Savva spat a wad of sunflower-seed shells out the doorway, aiming for the heart of a certain faded rose on the strip of carpet.

He missed.

The physics of a *poof!*

IN THE COMFORT OF A LIBRARY, the Omniscient spent the morning
fondly observing his latest, who had been writing like an author
should, not letting anything get in the way of truth, not letting
excuses such as paid employment distract. Such a panicky type,
so forgetful (at *his* young age)—there was something to him
that appealed to the Omniscient, who was glad to have chosen
an unknown, Giles Moneyfeather (*good name*) to give story
#*78JJJ* * * (a murder that the Omniscient had witnessed, and
the subsequent travels of the incompletely dry skeleton from the
Urals to the village of Little Bloxwich, Walsall, some centuries
ago). The Omniscient planned (a fantasy?) that, having inspired
Moneyfeather to find the written account (only mildly distorted by
human error), he (the Omniscient) would enjoy a long-earned rest,
no longer needing memory to do his job. He would be able to spend
time in his favourite places, blotto between the leaves.

So, unobservant of the discontent sprouting in the aspiring
author's soul, the Omniscient spent the afternoon in *The History
of One Day out of Seventeen Thousand*. When he emerged
refreshed, he only glanced at Moneyfeather, whose back was bent,
whose fingers clutched a writing instrument. The Omniscient
commended himself. He idly surveyed the room, and observed:
a snooty lady novelist who had never asked for his help; and a big
muscular man, not what the Omniscient would have called bookish,
but who was ogling at 6 pt reading range, a splayed-open tome.

The Omniscient wafted over. And this curious man surprised him again. So solid, yet spending his interest in myth. *Nonsense pictures and hocus-pocus formulae* (typical rubbish that the Muse handed foolish swains). The Omniscient was thinking of leaving when the man bent even closer to the book and kissed (?) the page.

Poof!

His clothes collapsed.

The Omniscient rushed to the book. Yowks! What a passionate kisser. The page was ravished. The Omniscient weltered with emotions. Never had he seen anything of his treated to a love so fierce.

Crandolin! A medusa of a Muse fancy. The Omniscient hrrred at the way Her creations interfere with the process of thought. This crandolin distracted him now, just when he needed to sharpen his mind to fathom the phenomenon of the disappearance.

The library is silent. The librarian has been so self-absorbed, he hasn't lifted his head—same as the lady novelist.

Indeed, they were both as oblivious as if there had been no *poof!* To be fair to them, what he had observed was an absence of something, not a something as such. No actual poof. No bang, puff, swirl, nor cloud. *None of your logickless magic that you shove down their gaping minds.*

The Omniscient, though still affected by his time between the leaves, knew without a doubt that he had witnessed *an extraordinarity.* A man was as thoroughly *not there* as the missing riches in a pilfered tomb. The Omniscient had seen much, and told it in countless stories. But *this!*

He studied the page again. Crandolin? *Like love poetry.* The Omniscient had never followed the Muse's balderdashes. *Why should I? How couldst I?* She was a fripperist, a serial fabricator. When he thought of how many men happily spread her lies for a gaze from her violet eyes ... In his increasingly rare times of sobriety he admitted to himself that the Muse's relationships disturbed him. *She is to blame.* He didn't detail what he blamed her for, but if he were a fictional character, a narrator might have mentioned his forgetfulness, his crisis of confidence that had made him escape ever more till he had sunk to the depths of referring this Moneyfeather to a *book*—and if the narrator had been opinionated (perish that sort), the book idea might have been pejoratively referred to as a 'dodge', or 'the ultimate abdication of responsibility'.

Gazing at the vacated apparel, he felt a surge of the unexpected—a jolt of confidence that he hadn't felt since *what did they call it, that excellent bunch that argued so ... the Age of Reason.* No, they didn't call it that. They assumed that truth was the only tale worth telling...

Bad habits. Such wandering lately.

Below, slumped Renewal—a Conundrum as bracing as an apocalypse.

The book was probably a coincidence, the spot of moisture glistening on the page: cerebral sap exuded when in a perfectly natural though rare phenomenon, the corporal man imploded into a dimension that ... *I need to ponder.*

These days *real* was getting so tenuous. What had he given out to whom? *Memory makes reality as real as the animals and tales that the Muse invents.* The Omniscient shuddered. *To believe in fantasies!*

At last, however, he had an anomalism to explore. Modern science would be able to explain. *It's high time I get back into science again. To observe is not enough. To extrapolate makes me great.*

The Omniscient felt young again. He was rusty, however, in extrapolation, so he didn't mind communing with human minds (He had never, to tell the truth, been able to get beyond them). So: *To science minds, at once!*

He was just dithering, preparatory for embarking on the quest, when he guiltily remembered his protégé.

"I'll be ba—"

Out of the corner of his sensibilities, he saw a woman in red rush towards the book and snatch it up.

"You!" he roared, infuriated and hurt.

"You!"

She dropped the book where it had been and the pages opened to the same place as before and at that moment Giles looked at his watch and smiled for the first time that day. They watched him close his notebook and perform his paid-for duties and the minutes dripped stickily, one by one, till he discovered the Disappearance down to the shoes with the sockfeet still in them—and fell: a faint or heart attack. Whatever, the Muse grabbed the book and ran.

A meeting of minds

THE OMNISCIENT RAN AFTER HER, a random mess of flesh and blood, mismatched apparel, and waftingness. "Against the laws," he puffed.

"What are laws?" she laughed, her high heels clacking on the pavement like any mortal woman's.

The Omniscient had not chased anyone before but he *was* the Omniscient.

The Muse had been chased by many men, but never the Omniscient, so after circuiting London for a moment, she stopped. "What do you know about this?"

"It's *your* crandolin. And who was *he?*"

The look on the Omniscient's face was not what she was accustomed to. A sneer? And who *was* he—that guy whose black shoes, socks, black jeans and black limp t-shirt lay so insouciantly on the floor as if they didn't miss the body that had just so recently given them a reason to exist?

The Muse and the Omniscient raced each other back to the scene. The Omniscient won. He had witnessed far too many faints and deaths to waste a glance at the librarian/writer crumpled beside the epicentre of Disturbance. He sped instead to the sprawl of raiments with no body in them. In he darted down the neck of the t-shirt, in the manner that an inspector would—*if*, he chuckled gleefully, *an inspector could waft like me.*

As he expected, the t-shirt was just as hollow as the socks, the legs of the jeans as hollow, too. But just as he *ahh*ed upon entering the bulging lefthand front jeans pocket, the Muse barged in.

"Why are you so interested?" he demanded.

"Why shouldn't I be?"

Why should you be, you fabricator? he thought, but was too polite to say.

"Who is he?" she said, thinking *I'm not myself. Was it something I drank?*

"Don't crowd me so." He inspected further.

That did it. She dropped the book on the table and shoved herself in beside the Omniscient in the wallet, where she met the credit cards of 'Mr Nicholas Vin Kippax'. *Anyone but him!*

Panicking, she slipped out of wallet and pocket. The Omniscient followed her. They hovered over the table. She was so flustered, she looked uncertain—and rather touchingly old, like something in a roadside diner story—that cloud of cigarette smoke suspended over a plate of bacon and eggs.

She tried to think but couldn't think of something nasty to say, something that might restore her dignity. *I've never been observed. This is intolerable!* She wanted to flee, but that would look, *O! Where's my goddessness?*

"Why did you take that book?" The Omniscient sounded suspiciously solicitous.

I don't know. She grabbed the book—only to fumble the snatch. The thing fell out of her hands and hit the floor with a sharp noise, and then a sussurance of heavily put-upon pages, not that she stooped to notice. *I want to be alone, home with my face and shoes off. I want to cry like a woman and damn the world.* Even escaping in wine prose had just lost its appeal. *I'm so very tired.*

"I was tired, too," he said. "Until this extraordinarity."

"How dare you to listen to my thoughts."

"Young lady, at your decibels, I could hardly block my ears. I say again: Why did you take that book? And why did you put it back as if you hadn't picked it up? You cannot change that fact. You know we are not to interfere."

"Gorgonna! You critique *me*. Do you know how much work you've given me from your failures?"

They glared at each other. It was all he could do to glare in a dignified manner. She didn't know whether to be flattered or insulted by the 'young lady'.

Two clouds approached and caught up to them. Hers was a hot sticky swirl of love and need and pleas from millions of Richard K. Stubbses—all variations on a theme of *Come, I need you. I can't live without you.* The Omniscient's cloud was a black whirlwind: *I asked for the straight stuff. This is bullshit.* and *You bastard. You've left me hanging.*

"Anything but that," they both thought at the exact same time.

"This is indeed an extraordinarity," he said, gathering up the book and laying it on a table. "We should secrete ourselves where we can unravel this mystery."

Escape!

Maybe they both heard that, maybe not.

She caught herself in the act of reaching into her pocket.

"An extraordinarity," she busily thought. *Excellent description. A crandolin, Nick Kippax... Perhaps the Omniscient has a use. He's dull as a rational explanation, though...*

He smiled at her, all uncle-ish. She considered inviting him to her place. *A crandolin, Nick Kippax... Escape* ... and she said what popped into her head:

"Do you like trains?"

70

Since my office is in the Whitefield area (eastern suburbs) in Bangalore, I planned to board from Krishnarajapuram, known locally as KRPuram (close to railfan Karthik's home). One of my office friends dropped me at the station at 1610 hours. The approach to the platform is pretty bad. Lucky if you don't sprain your ankle! 4 platforms in all, 8004 was to come in at Pf 2. As I made my way there, a 10-coach passenger came in hauled by a WDM2 at Pf3. No boards, but, likely to be Madras-SBC Pass. On Pf 2, there was an outdated board (no mention of AC), fortunately in English, mentioning the coach sequence of the Expresses stopping there. Very few respectable trains do.

—Arnab Acharya,
from *Indian Railways Fan Club Trip Report 8003 Trip No. 2*

Look a mirror in the face

NICK KIPPAX, such as he was also, stared at himself in the mirror. Galina applied a thin paste she'd made of cold potato water and smooshed rye, clouding his view. It looked like she'd applied a paste of exactly that, if you knew your ingredients, and if you didn't, it could make you want to cross yourself.

For the Adwentoursomme.

"Some adventure."

Nick howled his bloody head off, threw pans across Galina's galley, slashed the seats with knives, all after he'd choked the life out of that jerk, Valentin, and threw up at the sight of the pignosed Savva—all figuratively speaking.

Galina felt none of his angst. He was a disgusting, disfiguring rash on her otherwise blemishless, cherries-and-cream face. Nothing personal, but Galina hated that rash with all her passionate heart.

Nick didn't take it personally. He did, however, feel her heart beat. He felt her moods. He felt the soul of Galina, her hopes, her fears. Her vagina, from inside.

"So much for ancient virgin blood."

Two steps back

A GUST OF FOUL WIND hit Nick Kippax, or more properly speaking, another part of what Nick Kippax had become. Then an evil spray made him try to shrink into himself—impossible, stuck as he was in a matrix of honey. Nick had never been so close to a mouthful of rotten teeth. He cursed his state. *What good is seeing and smelling if I can't strike him dead with a wish?*

Ekmel the honey merchant slurped back a gobbet of drool. The night before had been that kind he most wanted to remember. His head felt like a pressed radish. And his storeroom!

"How could I leave it like this?" He knew, though the details were as water poured upon sand:

Last night, at the height of mundane happiness (always the madness smote him at those heady heights) he pulled his robes back on and ran free of the importune of soft arms, singing companions. He ran to his storeroom where alone in the dead of night, he opened all his jars and boxes—to coo to them, to appreciate them with the pure emotion of a true connoisseur in private communion with his loves. They drove him crazy—he never knew what for, but he always fainted at one point in the rapture of stocktaking. *Joy and Worry, two beasts hobbled together for eternity, by Desire.* He always remembered that much. He'd opened his eyes to see the ceiling of his storeroom, and daylight gazing back at him with the coldness of his wife.

But this morning, rat droppings bold as his wife's demands

sat where a honeycomb had stood. In a wide-mouthed crock filled with amaranth honey from Çis, a mouse hung upside down, its fur encrusted with golden bubbles. Sample jars gaped everywhere. Strawtips poked from one, a glob of cobwebs clogged another. Easily sieved, both.

The third sample jar, however (isn't it always the third?) ... "Hoo," he coughed. He peered closer yet. That remarkable colour that was not like honey, but was like ... a chill ran up his spine.

"Like a disease." Yes, he talked to himself. So? *A wise man is quiet in public and talks to himself alone.*

"Or (he shuddered) the hue of a young woman's cheeks at a certain time." *Disease and women are best kept away from home.*

"Fool!" When he was sober and unhung-over, Ekmel scorned superstition. He ladled a pitcher of water, drank half, removed his cap and poured the rest of the frigid water over his close-cropped scalp.

Yesterday he'd filled that sample jar with the cheapest, ordinariest, most insipidly *colourless* clover honey. He dried his head on a towel and stuck his face (revoltingly) close to the jar again. (Some nostrils are not made to be looked into.)

The honey shimmered redly. *Defiantly?*

"Unsievable."

The jar was worthless, the honey contaminated beyond redemption. Any other merchant would have tossed the jar into the street to be picked up by an urchin. Not Ekmel. *Waste not*, people said, a lesson stinking of misers and paupers.

Instead:

Waste nothing on the ordinary man.

There is no such thing as spoiled.

And *Quiet.*

Those three keys, a client list, a collection of unpaid creditors and a donkey were all the wealth he'd inherited. His father, a great carouser, had said:

"With these keys, if you have watched me, you will grow richer than if I left you a house of gold."

It is bad luck to curse your father, and anyway who was Ekmel to disagree? He worked too hard to think in those early years, but he constantly used the keys. Indeed, he grew richer (and rounder) than his father. His father the unfaithful, contrasted mightily with the son, who never cheated on what he called his two loving wives, "Honey" and "Intelligence".

"What happened to you?" he said to the honey in the jar. "I'm sure it's nothing serious." *Not sure at all. Use the keys.*

The honey glowed. So does fish on a hot day. So do rubies.

"Who did this to you?" Ekmel asked, thinking at first, that the answer needed a great detective, or a wizard who could spy on time.

At first Ekmel wasted time thinking of who he knew who could solve the puzzle, till he, in thinking of the smartest person he could think of, solved his own puzzle, for the smartest person also had the motivation, the sneak.

"Burhanettin!"

He had to have done this, but what did he have to gain by turning what was honey in this little pot, into something else? Ekmel didn't know, but he knew that only that *helvassia-i-dukka* Burhanettin knew honey as well as a bee. Only Burhanettin would know that Ekmel's heart would spasm at this lurid glow, and that Ekmel would not be able to sleep till he knew how to deal with it. Only Burhanettin belittled Ekmel's integrity at their every meeting. Had Burhanettin, the celebrated confectioner, been so turned by his perverted pleasures that he craved new heights, planting this evil shock to further plague the poor unsuspecting honey merchant?

Ekmel couldn't fathom, but the insults Burhanettin had always tossed to him made his ears burn now. *This has gone too far. To come into my own storeroom, my sanctum. Why, I'll have to get into his workroom and dye his nougat blue... Better yet, I'll drizzle it with mustard oil!*

Nick heard all this, and like Eve to the snake, the pussycat to the owl, Nick understood Ekmel's every spoken word, *whatever his language, whatever the place; whatever the hell, the century.*

Nick breathed a mental sigh as Ekmel removed his face from the jar's proximity. Then Ekmel rammed a stopper in the jar's mouth.

Three steps forward, to the master of the lips of love

FROM THE GLASS, Nick Kippax watched Burhanettin beat, stir, chop, pour, measure, pour, boil, slice into patterns and roll into shapes as varied as snowflakes. Gild, silver, box, pile into breast-shapes and pyramids. Nick could smell and see, and he could imagine the taste and texture of each sweet that Burhanettin created. He didn't know anything about the *helvassian-i-dukkan*, specialists in honey-based confections, but he always reckoned he'd know a true master chef if ever he met one.

Nick was more than awed. The man he watched was a moustachioed, mighty-muscled genius who bore conditions so primitive they made Kippax feel smaller than ever about his own renowned skills.

Too soon Burhanettin cleaned up, scrubbing his sticky pots till they shone. He wrapped one large load of nougat and dropped it into a sack. Nick tried to imagine the addicts who depended on Burhanettin—how many this production would satisfy for how long. He was moved when Burhanettin decanted every drop of what Burhanettin called *Kirand-luhun* from the little glass to a small and sturdy glazed jar like Ekmel's.

Then Burhanettin stoppered the jar, *dammit.*

Nick heard a thud—*that sack being slung over a shoulder?*

Then he felt himself picked up and dropped a short distance, and joggled. Warmth. *A sack hanging from his waist, against his underclothes. He's on the move.*

The heavy kitchen door creaked opened, latched shut.

"Uncle," Burhanettin said. "Take these keys."

Nick heard the sound of a crotchety old man unwrapping himself from a rough blanket, the slip of a reed mat.

"Impossible! What is this?" A voice that had lost a few chords. *He'd be good with a cane across a boy's back.* "The helvas!"

"In the cabinet," Burhanettin assured, "just as you left them."

Nick heard a slap of feet, the creak of glass sliding in wood. Perhaps the old man was counting.

"And in my room," said Burhanettin. "Enough to fill you with joy."

"And you?"

"I'll be back when I return."

"Hmph. May your—"

"Yes yes," cutting short a quarter-hearted blessing. "And you."

Nick heard the door to the shop open and Burhanettin call back, "Don't just guard them, Uncle. If someone pays you, let them escape."

No love match

NICK KIPPAX, SUCH AS HE ALSO WAS, felt as irritated as the bladder-pipe. Of all places to be stuck.

She's bad news, mate, Nick told Faldarolo. *What do you see in her?* Not that Nick really expected the man to be able to explain such execrable taste, even if he were sensitive enough to know that Nick was anything other than just a pain in the bladder-pipe.

A syrupy story

THE WOMAN IN RED caught the train with one hand and swung on, her long hair snapping. The cuddly man in the gorgeous paisley waistcoat was next. Only a passing lark saw them board but the facts that the train had not slowed and that Pshov station was the closest (and it, two hours away) were of no interest to the bird any more than the speed of the sun. Instead, the lark did notice that the female toted a case covered in spiderwebs; the male, a yellow portmanteau. Neither case leaked seeds or worms, so the lark flew onwards.

* * *

"Luxurious accommodation," said the Omniscient.

From their bunk/seats (across from each other at the window table in the first compartment that the Muse had opened the door to—"3C"—a 4-bunker with no other occupants, that the Muse and omniscient somehow filled within moments, as any mortal would), the Muse and the Omniscient watched the snow-clad land flow by—fast as a river of milk so vast the opposite bank lies in another horizon.

"Have you ever travelled by train?" she said.

"The Americas were once excellent for copy," he answered wistfully. He ran a thumb over the pattern ingrained in the red leatherette seat cover. "I've been on this train before," *I think.*

"In what form?"

The Omniscient didn't say, and the Muse didn't press the matter.

Every so often, a village would float by. Fanciful carvings, brightly painted romantic fripperies—swirls and hearts and animals and flowers, poked out from snow-capped cottages made with logs. In their seas of snow they looked half sunk, and they listed drunkenly. Their front doors were half the height of a man and the windows looked only half as big as they should be, scrunched but twinkling as a fat woman's eyes.

The cottages' cheerful, sagging shapes reminded the Omniscient of a story... *One snowy noon, a cart filled with sweet-boxes was boarded by three men. They slew the driver and tossed him into a drift. A short time later, the snowfall turned into a blizzard. At first the men argued, but soon enough crawled under the cart together, agreeing to sleep there for the night. But before night fell, the wind died, and one of the men crawled out. Making many exaggeratedly quiet movements that proved he was up to no good, he unharnessed the horse.* The Omniscient watched, wondering what would happen next when *suddenly the two other thieves jumped on the stealthy one's back, and the horse neighed, and with the ease and speed of a fish leaping through waves, the horse raced away, its bells jangling, through fields too treacherous and deep with snow, for men.* By the time the Omniscient directed his attention back to the thieves and cart, *they were nowhere to be seen, their footsteps disappearing within metres, but soggy sweet-boxes were strewn all over the snow.*

He remembered the boxes specifically because they trailed ribbons and bled red and green on the snow. They made him hungry for Roman ices, so he had dictated, "like Roman ices" and the author took that down, only to delete it the next morning, muttering, "Where'd I get this crap from?"

Like syrups on snow the Omniscient had said at another time. Was that kept?

He tried to recall the last time he'd been here, *if* he'd been, but instead, the song of the train's wheels made him need to *do* something, before their lullaby put him to sleep.

Shivering whispers

SAVVA WAS SO HAPPY that if Galina had asked him to turn up his nose at vodka, he would have forsworn that balm for her. Blissfully, she was ignorant of her newly-acquired power.

"All my beauty ruined," she sobbed into his hollow chest.

The railway carriage rocked and clucked in its motherly way as the train raced ever forward over vastness lit only by the train's eyes and stars shining on snow.

He repositioned the tossed blanket so that it covered her, and his sides. She was better than a quilt.

"You are beautiful to me," he said for the hundredth time.

"You only say that."

What can a man do? He shrugged.

"See?" She pushed herself up and the V of space acted like a bellows, sucking in icy air. "You think I'm ugly."

Before he could wrap his arms around her, she collapsed upon his chest in another spasm of grief. When his breath returned, he repositioned the blanket again. It didn't reach past his feet, but she did.

Two cars down, Valentin shivered and cursed. He always consumed alone in bed at night whatever casual pilfering he'd brought off that day. Tonight, it was a bag of Smith's crisps.

A hellish night, the bag had spilled its sharp, delicious contents between his sheets.

Faldarolo's nose

OH, THE STONES! Oh, the steepness! Oh, Faldarolo's heart, thudding as if *it* sees the depths of the ravine when just moments ago, a laden donkey passed on the inside of this path wide enough for two flies.

Faldarolo would sit against the mountain to compose himself, but he cannot stop. Cannot rest.

Oh, the curses of the bladder-pipe!

The strawberry-mark is livid as ever. Faldarolo's feet bleed, and he starves because of her. She travels strapped to his chest, his belongings on his back, mostly medicaments for her condition (not that they work) and the last dab that he possesses of the ass's butter emolument she demands.

At the top of the ridge he stops. To his right, the path drops down to a valley and the first town he has seen since he was driven from home by the torments of the bladder-pipe. Perhaps she will play.

Always Faldarolo hopes, but in the meantime, a scrawny tree stands unluckily beside him.

With apologies, he strips some bark and eats it.

* * *

Sweet-smelling town-smoke enfolds Faldarolo. He swallows.

"A musician?"

The bladder-pipe in Faldarolo's arms wears her blue velvet cloak with arrogant modesty, exposing a bit of neck.

"A musician for the Haczi!"

"Come, musician."

"No, come with us!"

Faldarolo lets himself be led by a band of boys to a house with great carved and studded doors. He is silent, but his eyebrows are busy, and his ears.

The head boy bangs a knocker in the shape of a cat's head and in a moment, Faldarolo is in a courtyard filled with roses and orange trees.

An imposing man comes forward. He must be the Haczi, whatever that means. "Water," he says, to Faldarolo's relief. A servant scurries forward with an ewer and towel. Faldarolo washes his hands and face and the servant leaves. The sweet music of a fountain tinkles maddeningly.

"You will play here tonight?" says the Haczi.

Faldarolo is weak with hunger, parched as a rusk. "I would be honoured."

The Haczi, a well-oiled man who would dwarf a buffalo, turns to leave when Faldarolo speaks. "My pay," he asks humbly. "What will you pay me?"

The servant reappears carrying a glass of water. Faldarolo wishes he had not asked. So crude, and now it is too late.

"Why, half before," says the master, "and half after. The usual." And he sweeps away.

The servant rushes after him. Drops of water fall from the glass.

The roses emit their perfume while Faldarolo stands in the courtyard feeling stupid as a post. Half before? He hopes he has not offended. The bladder-pipe's behaviour has been a blessing, forcing him to leave the place of his birth.

Faldarolo tries to listen past the fountain. Somewhere in the house a woman wails, sweet and bitter. Faldarolo cannot make out words.

The servant returns with the glass, now half-full. Faldarolo drinks politely.

The servant leaves and Faldarolo remains standing, waiting for the half-pay. He hopes, selfishly, that it will buy him a piece of bread and a glass of tea.

* * *

The wailing continues. He dare not sit, but he wavers faintly like a distant tree in the desert.

* * *

Billows of smell envelope him. A great feast is being prepared, and his tongue prickles. Sputtering lamb, quince, cinnamon, rice, almonds, honey, fresh loaves of toothsome bread. Sizzling butter, roast pistachios, fried spice.

The wailing continues and the smells increase. Servants carry things back and forth.

Finally, Faldarolo can stand no more. "Please ask your master," he says when he sees the water-carrier, "for my first-half pay."

Haughtily, the water carrier rushes off.

"Musician!"

Faldarolo looks up. The master of the house leans over an inner balcony. "I am paying you now."

Faldarolo waits, the smells getting ever stronger, richer. No one, however, appears with the pay. It will soon be night. His stomach makes sounds like a beaten gourd. Though his thirst was partly quenched, these smells have filled his nose till he must not breathe. So Faldarolo asks another servant to remind the master, in case the master's message has become lost.

"I am paying you now!" the Haczi bellows from somewhere.

Faldarolo trembles and bids himself to be patient.

A great many people arrive. Through their babble in what must be the banquet room upstairs, Faldarolo hears the fountain and the woman's wail.

Finally, the master appears.

Faldarolo removes his bunched-up sleeve from his face. He had been breathing through the thick, coarse cloth ever since the smells became unbearable.

"Come," the Haczi says.

Faldarolo, *experienced* Faldarolo does not 'come'. "My pay, sir," he says with dignity.

The great man stops, stunned. "You've *been* paid. Half before—"

"That is what we agreed."

"And now you want to change the agreement?"

"With respect, your Eminence, no one gave me—"

"I saw you take!"

Faldarolo answers with as much dignity as he can, given his honesty and his dress. "I took nothing."

"You stuffed your nose till you were full!"

The Haczi mounts the first step. "You are worth it, aren't you?" His eyes glitter with *tears*.

Faldarolo doesn't know where to cast his eyes. They settle on the man's fleshy hand clutching the banister.

"I am an honourable man," he says "and my bladder-pipe is a treasure above rubies."

"You're greedy," the Haczi sighs, "but you're all we have at the moment."

And you are all I have.

At the entrance to the banquet room, the master of the house pauses. "Sniff and chew, eh? No more of your nonsense?"

Faldarolo nods, confused as ever, but what else can he do?

"Good. Never before have I seen a man fill up till he couldn't take any more first-half pay."

* * *

The room drips with love.

Faldarolo and the bladder-pipe are as-one.

The town's most celebrated eaters swallow without tasting, or sit with their hands in their laps.

Faldarolo's eyebrows move like caterpillars in honey as the bladder-pipe moans in his hands.

A mouse stands on a tray, eating the congealed sheep-fat off the sides of a mountain of pilaf. The men sigh, shift their buttocks, hum, sway, tap their knees, rub themselves under their robes, puff out their moustaches as they breathe. Only the mouse's eyes are open.

The wailing has stopped.

"I should have paid you twice as much," the Haczi exclaims. He rushes out of the room, returning in moments with a huge apricot cat.

The cat sits on the master's lap and stares at Faldarolo.

Faldarolo's eyes are glazed, his breath and soul consumed by love. Thirst and hunger are forgot. And She! She has blessed him tonight. *What hearts can make together...*

Under the bladder-pipe's elegantly worn cape, "Twice as much of nothing is nothing," Nick screams.

Back in Faldarolo's birthplace, when Nick first realised that his struggles to escape the bladder-pipe hurt her and therefore Faldarolo, Nick stopped struggling. His second revelation was that maybe he could help Faldarolo, so he had decided that tonight he would keep the bitch in line if she decided to play up. "You hurt him, and I'll hurt you." He hadn't needed to do anything, and frankly, had been as seduced by her as everyone else (except the mouse). Finally he saw what Faldarolo saw in her.

But shysters, this is crook. The man's gotta eat.

Nick thinks of all the times in the restaurant trade that seedy deals were tried on him, and remembers an old story. "Half-pay now, and half-pay later." — in *food*, the first half being smell. Nick adds up all the evidence against this Haczi character, who, upon closer examination, looks like an "all you can eat" abuser. The fur-covered blimp, too.

Nick twitches. *You* couldn't see it, but the bladder-pipe feels punched.

"Eeooh," she squeals.

"Sorry, my love," Faldarolo mumbles, thinking this chapped lips have pinched her. He smears forehead sweat onto his lips and takes her into his mouth again.

"Yuchgh," she blurts. "Chrrghhhhhhhhh."

Faldarolo cringes, and blows down her throat with the most soothing of—"Chxxxgggheeee!"

The cat sits up, and wails.

"My beloved!" cries the Haczi.

The bladder-pipe screeches.

The cat shrieks.

* * *

Nick is satisfied that he saved Faldarolo from a worse humiliation: being a joke. *Can he even add*, Nick ponders as Faldarolo contorts himself for sleep in a field of stones. Unbelievably, he falls asleep, the bladder-pipe strapped to his breast, *completely unsatisfied*.

Back in town, the Haczi cries.

"Who *now* will soothe your cares, Kishkish my sweet?"

Servants squat in the dark gorging on the feast: meaty pilafs and stuffed eggplant, cold and soggy fried fish; custard-oozing "nightingale's nests" and sticky "sweetheart's lips"—the great bulk of the feast, and all the half-down-the-throat that Faldarolo forfeited when he ran. Although he had failed (and ruined the party), this is an honourable town. *An agreement's an agreement, even with a prostitute or musician.* Faldarolo had indeed managed to smell more than the Haczi had ever seen a man pull up his nose, so the second half of his pay would have challenged the biggest glutton.

"If only..." the Haczi sighs to the apricot cat. "He's greedy, but if he could make you happy, I would be willing to pay him anything his greedy heart desires."

Quaintnesses

THE OMNISCIENT'S QUESTION broke into the train's lullaby.

"Do you miss them?"

"No."

If Savva had cracked open the door to 3C, he would have seen the man with the paisley waistcoat lying on one top bunk and the woman in red on the other, both as stiff as Lenin.

The Omniscient spoke again. "What do you think yours are doing?"

"Killing themselves."

She didn't ask about his.

Time passed.

"Have you ever met a man in which you were truly interested?"

"Whom."

"I would have thought that, with so many—"

"If I'd have known you would be judgmental I never would have let you come along," said the Muse.

"You wouldn't have thought to come."

A frosty silence reigned for so long that anyone listening at the door would have wished for a blanket.

"Come now," said the Omniscient, "Have you ever met a man—"

"Nick Kippax. I told you."

"An unlikely coincidence," he said drily. "Tell me about the crandolin."

"I don't know what you're talking about."

"The crandolin portrayed on that page ... on any page. "

"Ask yourself," she laughed. "Or change your name."

"No need to be snide, oh revered one."

She turned on her side to observe him, but his arm obscured his face.

"Especially," he said, "when I'm *trying* to examine variosities. And your interests, and the products of your fecund mind, might lead to—"

"A plague."

"I jest not."

"No, I suppose you don't know how."

"No need to cut," he said, hoping she didn't know how close to his heart she'd thrust.

"No need to call me a fripperist."

"I'm sure there's value in your quaint creatures and unlikely tales."

"Quaint?"

"Isn't a cyclops quaint? And wolves that eat little girls, etcetera?"

She could *feel* his tolerant smile, the gloat of it. "Verily," she agreed. "I'm always going on about them."

"Naturally."

"Did you hear the one about the Cyclops who ate the little girl?"

"See? We succour different tastes. I am not disparaging your rejection of truth, your light enter—"

"As fish that walk on their hands are fripperies, and left-eyed flounders are archaic. And noble rot is the mould on that statue of King Arthur. And nuclear fission is my fancy. And the big bad Cyclops opened its mouth with such a *big* DNA expression."

The Omniscient sat up and turned on the light. "I was not aware of this facet of your structure."

He was so embarrassed that his stiffness of expression only

made him more ill at ease. He snapped off the light but that gave him no protection. The new day had dawned.

"A common misconception," she said. *Gorgonna! He's like a sack of concrete that's set in the bag. One knock on the paper and he shatters.*

"Look at me," he said, bravely facing her. "Rejected. Who is interested in a giver of truth, I ask you?"

So that's what you call it, she thought, but said, "The ones—"

"It's a fascinating truth," the Omniscient cut in, "that flipped the wrong way, 'fecund' is 'defunct'..."

Both of their faces worked away at something till they said at the same time, "No it isn't."

"The ones you helped," said the Muse. "Do you have a private name for them?"

"My students?"

"That's the problem," she said gently. "Clients pay attention."

"Did you have a private name for them?"

"Let's change the subject." She jumped down from her bunk. "I swear the crandolin is not something I created."

"It's too impossible otherwise. But I don't blame you for forgetting," smiled the Omniscient.

"Like I forgot the Bothidae?" she smiled.

"Like your Bothidae, I'm sure, and though I confess I have never kept up with your creations, I would have thought you did. But as I said, you are so fecund, it's no wonder you forget."

The train's brakes squealed.

"You're a fine one to talk about memory," the Muse shot, just as the train drew into a small station.

You deserve that, the Omniscient chided himself. *Would you be here, but for her? Would you be having that unnatural emotion—jollity—despite yourself, but for her? Is it her fault that you're a teensy jealous—yes! You're as stimulating as a breath of stale air.*

She pushed up the window and hallooed the single hawker,

an old woman who was waving a large army-green gherkin. They haggled, the train jerked forward, the old woman scuttled back, and the Muse shut the window with her elbow. Her left hand went to a pocket in her dress. The right held the dripping pickle.

"What did you use for money?"

"Baubles. I traded for this and cash."

The Omniscient smacked his forehead. "Beads and mirrors."

"I couldn't think of anything else," she said defensively.

"I deserve to have my ears boxed," he said. "Truly! Your action was not only capitally efficient, but historically pungent in the extreme."

"It wasn't worth *that* much," she said, but her eyes sparkled.

She held out the pickle. It smelt sour and fresh at the same time. "Want some?"

He shook his head *No* politely, though he wanted to say "Yes," and eat it from her hand.

Krelch went the pickle as she bit off its top. It must have been sourer than a fairytale witch.

The Omniscient exploded. *Those adorable wrinkles!*

He laughed as no man ever had in the Muse's presence — fruitcakily. There was no arrogance in it, no treacly worship, no begging with that taste of bitterness. His laugh was gloriously deep and rich and unseasonable and redolent of fruits that no one in eons had eaten; and a whiff of cat piss. A fruitcake for a goddess. A fruitcake for keeping.

The train sped through lands unknown with neither of them noticing.

She looked over at him on that other bunk, at the swell of his stomach in that relict of a waistcoat. He looked rather like a grape clothed in *Botrytis cinerea*, with vines coming out both ends.

"Would you like to taste my little efforts as a vintner?" she said in an offhand manner, reaching for that case she'd carried on — the one covered in spiderwebs.

The pain of baubles

BY A HUT IN A VILLAGE so small that it is on no map, an old woman digs a hole and curses her luck.

Haste caused me to make this bargain.

What is she to do with a pair of diamond earrings?

The kind of people who would know won't pay me. They'd just murder me.

She'd traded all the cash in her skirt for it, and one excellent pickle.

In her wish not to have the earrings, she wasn't alone.

The Muse had hated them since the first time they had come into demand. She had always dressed professionally; grinned (so to speak) and borne her various costumes, but sometimes she'd almost hated herself for acquiescing. When she'd arrived at the library, she hadn't put them on yet and had even been considering brazening out the session as if she didn't know he wanted them. Their American 1950s clamp style hurt her earlobes something awful. She was sure this was the reason for their popularity.

Good riddance!

* * *

The Muse unbuckled her spiderweb-covered case. She took out a bottle and displayed it to the Omniscient. Their eyes sparkled as she expertly, without looking at it, made the bottle go pop!

Party of three

EKMEL LIES ON A SOLID-GOLD COUCH. The mattress is a soft woman. "Another lips of love," he says, and she places his favourite helva upon his tongue. His strong white teeth crush—

"Oooh, Ahh. What—"

Ekmel's eyes could not pierce the darkness, but he smelled Burhanettin, and that grip!

Burhanettin pulled Ekmel out of bed. A scuffle ensued (a misunderstanding really, Ekmel having tripped over his own feet), ended when Burhanettin rolled Ekmel in a rug.

Burhanettin left Ekmel's house as stealthily as he had entered, yet he could have sung. Everyone's ears were stuffed with cotton.

* * *

The baker's first loaves of the day were perfuming the town when the stork couple looked down upon the man and donkey on their way out of town, not that the storks were interested in these two who were steps from the just-opened town gate.

There! Behind the donkey, a rat skittered. The male stork swooped, plucked the rat before anyone else got it, and dropped it in the nest, where she shredded it for the chick and lost not a drop.

Soon enough, it was day. Burhanettin was a strong walker, and though the bag slung over his back was filled with heavy nougat, it might as well have held whipped eggwhites, such was the burden he felt.

They travelled up and down and up and down till they were so far from town that the sheep spoke a different tongue.

When they reached a stream shaded by willows, Burhanettin halted.

The donkey rubbed the small of his back with her forehead, and reached for the sack of delights.

He turned to her. "Do you love me?"

"Rwlzghooee eeeyytt," said the carpet. Really, it was impossible to make out words. Burhanettin unstrapped the roll from the donkey's back and laid it on the ground, where he restored Ekmel with such a flourish that the round little man rolled into the stream.

"Fputh!" Ekmel spluttered—outraged, terrified, and in his nightgown.

Burhanettin threw Ekmel a robe, slippers and cap. They were Ekmel's.

Ekmel dressed with his back to Burhanettin. He trembled so much that he didn't know what to do, so he kicked the donkey.

Burhanettin kicked him, and then the donkey kicked him into the stream.

"Enough!" cried Burhanettin. "Nough ough," repeated the hills.

He pulled Ekmel onto the bank with one hand as his other hand reached to the donkey's mouth. A crunching sound tickled the hairs in Ekmel's purple ears.

"You will lead me to the Kirand-luhun," said Burhanettin.

Ekmel opened his mouth, and closed it.

"Excellent," said Burhanettin. "Lead on."

Ekmel felt himself being pulled upright, not roughly, but as he imagined Burhanettin pulled toffee.

A bird called from a tree across the stream, so Ekmel picked up the dripping skirts of his robe, and led that way—as good as any.

* * *

Nick joggled to the rhythm of the donkey's steps, the roughness of the trail. He cursed his lack of sight and smell, but he could hear, and finally, communicate — a blessing and another curse.

Before Burhanettin had kidnapped Ekmel, he ransacked Ekmel's storeroom for the stock of Kirand-luhun. All he found was the half-full one-occa sample jar, so he took that and packed his half-full sample jar and Ekmel's into one of Ekmel's baskets.

Nick and Nick felt their proximity, and were overjoyed to almost meet again. They compared notes. What an adventure! What secrets Nick had learnt (especially about nougats), what travelogues they would be able to write, if only they weren't *confined*.

Soon:

"It'll be impossible to scale up the production if we don't get equipment made for each type. Very expensive."

"That goes without speaking, so I trust you noted down all we need to know about timing and all."

"Of course," said the one part of Nick, now very uncertain. "Of course it all depends on you having paid attention to the honeys. Did you?"

"Probably more than you did," said the other part, not being sure at all, "So if the venture fails it'll be all your fault..."

Lost for good

TALON TO TALON, beak to throat, two birds tumble through layers of wind. Teetering above the cinnamon sticks in the nest, the ungainly head and selfish squark of the cinnamologus chick belies the grandeur of its father, the dedication of its parents, though it smells incomparable. Nick is barmy with desire since the hatching of the two eggs. The day that this chick killed its brother (sister?) and ate it was the worst.

This is a terrible time for the parents, too. There are others who smell the chick, who crave the precious red fluff.

The female cinnamologus stands guard on the edge of the nest, her wings outspread, but she's no sunning cormorant. At the base of the tree, a dragonish creature has settled into the sand. Only its eyes are visible, and only when it blinks.

Above her, the male throats victory. Two feathers float gently to earth, and a body plummets. The female swoops to pick up this meal for their voracious chick. It only takes a moment, but so does a gust.

The little gust of wind plucks a piece of fluff.

The mother lands back on the nest to the sound of the chick's hoarse cries. She is tearing the warm heart when the male lands with a cluck. He neatens the nest all round again, and takes out the trash.

* * *

The little gust raced away between thorn trees, over stones that look like tortoises and tortoises that look like stones, its prize held to its belly. When it came to a cleft between two mountains, it rested, rolling just high enough to keep the fluff from touching the earth.

On the two mountains, rival winds huffed. They roared as they raced down to the base of the cleft, where they smothered the gust and fought over the prize.

They attracted other winds, and in the tumult, sand was thrown into the sun's face. And then it was over and the sun looked down upon the familiar earth again, the same mountains, clefts, trees, more or less.

Somewhere here and there, a wisp under sand, a glimmer under a rock, was the bit of fluff, as vulnerable (and lost) as a word once spoken.

Nick had felt the gust rip off a piece of him and saw the gust race away with it till all he could see was pitiless-blue sky. Then he felt that piece of himself being jerked to gossamer shreds.

Until then, he'd spent countless relatively-happy hours pondering:

A) *When is this trip going to end—talk about hallucinogens!* and

B) *If it's not a trip, how much will I be able to take back?*

Now he cowered on the edge of the nest.

How much have I lost? Percy? a hand? my tongue?

Unbound

"I'M DEEPLY SORRY," said the Omniscient. "I've no taste for wines."

"Don't mention it," the Muse replied, too lightly.

"Never could tell a sack from a malmsey. And as for worth?"

"It matters not," she snapped.

"I'm sure that others who are experts, such as your Nick—"

"Gorgonna!"

A sound like a coil of ship's rope hitting a dock made Savva bite his tongue as he tiptoed backwards from the other side of their door. He busied himself over the carpet, picking up sunflower seed shells one by one. He'd learned that often, after that sound, the door to 3C opened dramatically and the woman in red swept down the hall. He didn't know that the sound was of her tossing her head, her hair hitting the wall in a writhe.

The mysteries in 3C

THE DRUNK from another carriage stumbled as far as the open doorway of 3C, reeled in, slapped a dried fish down on the window table, and staggered out into the hall, walking quite straight by the time he got to the far door. Savva, watching by the samovar, had heard the slap, and waited. Sure enough, the fish flew out and landed on the carpet. He scurried over and picked it up before anyone else could grab it.

He flipped the carpet and put fresh newspaper scraps on the toilet hook and refilled the samovar, all in record time, keeping an eye on that doorway.

He was rewarded. She sauntered out past him and left for the space between the cars. He screwed up his courage.

She had just lit up when he arrived. Never had he seen anyone smoke with such hunger. He almost felt embarrassed to approach.

"Could I interest you in —"

"How could you?" Valentin laughed. He must have followed.

Valentin clicked his heels at the woman. They matched in beauty. She reminded Savva of a cover heroine for *Onwards!*

Why did I try? He went back inside. It was busy as a train station in the carriage. The oddest collection of people strolling through. The door to 3C was closed now, though the only working heaters were in the hall. *And look who's here?*

"Galina!"

"Where is she?"

He glanced to his right.

"Is she too good to eat?" She shoved Savva aside and flung open the door to the smoking space.

* * *

The Omniscient took the opportunity to close the door to #3 again, and stretched himself on the top right bunk. The door was a nuisance. They had to keep it open most of the time as per custom (not that an unheated compartment could have affected them), but "We don't want to attract attention to ourselves, do we?" she'd said when they arrived. Quite true.

* * *

Despite his every attempt, she resisted telling him why she chose this train for their singularity. "This *is* a singularity," he kept reminding her. "Our travelling this way, and as the *rubberies.*" She was uncommonly incurious. She made indecent faces when he called people 'rubberies'. Yet for some reason, she had chosen this train, this time in history. He had never invaded history before, thought time travel another of her fripperies. Yet here they were in the twenty-five-years-ago. Twenty-five years till the *poof!* in the library that set the Omniscient on his quest. And did she care? She didn't even know what year it was, it seemed. It was the Omniscient who observed, the Omniscient who yearned to know the how, the why. "The future?" he asked her. "A frippery?"

"You are tiresome," she yawned. "I just thought 'trains', and here we are. How, I tell you, I know not. Can't you just enjoy?"

He'd hoped to educate her in particulars. She was so set in her ways, so intellectually vacuous. She wallowed in her mire of ignorance—even at this unprecedented time when there were mysteries of the universe to solve—when they both had finally met, being to being, and were ensconced in a joint temporary abdication of their respective responsibilities. At this chance of a lifetime, as the rubberies say, when she could avail herself of wisdom instead of slopping out fantasies to men who ... how could she waste her time on those failures?—the Omniscient *was* a trifle disappointed that she was even shallower than he'd thought. Now that she could learn from the world's most experienced teacher, change her ways and serve truth, she had as little interest in learning as she did, facts. Disappointing, but hardly important. *To science!*

The Omniscient fluffed his pillow. She couldn't dampen his thrill of being here disguised as a rubbery. She didn't impede his quest. And as a travelling companion, she was no trouble. He'd seen many companions, not that he had ever *had* one. She had habits that would annoy others, such as reaching into some concealed pocket in that red dress and making that flicking sound—a nervous habit of hers.

She is irrational, of course. About the crandolin, quite unnecessarily she had thrown at him, after only a preliminaria of questions: "Anything you want it to be!" She remembered not one detail, not that it mattered. The Omniscient had supposed she would want to remember her fantasications—after all, they were her work, and as such, he would have expected her to use them again, just as he had always done. When the Omniscient reminded her of a truth that the rubberies put well: *There are only so many stories*, she laughed—cruel Muse. *Why can she invent rubbish (that is loved—oh, perpetually unfair world!) without any effort, whilst I...?*

He turned over on the bunk. *Think not of this, for I am a gyroscope spinning in the joy of discovery, whereas she...* Despite her lack of substantiality, she wasn't easy as rubberies to divine, but the Omniscient detected flecks and blobs in her: remorse and embarrassment. "Quite understandable." Just when her eyes would be their most unfocussed, giving her the appearance of a thinker, she would jump up and escape to the space between the carriages to smoke cigarettes like a common rubbery. She was there now, when she could be... Disappointing, but hardly important. *To science!*

The Omniscient tossed a *Nature* to the bottom bunk, and

opened a *New Scientist*. Just as he found something interesting, he was jarred by a knock on the door. "Come in," he sighed.

Savva entered with a glass of tea on a saucer that held two lumps of sugar. "You must be thirsty, sir." He swept his eyes over the books and magazines.

"Capital," the Omniscient proclaimed. His attention had been broken, but tea was something good to learn. He'd seen it drunk so many times that he knew he should blow on it first. He jumped down from the bunk with a grace that belied his bulk, and pulled out a little roll of suede-textured roubles.

The elaborately dressed tourist in 3C paid Savva just what a Soviet citizen might, if Savva were ever to make a comrade a glass of tea. Worse, the man was not a capitalist but an intellectual parasite. There was no food that Savva could see or smell in the compartment. No walkman, no spare pair of jeans lying to hand. Only a bunk piled with tossed magazines and books ... of the sort that are burned for warmth. Not an Impossible Virgin amongst them, but Savva read 'Science' in the title of some. Savva noticed one magazine cover that showed a woman less sexy than a bust of Lenin. So much for the decadent West!

The foreigner spoke: "You are interested in science?" No sneer! Indeed, the man was more polite than anyone ever had been to Savva, and spoke such beautiful Russian. A worthless curiosity; he didn't even smoke. "Improve the mind, I always say," Savva said.

The tourist chuckled. He gathered up an armful of magazines and presented them to Savva as if they were, say, packs of cigarettes.

Another disappointment in a lifetime of them. Savva went back to his compartment where he threw the magazines on his bunk. He made a glass of tea and locked himself in, to suck noisily through his last sugar cube for comfort and chew salted fish for revulsion.

On consideration, those two passengers in 3C weren't worthless. Galina hated that beautiful woman sleeping in Savva's carriage despite his insistence that a woman with a figure like that could hardly be beautiful, let alone be worth anything in winter. And Valentin had sneered to Galina that the couple in 3C were 'wasted on Savva', that they were smugglers of a superior sort. Valentin was livid with jealousy.

Savva unlocked his door, smiling grimly. He'd have to get Galina into 3C to see for herself, how much Valentin knew about value. *Sweetness almost as good as a sugar cube.*

Then he remembered the magazines. He might as well cut them up for the toilet hook. But they were worthless for that, too. Thin, hard, shiny paper.

He unflapped his fake fur cap and tied it under his chin, narrowed his eyes against wind and snow, and pushed down his window. He tossed the magazines out, to flapping obliteration.

Why backless slippers
are called mules

EKMEL AND THE DONKEY watched Burhanettin pick his teeth clean of every piece of olive and fig. Then unbelievably, he brushed his teeth. He did this after every meal, after each glass of tea, not that his audience complained. Burhanettin's lengthy grooming sessions shortened the time spent journeying each day. He was a man of contradictions, feverish to reach the source of Ekmel's Kirandluhun, yet he could not pass a stream without stopping to wash himself, even his underarms.

Burhanettin dried his beard. "Your eyes are like twin moons that clasp the sun in their loins," he sang, and noticed his companions.

"Lead, fool." He pointed a staff at Ekmel that he'd made some days before by tearing a tree apart. "You and your shorter route."

Ekmel swallowed and stumbled forward. There were hours of daylight left. He narrowed his eyes at the path ahead. It was so steep that he'd slip out backwards from his slippers and tread on pointed stones, as he had so many times that he'd tried walking up backwards, till poked in the belly.

Burhanettin reached into his bag for a piece of nougat that he held out for the donkey, but Burhanettin's eyes were on Ekmel's back, so the donkey hesitated. Burhanettin dropped the nougat and strode away.

The donkey's ears sagged. She picked up the nougat with her lips and cantered after Burhanettin, but she didn't crunch the sweet. She held it in her cheek, where it degraded to base honey and bitter memory.

You are not alone

NICK MOURNED the loss of part of him from the cinnamologus' nest till the chick was as tall as its parents, when another piece of fluff went the way of the first, torn to insignificant shreds and scattered in the glitter of a desert's dust.

He first reaction was to panic—an unsatisfying emotion in his static state. So he obsessed upon his loss through the most delicious time of the chick's life, but one day when the cries it made to satisfy its appetite vibrated with the monotony of a religious chant, he experienced a—revelation? Whatever, the word 'converge' popped into his mind, and then that hackneyed: 'You are not alone.'

"Converge!" he repeated. "I am not alone."

Others would have been comforted by the 'not alone' thing, but Nick felt it in a higher sense. "I'm not just here."

The male cinnamologus continued tucking Nick neatly amongst the cinnamon sticks while the mother picked apart an eagle for their babe.

Nick tried to communicate in the only way he could, feeling that there might be other parts of him stuck on other nests. The attempt reminded him of the time when he was seven and stuck his hand up his sleeve, trying with all his seven-year-old powers to make an egg materialise.

He communicated and communicated and communicated, till he was sick of the attempt. But what else was there to do?

And one day he knew: *There are parts of me scattered in many—no, several places—and ... times.*

And then, one day, Nick besmirching the Bladder-pipe knew it too.

And Nick as the blemish on Galina's face.

And both parts of Nick in the side-by-side pots—they were shaken at first, having thought that they were the only two parts of Nick, easily merged *if Burhanettin would only get on with it.*

Then Nick on the nest felt as hard as he could, "Converge!"— and he pulled. That part assumed that it was the real Nick, and the other parts just accessories to the fact. But each other part must have felt that he was the real Nick, and certainly the brains.

Each part pulled till one day, something amazing happened. None of them were closer to the others, but they each knew where the others were.

"Bugger!" said Nick on the cinnamologus' nest. "Whatever made me suck that bloody book?"

A blood-filled tick crawled up to him and over his fluffiness to burrow itself in his protective midst and digest its meal without being swallowed by a cinnamologus. Such was his preoccupation with converging (all mixed up in his mind with returning to what he still called *real life*) that Nick didn't even smell the fragrant morsel. So many changes, so fast. Only recently he had nearly gone mad, craving those little blood puddings.

Revelation

"Eureka!" shouted the Omniscient.

Refreshed by the glass of tea brought by that curious little science-loving train attendant with the turned-up nose to whom the Omniscient had given an armloadful of magazines (that Savva had tossed out into the vast, incurious, snow-bloated night), the Omniscient set to work again to discover the Why and Wherefore of the Disappearance. Perhaps it was the mind-stimulating properties of tea, or Chance, or Fate, but in the middle of the next magazine he picked up from his pile, dated only one week later than the latest in that armloadful (but about a quarter century earlier than the present in this train) "Eureka," exclaimed the Omniscient, again.

"How unoriginal," remarked the Muse, who had just returned, smelling of snow-laden air and tobacco.

"Listen to this." The Omniscient's eyes were shining but he looked only at the magazine. He cleared his throat and stood, but fell heavily back on his bed when he unbalanced himself, brandishing his right arm Socrates-style.

" 'The string theory landscape is populated'," he read and paused to look at the Muse significantly.

She folded her hands in her lap, composed her face, and prepared to count unicorns in an attempt to stay awake.

"This will not be drearisome," the Omniscient said.

"Promise?"

"Populated, the string theory that is, it says here," he said, tapping the magazine as if it were the Stone of Qanxor, " 'by the set of all possible histories. Rather than a branching set of individual universes, every possible version of a single universe exists simultaneously in a state of quantum superposition.' "

He stopped and gazed at the Muse with rapture. "The climax is coming," he said, and dropped his eyes to the page.

" 'When you choose to make a measurement, you select from this landscape a subset of histories that share the specific features measured.' "

He stopped reading. For a while, the only talk that could be heard in 3C was the chatty song of the train.

She broke in. "Is that yours?"

"It's the Phenomenon."

Kulakity lak—

"You know. The library. The Disappearance!"

"Um," she said. "That. But what does that—"

"All good things..." he said, putting a finger to his lips.

She pursed hers, but he was already reading aloud.

" 'The history of the universe'." He looked up, lifted a finger in the declamatory stance, and lost his place.

" 'The history' "

She stood and reached into her pocket.

"Please wait," he said. " 'the universe, for *you*, the observer' it says here, and that means you, as you saw it. Sit, please."

"How ripping," she said, but she sat.

" 'is derived from that subset of histories.' "

"No wonder," she murmured.

"Without interruption," he said, "hark: 'The history of the universe, for you the observer, is derived from that subset of histories.' "

"*What* subset?"

The Omniscient muttered something that sounded like *What can one expect?* He felt more exasperated than he had with his dullest writer. "Don't you want to save your wasted mind?"

The muse's hair writhed. "You mean put to sleep. No wonder so many left you."

"I say again, I did not write this, but truth is beauty. You are too truth-deprived to—"

"There's no beauty in the obtuse."

"This is not obtuse!"

"Then what does it mean?"

"What it says here: 'In other words, you choose your past.' "

"Then why didn't you just *say* it?"

The Omniscient smiled perseveringly. "I was getting there."

The Muse smiled back. "Did you, Knower of All, fathom any of that opaquity before that four-word statement, 'You choose your past'?"

"Of course," sputtered the Omniscient, like a kettle boiled almost dry. He couldn't remember, but her snide inference could have been correct.

"And this *revelation*." The Muse's tone was aggressively interrogative. "You choose your past. You believe it?"

The Omniscient's arms drooped to rest on his skinny thighs.

"You make your own history," said the Muse gently. "That's one of mine. Why didn't you ask, if you wanted me to tell you a story?"

The Omniscient had never before been subjected to her charm. He was so flustered that he had no reply. Instead, he fondled the top button of his waistcoat, harrumphed, and dropping his gaze to the magazine, read the article verrrrry carefully once again.

It gave him so much of the strength he needed that he guffawed. *Who would have imagined? Me, falling under her spell.*

He laid the *New Scientist* on the window table. "I know it has not been your experience," he said in his most eminently reasonable tone. "But try to expand your mind."

"Ex—" she exploded. "Thou fow—"

But the Omniscient was ready for emotional ballyhoo. He

tapped the magazine. "Think like a physicist!"

"A phys—"

The Omniscient's eyes sparkled. "Only known as the greatest since Newton."

The Muse's eyes almost leapt from their sockets. *The old man is serious.* She suppressed a smile and put on a face that she'd never worn: *Please, tell me more.* Behind that mask she was more dismayed than she cared to think possible. The Omniscient was overly neat and no oenologist, but in the throes of excitement, not unattractive. But, *to believe in physicists!*

Biliousness will out

OUT OF THE BLACK NIGHT, another h'mph erupted from the Omniscient's bunk, regular as hiccups.

The Muse sat up violently. "Out with it."

"With what?"

"If you've got a complaint, make it or get off this train and go back to your cave or wherever you normally groan."

"I didn't know it showed."

"Only as bright as the sun."

"As your smile," quipped the Omniscient in embarrassment.

"I get that from *them*." Now she sounded hurt.

The last thing he wanted to do was talk. He was frightened of what he'd say.

"You hold something against me," she said. "Don't you?"

"How can you tell?"

"My supernatural senses."

"I should have known." *I wish I had them.*

"I was joking, you idiot. You're as subtle as a foghorn. You were saying?"

He sighed, but was cut off by "Enough."

"I'm waiting patiently," she said after he'd barely taken breath.

"I was thinking," he said.

"That can be dangerous," she laughed.

"Of a paranoid schizophrenic psychopath I met once."

She scraped a match against the wall and for a moment her

face was lit, cleaned of expression.

"You might remember him," said the Omniscient. "It was some time ago, before such diagnoses. He heard a voice."

"Let me count the cases. What does that have to do with me?"

"It told him to kill his son."

"So you think I whispered in his ear? Why do you care?"

"I'm not saying you did anything, or that I care. But don't you remember what happened next?"

"Let me see. The father slew the son by having him ground between two stones, and was in turn scalded to death by his wife the son's mother and lover, who took over the kingdom and lived extravagantly ever after. Is that the one? Really, there are so many, none of which add up to anything with me. Or do you think I moonlight as an accessory to murder?"

"Of course not. But you don't remember the one to which I refer?"

"No, oh vague one. Humanity is a nutcake that I've never cared to plumb."

"Nor the ram that was murdered instead?"

"Not a chicken? It's usually a chicken. Are you *trying* to exasperate me? Now you're saying the murderer didn't murder, but you blame me for his insanity. You've picked up indigestion. Sleep it off."

"You don't remember your role? She really doesn't remember."

"She is *here* and *that* is rude. She didn't have a *role*, you ... you false *accuser*."

He couldn't see her hair but could hear it slither, which only inflamed him more.

"You falsifier! You can't claim that you didn't dictate that best-seller."

Their breath came in gasps. His. Hers. Little laboured gulps.

"That," she said. "I didn't know it would be. A moment's diversion."

"Did you have to make him a hero?"

115

"I must remind you that he was centuries before Freud. I just gave personality to the voice. It was genre of the time. How did I know he would be a hero, and that book would be a hit? Neither of us controls the readers, do we?"

"So you knew Freud?" he sneered.

"Never had the pleasure. You're just jealous."

"No I'm not."

He dug his fingers into his stomach till he felt physical pain. She shut her eyes so hard, blackness turned into rainbows that burst into swirling shards.

"That book," she said quietly. "I never got a thanks, not from any of the writers."

"Good," he said before he could stop himself.

"If it'll make you feel better," she said as if she never heard him, "I never got a thanks from any of the authors of my top three books. They not only used me, but said that someone else dictated the works."

His bunk creaked as he shifted, making more noise than just turning over would. "I am flooded with regret," he said. "I overflow."

"Don't be."

He could hear a sad smile in her voice, or maybe he just wanted to. What he was sure of was the sound of his heart, cracking.

Faldarolo and the shepherd

A STONE SHELTER, a sheep's head, and a lively fire of pine cones dribbled with rosemary-scented sheep's fat. What more could Faldarolo wish for?

Sleet swirls into the shelter's open side. Visibility is so poor that it would be impossible now for the shepherd to hail Faldarolo, as he had only two hours ago. Faldarolo was touched by the generosity of the old man who offered to trade shelter and a sheep's head for a concert.

The shepherd sticks his knife into the sheep, then slings it off the fire, onto its fresh skin. He cuts off the head and motions to Faldarolo. "And that ewe. It was her second lamb, see, and guess what it weighed? Young man, you would never know..."

Faldarolo motions his thanks and his blessings upon his host, but does not stop the flow of the story. He eats without seeing his food. He tears small pieces off and chews them slowly, keeping his eyes on the old man's mouth as any polite guest does. Often Faldarolo stops eating to laugh and smile and sigh and shake his head at the demands of the story.

"And that other ewe, the one I was telling you about..."

He eats the second eye, and gnaws the skull clean. Still, he is starving, but a prized titbit remains to be delved. He taps open the skull with a stone, all by feel. His host's eyes are livelier than the fire.

The delicious creamy brain, he pulverizes. He takes the blue velvet cloak off the bladder-pipe and lays her naked in his lap. And there he massages the brain into her pipes and her bladder till the wood is shiny and dark, and the bladder is supple and glowing pale cream (and bright blemish red, not that he looks).

His fingers touch her lovingly. He cannot stop his body from swaying as he rubs the unguent into her skin, till *Do not close your eyes!* Without looking at the bladder-pipe, he cloaks her again and lays her in his lap. His stomach makes a rude noise: *More!*

No food has passed the shepherd's lips. His jaws are too busy otherwise.

He had lied to Faldarolo, of necessity. Trapping an audience had been a tricky business at the best of times, but on this frigid night, a young strong wanderer was nothing less than two birds in one. Not only could the guest serve as an audience, but, come dawn, as a helpmate with the wayward sheep. The shepherd had endless fascinating tales to tell, all about the ways of sheep...

* * *

Sharp dawn outlines the straightness of the shepherd's back. "You wouldn't like to guess the weight of that ram, would you?"

Faldarolo shakes his head.

The old man laughs, as crackly as the fire had been. "Wise choice, young man. When you know nothing, say nothing. But you'll know soon enough, thank fate—"

A lamb wanders into the shelter. "Where's your mother?" asks the shepherd. The lamb jumps backwards, and runs out as if it saw its fate. The shepherd jumps up and follows.

Faldarolo stands, trips on his robe. A horrible, muffled sound reaches his ears. The blue velvet cloak writhes on the piled-up coals. The bladder-pipe? Slipping off the cloak.

Faldarolo leaps over the fire. He snatches up the bladder-pipe—cheh, she was so close to being burnt alive that Faldarolo's knees shake.

A stick clatters against a stone, and here's the shepherd again. "What's keeping you?" The old man starts out upslope. "Did I tell you about the time when..."

Faldarolo follows the shepherd.

He doesn't know how, without interrupting, to begin his concert. He cannot think. He cannot see the sharp stones before his feet as clearly as he sees what could have been: the bladder-pipe falling into the fire's mouth. He cannot hear his host's never-ending story as well as he hears his imagination: the cry of the burning bladder-pipe.

* * *

"And the weight of that ram from her." The shepherd pulls himself up a boulder. "What do you think... Hiya! Where are you?"

Faldarolo's arms are locked around the bladder-pipe, held safe.

"Drop that useless—"

The shepherd brandishes his crook at the beloved.

Faldarolo steps back, closes his eyes, and puts the bladder-pipe to his lips. Finally, he is business-like. The concert is now, whether the shepherd listens or no.

He blows with a will. He hopes (may his fault be forgotten) that the bladder-pipe is at her worst. He hopes she screeches to make all the sheep on the mountain run like water down its side, and the shepherd, cursing, after them.

"What! You—take that plaything out of your mouth and get to work. There's sheep to lead, you clod!"

The shepherd's curse fills Faldarolo's ears so that he cannot hear the bladder-pipe. He adjusts his lips.

Hhhhh she says—a startling, pitiful *hhhh* no louder than a snowfall.

"Obey me, you pile of sheep shit."

Where is her temper—those sarcastic, skin-stripping *scracks* that had forced Faldarolo to live as a vagabond? His eyes pop open as he blows, looking down. *Hhhhhh.* Her bladder is as wrinkled and flat as a crone's breast.

Faldarolo turns, just in time. A rock hits the back of his head. The old man screeches so shrilly that the sheep, fat with summer

119

grass but stupid as stones, run—not in a herd but in a burst, catching their legs in rocks, forgetting their lambs, jumping like goats onto outcrops.

Faldarolo runs, too—faster and more carefully than ever he thought he could. Love and urgency guide his steps. The bladder-pipe nestles against his chest hair, clamped in position by his right arm over his robe.

By the time he gets to the bottom of the mountain, he and the bladder-pipe are slippery with sweat scented with sheep's brains.

Sacre something-or-other

"MISTRESS!" burst the Omniscient as the New Dawn broke through the window and threw itself at the Muse, coating her face and figure with: *Sacre memoire!*

That hair, wild and unbiddable. That nose. Those chests. He coughed and averted his eyes. Ever since he'd met her in the library in what already seemed like another's life, she'd reminded him of *someone.*

She stubbed her cigarette out on the wall, and raised an eyebrow.

"You know of," began the Omniscient (trying to keep a bygone irritation out of his voice) "that ship you call the Flying Dutchman, which is resting at a depth of ... uh..." He tugged helplessly at his moustache.

"No matter," he finally said, airily waving a hand. "You know. As you also must, the latitude and..." *Memory, why do you forsake me so?*

Not that the ship's position mattered anymore. *Or ever had!*

That was my past life. Forever work. Why did I never question Why? My life. What an ending. He shook his head.

How did I not calculate? How many times when I got to the thrilling climax, did my author reject me, and call upon —

She smiled, and the sun broke through the window, killing New Dawn and tossing sparkle into her eyes. The Omniscient's mouth opened. He remembered sun tossing seaspray on —

That wooden figurehead of Mistress Fokke had inspired him ever since she rode her first sea. He'd never understood the vast incuriosity of his writers—their wish for her to be lost forever, their need to deceive. Why did they not see what he saw in her? Why did they reject his facts and leave her unsalvaged till she was a wormridden mockery of magnificence? Why did they *want* her to be another Tragic Lost, travelling forever in a fog of mystery, a mistress damned by association? He'd loved her, but he, only the Omniscient, could not save her. Only the rubberies could do that. He could not *make* history.

The sun ran its fingers through the Muse's hair.

You make your History!

His right hand flew to his chest where he felt something that he'd dictated so many times—a catch in his breath. 'Catch' was such a weak description for the grab at his throat from out of nowhere—terrifying and thrilling.

The Muse stared, bemused. Then, he wobbled, higher than safe for a human of that age and portliness (though he called them *rubberies*, rubberies don't bounce, and she'd learnt, after catching her finger in the door, that this form of theirs could be *hurt*) and his mouth closed and opened again ... and closed, his eyes caressing with the greatest delicacy: the lines of her face.

And she felt something also. Something ... what?

She dropped her eyes and adjusted the neckline of her dress. She climbed off her bunk.

"Would you like me to get you a cup of tea?" she said.

Some lordes wyll soone be pleased & some wyll not, as they be of complexion.

—Wynkyn de Worde,
The Boke of Keruynge

Failure is not an option

THE GREAT TĪMŪRSAÇI was not as creative in his punishments as his late uncle, once a Great but since his death, remembered as Tīmūr of a Thousand Pieces—but what the present Great Tīmūrsaçi lacked in creativity, he gained in the swiftness of his justice.

Munifer's imagination took him to the feet of the Great Tīmūrsaçi, where he had just dropped after presenting the new moustache made out of who-knows-what?

"Tap," would go the terrible staff upon his shoulder, and the chief eunuch would toss the first cord around him, and in the gulp of a throat, Munifer would be swaddled in ropes in front of His Greatness, who would rise and proceed, with Munifer carried like a baby, and the court following noisy as birds at dawn—to the Bridge of Dispatch and Divorce where Munifer would be tossed into the Pond of Sighs to the consternation of the assembled.

Would he be torn apart by Tīmūrsaçi's crocodiles, or taken down whole by one? Men would tear their beards and cry out in grief when the pond stilled. Much was wagered at these games.

With all his heart, Munifer wanted to die an old man, spending his seed in the warm earth of a woman.

So he smothered his imagination and steeled himself to become a hunter—a difficult change of role for someone who had only ever gathered. The village-of-no-name had been so honoured by the Great Tīmūrsaçi's mother, that they had no choice. They rendered unto Munifer, for the Great Tīmūrsaçi, and that was all. But now cruel life had intervened, and he could hardly go to Timūrsaçi's mother and ask her bestow the honour on another village, since her rage at her honoured village thwarting her could entangle him. And of course, this virgin hair was not something that you could find by looking any more than you could find that precious mushroom that grows under the ground. No, you had to sniff around their fathers, and ask without asking. And how could he obtain it? Money would taint it.

Hunt, Munifer! he told himself *and your quarry will reveal itself. You are a man who has been blessed, and this is a trial. A trial, not a sentence. Remember that.*

He set off on his hunt, a handsome, well-dressed, wily man. A smooth man such as you would expect, since his very smoothness lent its grace to the length of the moustache that was without precedent or equal—the moustache that gave the Great Timūrsaçi his saçiness.

A week passed while Munifer hunted.

Another week.

Another.

Another!

He forgot to bathe. His underarms became rank. His long black eyelashes turned white and his handsome head of coal-black hair grew shaggy and long and grey and when he saw a man who must have a daughter, his upper lip curled back and his teeth gleamed long and yellow, which was no help at all in his wily smoothness.

On the fourth week of his hunt in a tavern packed with foreigners he heard of a certain Mulliana, a virgin with a voice of gold (it was said, which didn't interest him), the looks of the sun (not that he cared), and hair so black and long and sinuous that it was said to coil around her at night and protect her from all harm.

She lived in a tower (they said) where her father had put her for safe keeping when she was still a child. There she had grown to a maidenhood so pure that no man had ever seen her, including her own father. Munifer overheard this from three earnest princes on a Quest. They had come from afar, as she was said to be a virgin without peer, for her skill at rugmaking would pay for all the years she lived, once her petals had fallen. They had apparently set out to woo and win her, *or* (later in the evening, with earnestness having slipped to the floor) *just win her* (brotherly sniggering) *by the book of Quest, or the hook of a shepherd, stilts and rope, or by the crook of a forefinger to the father, if she cannot truly be stolen, for what could he want but the highest price?*

Munifer was elated, and when they made their way out of the tavern, a serpent player could have followed them, braying his instrument at full obnoxiousness, and they never would have noticed. They fell in a heap in a field by the road, and woke when the sun was high—with sore heads but brotherly, youthful jest, and great energy to be on their way. He followed them, a tail that they never noticed, so loudly did they travel. They talked in yells, so the tales of their exploits were not only amusing, but wonderful for this lonely hunter who could otherwise be frightened in the strange wilds. They traversed mountains, a desert, and through the Cave of Sorrows. He followed the three princes there, too, having first held back. But that test they had spoken of so much in the days before must have been a doddle to them. When their shouts were no longer in the cave, but on the other side of the mountain, he just walked through with the most unpleasant part of his sojourn being: a stubbed toe.

Onward walked Munifer, behind the three princes. At night he slept as close as he could without making them look up from their fire with a "Hark!", and the inevitable raised swords.

Week after week they progressed, and amazed Munifer with their Quest. The further they walked, the more exploits they must have performed (Munifer safely behind them and ready to run the way he'd come), yet they carried on and on. At the site of each exploit passed, Munifer paused to pay respects.

That rock. No gold ring that could not be pulled from it, jutted out.

That river. They must have tamed it. Munifer had no trouble crossing the timid flow.

Etc.

One night as the princes rubbed their muscles, Munifer overheard:

"We draw near, brothers."

"A truer word was ne'er said."

"Near we draw, I trow."

"Brothers?"

"I think that I shall never see—"

"Fie, brother! Thoughts are virgins to the Evil Eye."

Munifer drew as near as he dared, yet he could not distinguish one prince's voice from another.

"I fear that when we come out of the Desert of No Return, I shall not be the prince I am."

"Neither I."

"Nor so."

"So we are three. We will have conquested," said one. "And then it is only a matter of fighting each other, for you, or you, or myself, to win the Singing Flower of Virtuous Usefulness, Mulliana."

"Truer words hath never been."

"Truly."

"Brothers!"

They rose—and made lustrous black by the moonless night and the fire that leapt between them, they noisily crossed their blades.

"All to the fore!"

"Though it be seven years more!"

"And possibly, a score," said the one who might have been the one who had earlier expressed self-doubt.

"Seven?" mouthed Munifer.

He slithered away in such sloppy haste that the next morning when the princes woke refreshed, the track that his body and his limbs made, put the end to the princes' Quest.

Each would have liked to have said that he would leave the Singing Flower to his brothers, and walked away, but each did not. For as each woke and went behind a bush to relieve himself—he saw, as he squatted, the spoor of a dragon that must have been watching them; and each ran as fast and silently and alone as he could, away from the dragon's Quest (and secretly hoping that, of the three brothers, his own spoor was the weakest).

* * *

The place where Munifer severed his tie to the princes was, he estimated, three months' journey from the Great Tīmūrsaçi's palace. Added to the time it would take him to create the moustache, Munifer had no choice.

In the first town he reached, he bought—yes, he was forced to purchase—a bag of virgin hair in the Quarter of Ill Repute.

Burden borne by a spy

HE BLAMED IT ON LOVE.

Mistress!

Master!

Coo coo coo

Sure, he'd seen what love did, and always dictated its illogicalities with the superior non-judgmentalism of the objective observer. Many of his writers had taken this as a license to be cruel—not that this bothered him *then*, before he was love's victim.

Twilight. She was lying on her top bunk making that flicking sound. Flick. Flick flick flick. Flick.

"Miss all those men?" he asked casually.

The flicking got louder. "I already *told* you."

"Don't you miss that life?"

"Gorgonna, no."

"I don't want to pry," he said, "but how many were there?"

"You should be able to guess."

"Millions?"

"I never counted."

"Did any of them treat you with as much respect as I?"

"They worshipped me."

"You, or—"

"Me!" she screeched, but she broke into a jagged sobbing that turned into hiccups.

"Mistress," he crooned.

"Master."

Verily, she *said* the right thing with its concomitant exclamation mark, but he'd had eons of being an observer. Her non-enthusiasm was too eloquent for words. She'd cut off his flow with a guillotine.

And now, clutching a pack of cigarettes, she left. She closed the door behind her as if she cared for his privacy.

He suspected, you see.

All those trips to that smoking section. She wasn't law abiding. Sometimes he couldn't smell the fragrance of that nice young man's wonderful tea because of the atmosphere in 3C—tobaccan smog. *There must be another reason.*

Motivation?

It was a curious fact that, since he'd taken on human form, he had gained emotional depth, and also lost. Now, in a cruel twist of history (*of my own making*) the Omniscient had to guess her motivations, and that guessing dug depth into him with a wooden spoon. *My companion for eternity? Pshaw!*

Love hurts.

Act like a man.

* * *

Alone in the cacophonic, wind-whipped smoking section between the carriages, she pocketed the cigarettes and reached into another pocket in her red dress and made that flicking sound (how many pockets does that dress have? None of them show and the dress swirls as much as a romance). She dropped her arms to her sides and the dress slid off to pool like blood around her feet. Her thigh-high red rubber boots unlaced themselves down to her alabaster toes. She kicked the costume to some corner that the Omniscient would have noticed in the old days, but couldn't see now. Besides, he had to concentrate on her (yes, there he was, like a common rubbery, furtively watching through a hole in the window's muck).

Her arms rose and a pure white Junoesque gown fell upon her, partly covering her perfect chests. She girded her waist; and silently, stealthily, infinitely treacherously, she vanished.

Retired, my foot!

If only the Omniscient could have followed, but the body he was dwelling in had trapped him, or rather, the History he had made (*and*, he thought bitterly, *she*).

Where has she gone? Who is she seeing? Why does she need them? And how does she return?

For return she surely had. This was a habit of hers that she had not kicked. *That sneak. That perjurer! She's not worth me saving.*

Truth hurts.

Now I know why spies and death go together.

"Watching 'em isn't a touch on smelling 'em."

"Eh?" The Omniscient jumped back.

An old man shuffled between the Omniscient and the door, and uncricked himself vertebra by cracking vertebra. He rubbed at a lower place on the glass and peered, but as the Omniscient could have told him, there was no one there.

Eventually, "Ahh," he said. He released his grip and subsided. "I also like to wait here. Why freeze?" Crisply, he saluted. "Your watch, comrade."

The Omniscient nodded. *What is he talking about?* Not that it mattered, for this was the second friendly rubbery he'd met. This warmth was just what he needed. The Omniscient's eyes dropped to his companion's chest: the fabric of the coat (cardboard and whiskers?) and its repairs; the stiff rows of faded ribbons and grey-faced medals. "Yes indeed, comrade," he agreed, to what, he wasn't sure, but he smiled expansively and was suddenly so happy that he began (not that he noticed) to pet his own comfortable, cuddly round stomach covered by that gorgeous paisley waistcoat.

His new friend noticed. His eyes jumped to the waistcoat—its buttons, its embroidered tear drops—as warming as a song, against winter. His jaw jutted out.

"It's an unregulated space. You can't stop anyone smoking

there, and if you report me for innocently smelling them, I'll report you for harassing a hero of the State." He raised a knotted fist to the Omniscient's chin. "Comrade!"

Manifesto delivered, he fled, fast as his bowlegs could scurry.

Blue velvet

UNNATURAL, a silenced bladder-pipe. The fall into the fire hadn't burnt her alive. Faldarolo plucked her from the lips of that disaster—but in the moment that she slipped from the cloak (which was itself consumed by fire) sparks spattered her skin (so richly massaged with sheep's brain). Each tiny spark ate its banquet, and expired.

To look at her, you'd never know that she was injured. Disfigured, yes. The red blotch besmirched her bold as ever. You couldn't see the holes, but who sees stars in the sky in day? Faldarolo's fingertips felt her voice fall through the holes to be lost as surely as water through a colander.

The musician hid in a cave for a day and a night. He mourned, tore fistfuls of hair, rent his robe, and emerged at last with so much confidence that he looked like a fakir: She was not dead. There were masters skilled in science who could restore the bladder-pipe to health. Faldarolo swallowed the truth, his bitter feast: he was now and until he could restore her, a bladder-pipe player with a silent bladder-pipe. How he would pay, he knew not. He'd never been anything but a bladder-pipe player, and this bladder-pipe had been given to him by his father (a man who had skill, but no sensitivity). Faldarolo walked out of the cave a determined man. If he had to be a slave to some master with a whip, he didn't care. He would offer himself.

In the meantime, however, he, the slave of the bladder-pipe, set out with a goal if not a plan. He made his way down to the path and walked till the path became a road. And there he sat cross-legged, the naked bladder-pipe on his lap, shrouded as well as he could manage with his hands. A dried-fruit merchant passed, dropping onto Faldarolo from each of his donkeys, a little dust. A shepherd passed with a flock of goats, their great udders swathed by kerchiefs knotted on the goats' backs. Many other people and animals passed, and though some glanced at him curiously, none stopped. He mightn't have seen any of them, such was his disregard. Eggs, he didn't seem to notice. A heaped donkeyload of freshly cut chickpeas. Feasts passed, and he, to whom one dried apricot would have been a banquet, looked past all of them as if he expected someone (perhaps dropped from the sky in a bubble).

Finally, his eyes lit with an unholy-man glow. Up he jumped, ran into the road, and begged, with preliminaries so respectful, to reveal them would be indecent: "blue velvet—only an arşin-length".

The cloth merchant was so intrigued by this starved beggar with the bladder-pipe (yes, the merchant saw the bladder-pipe, and the way Faldarolo tried to shield it) that he ordered his donkeys led off the path and hobbled, and camp to be made for the night. He promised to give Faldarolo all the cloth he needed on condition that Faldarolo tell him why.

* * *

Faldarolo had never eaten so well. "Another fig?" urged the merchant.

"Thank you, no." Faldarolo itched to hear what the merchant wanted of him. He had asked a number of times but been told to go on with his story, as that was "payment enough". He knew from experience that it could never be. He was a musician, not a story-teller.

"And now I am not a musician," he insisted yet again. He needed to feel the pain from that piercing truth the better to keep his resolution strong. *If only that fire had burnt holes in* my *skin*

135

rather than hers. "I would die a thousand deaths rather than—"

"And so you shall," the merchant laughed indulgently, "where I'm sure to meet you again."

Faldarolo dropped his eyes. Under the square of velvet on his lap lay the bladder-pipe. As soon as they were alone, Faldarolo would sew her cloak. He was eager to leave the merchant, who had been so kind that Faldarolo expected the punishment any moment.

* * *

The cloth merchant acted as calm as he could manage. He had never believed in Fate until now. What else could explain this meeting—this inspiration?

He dipped his fingers into the dish of rosewater wielded by his servant. "Make up a bed beside me," he ordered, then turned to Faldarolo.

"Your Effusionness," he said (a term known to expert appreciators of bladder-pipe music) ...

Cover story

"TEA, UNCLE?"

Savva entered 3C with a steaming glass and a smoothed issue of *Truth*. The cover story, "Women hide their wisdom beneath stupidity" drew a grim smile from the Omniscient, who pointed to it. "What do you think of this, young man?"

Savva closed the door and made himself comfortable. They'd become great friends, not that Savva would tell anyone, even Galina, about this camaraderie with someone who was an intellectual parasite, harmless but still a parasite. Who else had such a fine waistcoat and a sunflower-yellow trunk? Savva had had a difficult time hiding the yellow trunk and didn't know what he could do with it, but it was generous of the old man to give it to him once it was empty. Uncle, as the old man insisted Savva call him, had previously given Savva all the contents of the trunk once he'd read it all. Who but an intellectual parasite would travel with a trunk filled solely with stuff to read? Still, the parasite treated Savva with unbelievable respect, and it was a novel experience to be considered an intellectual. It felt good, too, to be able to share the joys of *Truth* with someone, and to discuss its depth. It had never occurred to Savva what difficulties passengers have keeping up with news and stimulating their minds till he caught the old man borrowing those little squares of *Truth* hung in the toilet. It particularly delighted Savva that of all the sections in that newspaper to choose from, they both enjoyed the same section the most: *Anomalous phenomena*.

"If not for this," Uncle had told him, "my studies in science, law and nature would have stagnated."

"Enquire Within" has an answer for every question you put to it.

—*Enquire Within Upon Everything*

Questions to a man of experience

"So, YOUNG MAN," said the Omniscient, "you're experienced in the ways of women. Do you think, as this cover story says, that they hide their wisdom beneath stupidity?"

"It's important enough an issue that it takes a second reading," said Savva, flattered and embarrassed at the same time. He often skipped the first page in his eagerness to read his favourite section, and once having turned to it, never got around to reading much else.

Savva stretched out on the opposite bunk, a model listener.

The Omniscient cleared his throat, utterly delighted.

"Women hide their wisdom beneath stupidity. That's the title, remember. 'First off', it says, and I'm just clarifying the voice here, 'the above statement'—meaning that headline, you see—Yes? Yes. 'The above statement used for identifying the nature of a problem is more complex than it seems. It requires a detailed analysis on the part of a full-fledged intellect, which simply cannot exist without examining something carefully and in detail so as to identify its causes, key factors etc. In other words, "pure reason" is prone to finding a problem in all places so that the former'—The former hmm," said the Omniscient.

"The former is irrelevant," he declared after moving the paper towards him and away. "As this says, 'Pure reason dah dum deed dum may be properly analyzed. As a result, it is also inclined to call into question all kinds of postulates including the above one ("all the females are stupid"), which is seen by many as axiomatic and self-evident.' "

Savva sat up. Otherwise he would not have been able to stay awake. He nodded sagely, thinking that in any worthwhile revolution, words like aksiomatic would be purged.

" 'First'," read the Omniscient, poising a finger in the air exactly as he'd seen Aristotle do, " 'what is a "female?" ' "

Savva only just suppressed a giggle. He twisted his lips into a tight frown.

" 'Second'," continued the Omniscient, mightily encouraged by Savva's knitted brows. " 'How can we define the concept of "stupidity?" Third, does such a high degree of generalization really apply in this case, at least theoretically?' "

Savva caught a yawn, turning it into the opportunity to raise his hand. "When you said 'stupidity', that was of course—"

"Of course." The Omniscient rubbed his waistcoat, making the paisley pattern of gold-embroidered bent-necked teardrops shimmy. "You are so perspicacious. So young, yet your mind is tuned to the nuances of all these nested quotes." And he continued.

Nested quotes. Savva balanced his chin in his hands just before his heavily pensive-looking eyes beheld Uncle turn into a matrioshka of quotation marks. Gold double-quotation marks curling around single quotation marks—then double to single, each enclosing a shiny black, individually carved group of letters, till the eye would never be able to find nor the mind understand ... 'what is "female" ' indeed! And in the pit of the nest, a tiny perfect question mark turns, every curve exposing a new facet of allure. On its top is perched at a rakish angle, a white cloth hat, for what first looked to be a question mark, is infinitely curved Galina. She is holding a knife to a potato, the peel dangling to her suckling toes. Importunate whistles and comments fall upon her, as men climb down the faces of every building in sight and fill the streets, each man running to join the stream of men, each intending to sweep all others away and lock this Woman of women into his arms to, first ravish her lips with kiss—

"And so, you see, young man—" Savva shook his head clear, hoping he hadn't snored. All that inked paper that Uncle had found so useful for his mind, was just the printed matter that Savva cut up into squares.

The stuff that this professor type loved so much that he couldn't see its sleep-inducing properties, was just the stuff that had always sent Savva directly to the Anomalous page, for actual reading matter. He didn't know what anomalous meant, but the articles there didn't waffle and ask questions. They were news, so they stuck to the facts. *Beheaded human body can stay alive and kicking! A mushroom collector came across an explosive device in a forest. The device went off in his hands. As a result, his head was blown to shreds. The headless body of the man kept walking some two hundred metres and crossed a narrow bridge over the creek.* Straight talk for the people. None of this impossible-to-understand theory so beloved of intellectual parasites. He was wondering whether *Truth* had been infiltrated when the old man raised his voice.

" 'Thus it can be concluded'," boomed the Omniscient. But like all speechifiers, he didn't conclude. He followed this false promise with so much more impossible-to-understand theory (except when it asked silly questions), that Savva was hypnotised yet again by that waistcoat.

He woke to Uncle announcing, "Here is the conclusion: 'all those females' "—and though the Omniscient tried his best to unwrap and highlight verbally each layer of the quotation matrioshka, Savva was soon dreaming again—this time Galina was crooking her finger in his direction as she writhed languidly on a soft bed of "s and 's. She wore nothing but her railway shoes, one thick black sole blemished with a pink blotch of American chewing gum.

"...'belong to' " continued the Omniscient, " 'the species of "rational man possessing reason." Let us then proceed to analyze the definition of "stupidity" ' " " ' " " ' " " ' " ' ' " ' "" ' " ' ' ' " ' "" ' " '

143

"So you agree, young man? Or do you need more time to ponder?"

Savva rubbed his face. "What do you think?"

The old man sighed. "I am a bachelor."

Savva laughed. "And I?"

"But you have experience where I have not. Do you opine, as the article says, that men and women have different goals, and that the differences feed a proverbial misunderstanding between males and females?"

Savva took his time. With this comrade, time meant intelligent thought. " 'Proverbial' could be questioned," he finally said. "But 'misunderstanding'? Certainly."

"I knew you would know."

If only I knew, thought Savva. *Why can't Galina accept that I would die for her regardless of that mark on her face that she is obsessed with? Is she stupid? Or...* The beast of jealousy raged through Savva's blood vessels and pushed against the skin of his face, turning it dark as a beet, to the tip of his little turned-up nose.

Does she want that mark removed because of others? *So that she can stroll again at every train stop and attract those thousands of men who would have thrown themselves under trains for her, pre-blemish? Compared to them, I'm just a little squirm to tread on without noticing, or laugh at, a worm compared to real men—those who stoke Galina's blood fires— men like Valentin.*

The door opened and the two friends' pursuit of knowledge was again cut short by that woman in red who, when the old man greeted her with, "I went to the smoking section to see if you'd like to take a stroll down the passage with me," acted both startled and stupid.

Love pops out like
pomegranate seeds

BURHANETTIN SHOOK HIS FIST at the fat-faced moon, then punched Ekmel.

Ekmel mewed. Sleep was his only joy now, and this monster denied him that.

"Rise before I bathe you." The punch was vicious, the threat cruel, but Burhanettin handed Ekmel a glass of hot honeyed tea, and tossed the donkey a nougat.

Some nights, Burhanettin doubted his sanity. This wild hunt for the source of Ekmel's Kirand-luhun would have been trial enough for any man. But Ekmel's snores. Mere murder wouldn't have been satisfying enough.

The only way to stop the rage that built up in Burhanettin's heart and pumped through his body—a body strong enough to snap Ekmel in two easily as breaking a toffee—was to wake the man and continue the journey. *The sooner continued, the sooner arrived.*

* * *

The path is covered with pine needles. Ekmel leads, Burhanettin follows, and the donkey comes behind.

Ekmel, little shiny round Ekmel, is almost unrecognisable now—thin as mountain air, and just as dry. His blistered feet have grown soles thicker than any shoes he's owned, let alone his worn-out slippers. His teeth are as disgusting as ever, but if he doesn't expose them when he smiles (and when does he smile?) he could be said, on such a moonlit night as this, to be as dangerously handsome as a brigand in a dream.

Burhanettin has also changed. He has obtained a mirror. He practices facial movements such as an expression that must be 'lovestruck' and another that might be 'The pigeons cry out my faithfulness so how can you be so heartless?' He plucks. He scrapes his tongue. He shaves his cheeks so often that you can no longer hear their rasp.

He collects the odd leaf and pod, and makes himself bitter tea that he drinks in a gulp.

He composes poetry. He sings it, booms it out to streams, his mirror, the night, the day. "My love pops out of me like pomegranate seeds. I shower you... I fly to your heart and affix myself to you like burning honey... My passion knows no bounds. Bind me, my torturess, my jeweldrop... I have come for you from so far away that we have worlds to..."

Often he stops mid-sentence.

And what of the donkey? Is this the same beast who Burhanettin called "dear friend"? Is this she who sucked Burhanettin's moustache, who shivered when Burhanettin stroked the insides of her ears? Is this the donkey for whom Burhanettin made his celebrated *helva-i-sabuni?*

This is the donkey.

Is this the donkey who thought she was loved by Burhanettin?

This is the donkey, but where is that Burhanettin?

Fluffy clouds spread across the moon's face and the whole landscape is softened to smudged greys.

The footsteps of the travellers are muffled but the sadness of two of them is sharp.

Heart to heartbroken

DARKNESS COVERED THE LAND except those places between the snow clouds where the moonbeams broke through. The Muse and the Omniscient were lying on their respective beds, breathing as sleeping people do when they are not asleep but pretending to, as, indeed, these two pretenders were.

The Muse climbed down without making a noise, and reached into her pocket. With infinite care, she pulled out a deck of cards and shuffled.

The Omniscient snored and turned. As she laid the first card on the table, he reached out his foot and with the stealth of a spy, moved his toes along the wall till the light-switch flicked ON.

"Gorgonna!"

"I didn't know you played solitaire."

"This isn't solitaire," she said, and bit her lip. *But what would he know?*

He put on his spectacles. "Upon my soul, you're right. Far be it from me, fair mistress, to interrupt your game."

"You already have," she said, sweeping Death off the table and into a pocket in that dress.

"Good night," she said.

"Don't you want to talk about the tarot?"

"What tarot?"

"You don't need to hide it from me any more," he said. "As a matter of fact, it must be fated that you would reveal to me this hidden talent, on the very day that I discovered the value of those tools in that inestimable newspaper."

"What tools?"

The Omniscient laughed that irresistible laugh of his. The Muse was alarmed. *Does he know?* Then she was smitten with that disappointment, that heartache, that tidal wave of unfulfilled desire that she lived with as helplessly as a thirsty butterfly on a beach. Squashed and drowned by the fact that he doesn't love *me! He just thinks of me as the closest thing he can get to some woman he never met and who probably never existed. A wooden mistress.*

"What does it matter to you what I do?" *No one ever has loved me.*

"Everything!"

"What could *you* know?"

"I know that they cannot satisfy," he said, hoping he was right.

"They don't." *Why did I say that?*

"You could teach me about the tarot," he said. "I only learned today how useful it is in predicting the future."

"This isn't tarot," she said. "But I do know tarot, of course. And it's like dragons."

"So you can teach me tarot?"

"Why?"

"To predict the future."

"I thought we made it."

"That too," said the Omniscient. "But I'm learning that there are so many ways to make the future."

"And the past. You forgot that."

"And the past," he said. "Thank you for reminding me."

"It was not a reminder," she said wearily. "But a joke. A jest. No, don't shake your head knowingly at me. I'll bloodsoak a wisecrack and shove it down your silly throat, you old fool. You who've seen the pyramids built, stone by slave-crushing stone. You! who've heard the greatest arguers of all time, who have witnessed triumphs and revolts. Loves and losses. Dreamers crushed and the crushers obliterated in a thousand ingenious ways. You! who have seen the magnificence of disease. Jumped on the moon. Run with the titmouse. What's card tricks compared to some of those marvellous animals you've described to me? The ones you saw at that water hole? That naked rat with no eyes? Shepherds walking on stilts through fields of sage and lavender?"

"I saw that?"

Her cheekbones stood out and bright red spots appeared on her cheeks. She was terrifying, ugly and beautiful as a consumptive, *utterly unworldly and yet so ... so real. So magnificent.*

"You, *master*," she said so nastily that he was sprayed with the 's'. "You are the greatest witness of all time. *Remember?* Tarot! Phht!"

She lit a cigarette and pulled a long drag, as if she wanted to choke herself. "Fantasy! The stuff you used to question my intelligence about. Don't you remember when you called me 'credulous'?"

"I never!" The Omniscient's voice trembled. "Did I ever, dear mistress?"

"Don't mistress me."

She threw out her arms in a *keep away* gesture of supreme tragedy and climbed up to her bed. He would not have had the courage to go to her anyway, but now there was nought for it but to stretch out his toes, turn off the light and listen to her cry. Her sobs were sharp and small—a mouse caught by an owl. Soon they stopped.

The train's lullaby did not put either of them to sleep.

He coughed, once.

"Yes?" she said.

"I understand."

"What, exactly?"

"You need to exercise your creativity. That's why you go to them. You don't need to sneak out any more."

"Gorgonnannanaaaah." But she didn't sound angry. "*My* creativity."

"I don't have any," he said sadly. "I never did, and when my memory went, that was it for me." The Omniscient broke into wet, walrussy sobs that tore at the Muse's heart.

"How can you forgive me?" he snuffled. "I have kept you from *them* in the vain hope that I could make you—"

The Muse couldn't bear the force of that wave poised to crash down on her, on her delicate hopes.

"Intelligent," she sneered, drowning out his timorous "happy".

The crash of words crushed what she'd actually said, but her tone was loud and clear.

He curled himself into that foetal position he'd seen people do, but it gave him no solace. He'd never been a foetus, never even had a childhood, and was now feeling not just old, but heartbroken as the tragickest of rubberies.

Çimçim

CLOTHED IN BEGGAR'S TATTERS that hide a purse of gold and a velvet-cloaked bladder-pipe, Faldarolo knocks on the door of the cloth-merchant's brother. Faldarolo has been paid more generously than he has ever known—and beforehand. His heart flutters. He hopes the bladder-pipe will forgive him the indignities she will suffer for her cause. The purse will not be enough to pay a master who could restore her to health, but it is a step along the way. What steps tomorrow, and whether he'll be able to walk or drag himself clear of this town—these are questions he cannot allow himself to ask. His only fear is for the bladder-pipe.

The great door creaks open. An old man holds an oil lamp to Faldarolo's face, and before the servant can slam the door in disgust, Faldarolo begins to work.

* * *

The town of Çimçim is home to the cloth merchant and his older brother. Your eyes can search every word engaged to every dot on any map, and never will Çimçim show itself. This affectionate or scornful nickname was earned for the town by its quarter devoted to the making of those big brass clackers known as Çimçims, the tuning of which has levelled a mountain (so they say).

Faldarolo's interrogator, the cloth-merchant's older brother, looks like a carob pod stored too long— his skin has darkened and pitted with age, and has dried on his bones that stretch his form out, curved and twisted, from desiccated hollows.

He has been roused from bed. Under his eyes, he bears the pillows of the habitually sleepless. His lip is curled up on the right side and his voice is nasal. He examines Faldarolo through a thick piece of glass.

"And what is your proof that you are The Effusor, Chief bladder-pipe player to the Great Tīmūrsaçi?"

Faldarolo throws back the cape.

"By the light of His life!" exclaims the cloth merchant in fright and awe. *That red mark is so hideous, it must have meaning.*

Faldarolo tosses the velvet back over the bladder-pipe. He slouches in his rags, looking not at his interrogator but at some place too mentally lofty for men.

* * *

"The scoundrel! Eat, eat!"

Faldarolo had just told how the cloth merchant had rolled him in a bolt of cloth and stolen him from Tīmūrsaçi's palace, of the trials he had suffered travelling with the man of cloth. Of how he had secretly collected rags along the way, and how when they arrived at the cloth merchant's house only this evening, he had disguised himself as a beggar and escaped, and naturally ran here. How he already knew about the cloth-merchant's brother from his reputation (by the heavens, yes. There are so few men of discernment and classical taste that their fame spreads like the sun's warmth in spring). He told of how he learned where to find the house from the descriptions given by the cloth merchant, for the cloth merchant's brother was the only other topic of conversation the merchant possessed.

If Faldarolo had let himself think, he would not have been able to deliver this sack of lies. He was no storyteller, let alone a liar. Love gave his voice tongue, his eyes candour. Unbeknownst to him, his bearing was that of a great artist. He found it difficult, however, to remember all the details and the prescribed order of telling, and eat at the same time.

His host nibbled an oriole tongue. "And why would he do such a thing?" Faldarolo had told him already, but the man was like a child with a favourite story.

"He swore you have never seen nor heard a bladder-pipe, and that you could never find a bladder-pipe player."

"And did he say why?"

"Because, he said," Faldarolo swallowed a mouthful of pigeon with walnut and pomegranate sauce and washed it down with a beaker of wine, "you never do anything."

And here Faldarolo seemed to remember another something he hadn't told.

"He said that he would shame you by finding not only a bladder-pipe player, but me."

"That..." the cloth merchant's brother spluttered. "That *trader!* More ass's butter?"

"No thank you," Faldarolo almost said. He had secreted a chunk of it under his rags. "Good man," he said.

The cloth-merchant's brother smiled shyly, an ugly sight.

"Have it put by my bed," Faldarolo ordered, and rose.

His host scrambled to his feet. "Yes, Your Effusiveness."

* * *

After massaging the bladder-pipe with the precious ass's butter, Faldarolo bathed and put on the luxurious set of clothing that was laid out for him. Then he slept the day away.

His host, the cloth-merchant's brother, spent the first hour gloating. Then he handed out orders and spent the rest of the day and early evening drinking tisanes to soothe his nerves. He was not frightened of the Great Tīmūrsaçi, who would never find out that *The Effusor himself is in my house, wanting to play for: me.*

No, thought the cloth-merchant's brother. *I won't let the Great Tīmūrsaçi know that his Great Effusor is here, not if I don't fancy being shoved in a bag and drowned like a kitten.*

Indeed, the cloth-merchant's brother considered that it was quite enough to produce a bladder-pipe player for the townspeople to hear—his very own bladder-pipe player who came looking for the famed connoisseur. It is true that he had never seen a bladder-pipe, but he had an old book with a description and picture.

It is true that the more the cloth merchant swore that his older brother didn't know the sound of a bladder-pipe from a goat bell, the more the elder swore that bladder-pipes had become his life while the travelling trader, his younger brother, was but a ragdoll, his head filled with cotton and silk.

* * *

The cloth merchant sits in the back of the room. He has snuck in without an invitation, bribing his brother's servants (who had been instructed to accept the bribe).

The drama of the two brothers employs all, and many necks will be sore tomorrow.

The introduction is long and flowery, the better to frustrate the audience, who delight in their torture.

Faldarolo looks the part of a celebrated arcane musician. He wears silks not seen by anyone here (except the cloth merchant's father who had imported them when the boys were young).

The bladder-pipe now wears an over-cloak of stiff brocade, to Faldarolo's specifications. The introduction finally ends and the host sits.

Faldarolo closes his eyes and puts his lips to the pipe.

My love, he blows. *Your constancy fires me. The brightness of your soul guides me. The very stars are but black holes against your firmament. Your voice is honey. You candy my lips. I drown in your sweetness...*

Not a sound comes from her.

The townsfolk should be forgiven for looking to the connoisseur. Many ears have been ruined by the çimçims.

His hot breath flows through her like water through a sieve. The skin of her bag is soft and supple, yet wrinkled and flat—its visual horror hidden under velvet and brocade.

Why do you torture me? he blows, a song that is so familiar that everyone in the room can hum it. His eyes are closed, his eyebrows moving to the rhythms of the song. He had thought that he would be tense, would have to pretend, but at this moment as in those best times with her, all he feels is love. His lips, his hands, his love do what they've always done with her—he doesn't heed nor care whether others can hear their act.

Faldarolo and the bladder-pipe are more as one than they've ever been before. His swaying, his eyebrow-dance—sights only. Not a sound.

For the first few moments, the cloth-merchant's brother looks disconcerted. But then the connoisseur's lips fall into that line of tight-muscled (down at the corners) pleasure that is the sign of true discernment. His guests read the look correctly as "What a master! I would give my lifetime for this moment. It is too perfect to contemplate a wrong note, yet I fear... Ahh, paradise!"

* * *

Faldarolo played the concert of his life. He played till he fainted. He played without remembering that he had strung at his waist under his garments, the purse of gold and the pot of ass's butter; that alone in the luxurious guest room, he had practiced tumbling with the bladder-pipe (as he would fall when kicked out the door); and that before the concert he had eaten as much as his stomach could hold.

Faldarolo's eyes were closed, so he didn't see the audience, who within a songspan, looked not at their master of taste, but to Faldarolo.

He didn't see a man begin to hum, only to be jabbed quiet.

He didn't see men begin to sway.

He didn't see thirty-eight eyebrows rise stiffly, and slowly bend, stretch, then leap.

He didn't see the tears roll down his host's face, the uncurling of the man's lip.

He didn't see the look in the eyes of those who watched through the filigreed wall.

He didn't see (and no one else noticed) the sneaking out of the cloth merchant.

* * *

The unconscious Faldarolo (clutching the bladder-pipe) was carried upstairs by two of the concertgoers, the town's foremost physicians. Beside his bed, all of Çimçim's five physicians argued noisily over his treatment while the master of the house absentmindedly tore his hair out.

Nightingales were killed for broth. Nougat was pounded to powder and mixed with gold, then rubbed on Faldarolo's lips. He was washed with rosewater, oiled with neroli, massaged, dribble-fed and sighed over. The bladder-pipe, pried from his fingers, lay on a pillow beside the bed, resplendent and intimidating and hidden as ever in her velvet and brocade.

For a week, Faldarolo hovered between worlds. When he woke, the physicians prescribed bed-rest and the building up of his strength.

So at his host's insistence, Faldarolo rested and developed that physical feature of the great artist—the little ball of a stomach. He was plied with fine drink and food, raiment, jewels (including ten magnificent toe-rings), gold pieces and cloying respect. No work was asked of him. The cloth-merchant's brother treated him with such delicacy that Faldarolo felt feared.

The only thing Faldarolo asked for was ass's butter.

He never learnt the name of his host. It was so like all the other names in this town. His host never knew quite how to address him, so meekly called him "Master".

On about his thirty-second night in Çimçim, Faldarolo stole away. He wore the most modest garb he had been given, though he carried secreted on his person, the velvet-garbed bladder-pipe, a pot of ass's butter, and more than enough wealth, he estimated, to find and pay for the one who could heal her, though his journey could take years.

And that day began the decline of the cloth-merchant's brother, who went mad asking himself *Why?*

Why did the Master leave? And why did he leave behind all the gold and jewels, and the specially specified brocade cloak? *Why* had he who had been showered with so much and could have asked for anything, eaten so much ass's butter, yet when he stole away, carried with him so little, he'd disgust a beggar.

The heartbroken connoisseur felt only one certainty. The great Effusor had not run back to the Great Tīmūrsaçi. Many of the town's çimçims were made for His Greatness's çimçim band.

The pot boils

Morning in the restaurant car.

Savva concluded to his audience, "She's such an independent woman."

Galina shivered dramatically. "She sounds dangerous. Who knows who she's working for? But first, how is it that you can hear so much they say? Aren't they foreigners?"

"They mustn't be."

Savva felt a little bad about reporting on them, but it didn't hurt his friendship with Uncle—and that woman often interrupted a lovely time he'd been having, all snug in 3C, door closed, feet up, talking up a storm with the old man, delving the secrets of the universe. Only this morning they'd been discussing the story, *Beheaded human body can stay alive and kicking* when that woman too beautiful for anyone's good had entered, and he'd had to scurry out like some capitalist worker.

"Maybe I should take over your carriage," said Valentin, earning him not so much as a scornful look.

(But it is a curious fact that the Muse and the Omniscient were lax in the languages they spoke, always grabbing the closest to mind. Not only that, but upon boarding the train they had fallen into the very human habit of speaking to each other at human frequencies.)

"Tell me again," ordered Galina.

"She calls him 'master'."

"No! What does he call her?"

"Mistress."

"That's the stuff!" She wagged her finger in Valentin's face. "Does she say 'Fetch me my slippers, dog?' "

"No."

Galina sighed and picked a potato out of her bucket.

"I've heard her treat him badly," Savva offered.

"Eh?" Galina's face brightened. "Go on."

"I once heard her call him All-Seeing-One."

"See, Galina?" Valentin laughed. "A man who isn't respected can't understand respect."

"She laughed when she said it," said Savva.

"Cruelly?" asked Galina.

"Yes."

"Aha!" cried Galina, tossing her knife in the air.

"But that was in the past," Valentin said primly. "Wasn't it, Savva?"

"Yes, but—"

"Tell me again," ordered Galina.

"She can kick me with those boots right here," Valentin said, striking his heart. "Did you see them? When she's got her hands busy lighting a cigarette and the wind—ouch!"

"You wanted boots."

"Not yours, Galina, and not on my foot."

But Galina, who didn't have a skirt to sexily blow up, nor any boots but train-work-unit issue, had turned all of her attention elsewhere. "You were saying, Savva?"

* * *

Valentin and Savva asked the same question at the same time: "What does it matter?"

"Everything," said Galina. "If he calls her 'mistress', it means she is an independent woman, a power to be begged to. But 'my mistress'..."

"My mistress," cooed Valentin, "the purvey of every bourgeois gentleman, tucked away in a little flat in Paris."

Galina snorted like a horse with a fly up its nose. "Exactly," she sneered, looking to Savva.

"Ahhhh," said Savva, who was so unworldly that he had to take Valentin's word for the secret lives of bourgeois gentlemen. But Galina's snort, and that sneer that narrowed her gaze till it was two shafts of ice, made him need to grab the counter. Every romantic heartstring in him had just gone *sproing!*

He'd never listened closely enough to these strange passengers to know, but answered Galina with all his heart: "He is bourgeois, who could deny with that blinding waistcoat, but he's not a purveyor. 'Mistress' he calls her. And ... I think... No, I'm willing to bet he loves her."

"As if you had anything to bet," said Valentin, in a tone to assure the others that he was above such diversions. "Fascinating. But what was that about the millions?"

"Millions?"

"*You* said that *she* said she'd been with millions of men."

"Did I?"

Galina turned to Valentin. "Did he?"

"Yes," Valentin insisted. "The first time Savva told it."

Galina poked a potato in the eye. "Tell me again."

"I can't remember exactly."

"Remember unexactly," ordered Galina. "And be quick about it, before you forget again."

* * *

"There can be no other explanation," pronounced the worldly Valentin. "He must be her pimp." His eyes glittered.

Savva wrinkled his nose. "Shameful way to make a living."

"Umm," Galina nodded. She fed herself another raw potato peeling from the side of her knife.

Savva and Valentin made way for her as she picked up the bucket of potatoes and tumbled some into her pot.

Valentin perched one pert buttock on a table and lifted his chin.

His eyes took on a far-off look—all wasted since Savva's eyes were on Galina's back and she was bent to her stove, where the other two heard a match strike that only partly muffled a filthy word.

"Millions of men," drawled Valentin. "At what? Sixty percent?" Galina twisted the stove's dial. "You're both liars."

"She's beautiful enough," said Valentin, and his eyes flashed. "For billions!"

"At your speed."

Valentin exited so fast, the door must have huffed dust in his eyes. Did he suffer? The answer must remain forever a mystery, as no one noticed.

"It doesn't take beauty," said Savva.

Quickly Galina turned.

She didn't take her left hand from her mouth—whenever it could, it took up position there as if she were posing for a painting titled "Contemplation".

But she did rush to the fore door, lock it and tape the CLOSED cardboard over its window; and she also secured the aft.

* * *

The soup bubbled ..., and burnt.

Ekmel twists his ankle

AT LAST EKMEL found the place he sought. Stretched out below, covering the valley between the hills, was a thick grey blanket that only partly muffled what sounded like thousands of goat-bells. Market-day tomorrow? The time now was the turn of afternoon's back, those few magic moments when, if you pick up a handful of dirt and toss it in the air, the sun gilds every worthless particle.

He heaved a heartfelt sigh and pointed. "Your destination."

"So, scoundrel," laughed Burhanettin in surprise. Dark thoughts had assailed him lately—that he was being led on an aimless wander. Now he almost felt remorse for beating Ekmel at those times of doubt.

After so many weeks on the road, Burhanettin could no longer wait.

He shoved Ekmel, and the honey-merchant stumbled and cried out.

Burhanettin threw Ekmel on the donkey's back, but she would have none of that. Burhanettin almost hit her, he was so incensed, but he caught himself as he balled his fist.

"Patience." *An angered heart clouds judgment.*

* * *

Kirand-luhun—
> *Take too little, and madness seizes you.*
> *Take too much, and Death swoops you up.*
> *Take just the right amount...*

"Come, friend," Burhanettin cooed. He pulled Ekmel up from where the donkey had thrown the extraordinary little man. The confectioner didn't notice the look Ekmel shot at him, but the honey-merchant's weight was remarkable.

"You're light as air, Ekmel! But soon enough you'll be your old fat self again..."

Burhanettin prattled silly nonsense as they made their way down the slope, his treetrunk arm supporting Ekmel, whose feet were constantly being knocked on stones and whose face was a study in grimaces, a study that Burhanettin did not attend.

The closer they got to the town, the louder Burhanettin had to speak to be heard above the din. *Odd* he would have thought if he had been thinking of such mundanities. *Such clanging, but no smell of goat.*

By the time they reached the town gates, darkness had almost fallen.

Burhanettin shouted, "I'm coming, my love."

* * *

At sunset in Çimçim the gates would close, the çimçim district quieten, and the town criers and lamp-lighters get ready to walk the streets. At sunset, the alleys clogged with homegoers, trudging labourers, bowlegged tradesmen, stooped porters, near-sighted students—all joggled by gossips who scurried, shouting whispers.

"He's over this way," Ekmel said as the gates shut behind them. "I can hold." He slipped out of Burhanettin's grasp and limped over to the first alley, where he gripped the stone walls with both hands and pulled himself up, step by step.

Burhanettin and the donkey followed till, at a twist, the donkey hawed, pulling and then standing still, a wicker pannier on her side, caught on a rough stone in the wall. Burhanettin was stuck behind the donkey.

"Hoy, skinny!" he shouted up the alley. Ekmel would be able to crawl between the donkey's feet and unhook the basket by slipping his wisp of a body between wall and donkey, if she didn't kick him.

But to Burhanettin's disgust, instead of Ekmel, a giggling little boy poked Burhanettin's behind, and the boy's grandmother cursed. Burhanettin agreed with the hag about the donkey. But his ears burned to hear himself also compared to a barrel, in physique— and brains! He might have clouted her if her grandson and her own impressive physique and basket hadn't been in the way.

* * *

Far ahead, Ekmel ran through the alleys with a delight he hadn't felt since he last crunched his favourite *helva* (not on this trip), or was it when he thought he had sold Burhanettin the spoiled honey for an unbelievable profit? No matter. Ekmel wasn't weighing delights against each other. He ran with thoughtless joy.

He frightened old women, grew a tail of urchins, slipped on spilt oil and laughed as he sped on. He was lithe as an eel and as shoeless.

He ran without knowing where he was going, but when he saw the cemetery, he turned into it, strolled till he found a nice tomb under a tree, and settled down to sleep. He wasn't afraid of ghosts, not after Burhanettin.

* * *

Dawn always broke spectacularly upon Çimçimmians. If you lived there, you were accustomed to it, but Ekmel had never heard of the place. The cemetery being surrounded by the çimçim quarter, Ekmel woke screaming.

"They're quieter than you," said Burhanettin.

A tombstone away, the donkey was grazing flowers from a vase.

Ekmel stood up. This scene was worse than his nightmare. But wait! A bear of a constable was approaching the little group, his eyes on the donkey.

Ekmel rushed forward. "Effendi!" He smiled with all his honey-merchant charm.

The constable reeled back. He had intended to fine the owner of the beast, but now that he got an eyeful of the group, he ascertained that the gentleman standing to the side would not be in the company of this foul-mouthed ruffian who must have kidnapped him. The donkey could only have been stolen, but who is the gentleman?

"Blessings upon you," yelled the constable to Burhanettin.

"And you," yelled Burhanettin, wiping his forehead. "I feared for," and he glanced at the donkey.

"Yours?" the constable stage-whispered.

"My youngest brother's," Burhanettin sighed.

The constable sighed along with him.

"At last," Burhanettin mouthed, giving the constable great eye-to-eye contact, and then dropping his eyes to his right thumb, which jerked ever so subtlety, at Ekmel.

The constable pounced on Ekmel with explosive zeal. He always found nothing so refreshing to start the day, as a good beating.

"Would you like to make a statement?" he asked Burhanettin, only to retract his question with a hasty, "Don't trouble yourself."

Scribes are for exploits, not embarrassments. The constable pulled at his moustache, prouder than he could say for having first, noticed a mystery, and then within moments, solving the case, a case which was complicated by the glaring fact that this ruffian in hand had stolen this gentleman's brother's donkey. *The gentleman's brother,* the constable concluded, *if he is at all like my brother, is a drinking companion of this lowlife. And furthermore, the kidnapper-thief is sure to have filled those panniers with the gentleman's own belongings, which will have to be noted in any report, and no gentleman should suffer that indignity.*

He shook Ekmel, a preliminary that allowed some frustration to escape. *This cockroach is sure to be wearing the gentleman's turnip-sized watch strung from his dirty neck.* The constable always wanted a watch.

"Would you like to press charges?" he bellowed at the gentleman.

Burhanettin hmmed and stroked his chin. Finally he glanced at Ekmel, who was convulsed in sobs as he hung like a dishcloth from the constable's paw.

"A hobble for him will do, thank you," shouted Burhanettin. "I must take him back to face..." He smiled with the sadness of the magnanimous at heart.

The constable smiled back (protector of the peace to upstanding citizen) as he felt with the skill of a pickpocket, for a pocket in Ekmel's filthy robe. When the frisk found nothing but a bony body underneath, he lifted the ruffian up high, dropped him on another tombstone, and stalked away.

Compliments

"IT'S JUST LIKE HOME," said the beautiful woman in red, smiling at the cook who, behind a protective hand over her mouth, gaped in astonishment.

Though game to eat almost anything, Galina drew the line on the mess she'd created today. Some of the potatoes had burnt so well that they had to be chipped from the pot with a screwdriver, so today's special (Borscht) glittered with aluminium.

The Omniscient was all a-simmer. He shoved his bowl away. "You eat hungrily, Mistress," he said in a low, husky voice. Her earthy appetite made him feel things he'd only ever reported.

Mistress! If only you noticed that I could no more eat for love of you than I can forget your perfidy. I forgive you! But come clean with the only one who can understand you, etc.

They were the only patrons in the restaurant car, the other nine tourists having left in disgust and the locals having decided to make do with their own provisions, or starvation. Not that any of the others had tried the borscht today. The stench upon opening the door was enough.

"Umn," said the Muse, gazing at Galina.

The Omniscient gazed at the Muse while she dipped her spoon in her bowl without once looking at what she was eating. Her eyes were glued to Galina.

Galina examined that nice old man with a waistcoat that she imagined putting her feet up on. *He can't be a pimp, but who is she?*

When that woman who Savva denied admiring asked for a fourth portion, Galina said she was sorry but there wasn't any left. The woman said she was sorry, too, and, "So delicious!" Lunch over, they left, but as the old man held the door open for her (*!*) the woman in red turned to Galina. "You have beautiful eyes," she said.

Galina couldn't lock the doors fast enough. Heart pounding, she yanked her mirror out of her pocket. *Maybe the old sayings are right.* She remembered her babbling grandmother's: "What's bad comes good whenever it would." *I've certainly had enough of what's bad.* "What's good comes goodest to those who cookest." *That woman likes my cooking.* Galina delayed looking for another moment: the delicious suspense made her tremble.

Then:

That horrible red mark. Still there, large and livid as ever.

And my eyes! She shut them tight, but they leaked as memories of childhood stung her—of being called Piggy because of those bright, but deeply embedded so-called windows to the Soul.

The immaculated maculation

IN THE TOWN OF L——, the grey-coveralled members of Work Unit 4 tear down the scaffolding and walk across the road to the pavement in front of the railway station, where they look up to their great work from the necessary distance to see the broad perspective:

They look first, to the eyes. Are they successful? As explained in the Art Production directive from the Central Institute, *Stance 1, Face Forward, Full Colour/ size G Facades and Banners: The focus rests in the eyes, which must be slightly unaligned. Colours: Brown 3 ... Interpretation for Commentators: His gaze is of necessity internal, focussed beyond the obvious, to Posterity.*

The eyes, which had needed 10 litres of White just for the glint of foresight, are satisfactory. The face is taller than 2 storeys, wider than a two-family apartment, and pink and smooth as a pickled pig's foot.

That famous (in other countries) strawberry mark is nowhere to be seen. Although other teams of workers have failed to erase the blemish in every frame of every moving picture of the man, the members of this Unit have, yet again, painted the President in the manner in which the People are accustomed.

Here on the pavement in front of the train station, a collective grunt of satisfaction passes through the Unit. The morning rush is over, but the day is young as a girl. Each plans to drink her health for the rest of the day—but at the moment, with no one about, the

169

Unit lingers, talking shop.

* * *

"And Lenin had a receding chin," the senior painter was saying, just as Savva rushed out of the train station's doors.

The night before, the train had stopped for longer than the usual quarter hour at L—— Station, because of a small *khu* that had begun to insert itself between the verses of the train's song, worrying the Chief Driver.

Upon inspection, the senior in Railway Repairs (which didn't make him senior anything else, L—— being a long way from District Headquarters) informed the workers of Railway Work Unit 675645 (Valentin, Galina, Savva, the Chief Driver, etc.) that the train would be held up at the station for 24 hours. On this gloriously sunlit unscheduled holiday, most of the Unit streamed out, following the normal procedure in cases of unscheduled stops for repair.

On no condition are schedules to be changed, except by Order of the Central Office.

This most important of all directives, in practice, meant that passengers were kept in the dark informationwise, so they sat in the train past the quarter-hour stop, and then longer, and longer ... and with the train being stopped so long, it was bound to speed off any second, so none dared even to stretch their legs on the platform.

In the recent past, Savva had spent these unscheduled holidays in his compartment, locking himself in with his daydreams, because, oh, *years and years* before when he'd hit a holiday in a town as big as L——, he'd explode out of the train just like the rest of the Unit, and spend his time cavorting down the wide avenues, spending wildly. First, he'd lift his nose to scent the nearest corner barrel, where he'd buy the largest mug of tart kvass and stand in the street drinking along with the other customers. Then he'd drop his kopeks into the pear-juice vending machine just for the thrill of seeing it open its jaws and spew juice into the clouded glass. He'd join queues buying who-knows-what, though he didn't need whatever it was. But that was not the point. The point was (the first one): he'd never bought anything anyone else would give something for. But worse, the point that hurt was that, even if he'd ever miraculously bought something that was worth trading for something good, he'd never had anyone he could give it to, for love. But back to what he used to do back when. Just before he boarded the train again, he always used to buy the day's issue of *Truth* (there was never a lack of supply of *that*), just like a civilian.

But that was years ago.

Cavorting in towns had been a false joy. The bourgeois urge to hunt for things to have for having's sake had withered in him. The train was home to him. Unlike the dashing Valentin who had a tie from Paris that showed the Eiffel tower, Savva never wore civilian clothing. He, who had never managed to buy or trade for anything better than a case of green plastic alligators with thermometers shoved up their backs, was no trader. And, besides, what could be as good as what he got from Galina? Now his pay, meagre as it was, had become a clump in his little hidey hole behind the samovar. And why waste money on *Truth* when he could (before cutting them into squares) read just what interested him amongst all the full issues left by passengers along with their spat-out sunflower-seed shells?

So, normally Savva would have hidden himself in his compartment while Valentin hit the town making better deals than any capitalist.

And Galina? She had only been in Savva's Unit for about a year, and this was her third unscheduled holiday. The previous two, Savva had spent in his compartment, daydreaming and absentmindedly grinding his teeth *while she walks the town—innocently, maddeningly, untouchably flaunting her unreachably high, pure beauty.*

Today was different. Valentin had rushed off, to be sure, his lithesome form bulked out by what Savva could only imagine.

But Galina had not rushed out into the glorious sunshine to

171

walk the wide boulevards where she stuck out her pink tongue and licked ice cream from a wooden slat, or whatever she did in these stops.

She was holed up in her compartment weeping, her eyelids puffy as mashed potato.

That was all she did now: weep. The love of Savva's life wept when she cut potatoes. When wrapped around Savva, she wept. His assurance into her pearly ear that she was still beautiful to him made her stop her weeping, only to break out into sobs that made his ears ring as the weight of her great chest drove the air from his lungs.

Love hurts, but it also ennobles.

* * *

Savva ran out of the train determined to find that pot of magic goo that Galina wished for—that paint that would hide the mark.

Valentin said it was called Girl Cover, but Valentin was too busy helping himself, to do something for Galina. *Very expensive imported stuff*, Valentin had said, *if you have to pay*.

Savva didn't care if it cost his savings. He was prepared to throw them away to the last kopek—for Her.

As he pushed his way through the crowd in the train station's waiting room, he would have laughed bitterly if he were destined to be a classic character, but he wasn't. Valentin had told him privately, with a shrug, that Girl Cover was no better a cosmetic than Galina's desperate smooshed-rye-and-potato-flour paste. Girl Cover's counter-revolutionary advertising always shouted *New* and *Revolution!* ... *so* (Valentin laughed) *those weak-minded women think it was created in their best interests*.

So:

As Savva burst through the doors of the train station on his tragic quest to track down and buy for love, a pot of paint with a false claim: *Works Like Magic*, fate perhaps caused him to almost collide with the unmoving bulk of the grey-coveralled group that crowded the pavement: Work Unit 4.

"And is it true Stalin had so many warts, the Units called him 'Warthog'?" the youngest, almost a boy, asked the senior who had revealed in so many words, Lenin's receding chin.

"Not warts," chuckled the white-haired man with the yellow-stained moustache. "Teeth. An extraordinary bite. He—"

"That's the reason for the moustache," the other white-haired man in the crowd interjected, turning his back on the senior's expression.

The young one's tender cheeks flushed, and he drew himself up into an unslouched position. "You mean," he said, "Stalin obeyed our, your advice?"

"Ha hahaah." The senior's laugh turned into a nasty, back-bending, hawking cough.

Into the breach shot the second-most senior—"He was hairless as an egg."

The boy wasn't the only one who goggled at this news.

"Who invented the moustache?"

"The great Berentsov," snapped the cougher, now recovered sufficiently to throw at his rival a look of two parts Yellow, one part Blue.

"Berentsov of the—" began the other.

"Excuse me," whispered Savva, respectfully touching of the elbow of the one who seemed to know the most. "Then is it true that he" (and here, Savva glanced significantly across the street, and up). Savva had heard rumours of the President having one ball and a wooden leg, neither of which mattered to Savva, but "that he has a red mark on his face?"

The one who knew regarded Savva sternly. "Where'd you hear that?" he demanded.

Savva broke into a cold sweat. "I'm just reporting to you," he babbled. He turned away casually, wanting with all his heart, to run.

The old man grabbed Savva's sleeve. "You can't believe what you see on television. Don't you know that foreigners infiltrate the moving picture frames?"

"I don't believe foreign infiltrators," Savva stated fervently. Actually, he'd never seen television, his home being the train, and he'd never wanted to watch television anyway, happy to get all his news from *Truth* and people who knew, like Valentin.

The second most senior slapped Savva's back, laughing. But the rest of the crowd (minus the one who seemed to know the most) was tittering, even the fresh-faced boy. The senior now smiled indulgently at Savva (who was, of course, wearing his Railways Unit uniform) in the same manner that railway workers do, of the question, "Does the restaurant car serve anything but borscht?"

"Let's say, young man," he said quietly, "if we were to paint him as he is, we would need forty litres of red number two."

CHRISTIE'S

A quantity of ephemera relating to Mstislav Valer'ianovich Dobuzhinsky including a drawn New Year's card from 1956, the artist's jacket, his snuff box, a photo of the artist, a printed New Year's card for 1912, a cigar box cover, a backboard, a pamphlet and thirteen bookplates for the artist's son, Valer'ian Dobuzhinsky (22)

Price Realized £125 ($259)
Estimate £600 - £800 ($1,243 - $1,657)

Sale Information: Sale 5131
Russian Icons and Pictures Including works by Non-Conformist Artists
29 November 2007, London, South Kensington

Provenance
Gift of the artist to his niece, Ewa Totwen
Acquired from the family of the above by the present owner

Department Information 19th Century European Art

Under the bees

FALDAROLO WALKED till he could walk no more, which was a very small way indeed. The only shoes he had were gold-embroidered slippers, and he couldn't wear them for two reasons: their resplendency and their uselessness. His formerly well calloused feet were almost as useless, soft as coddled eggs.

He stopped in a shady orchard. Great boughs laden with tight green leaves drooped so low that a child could have picked their fruit. A blanket of white blossoms covered the ground. In every place on every bough that the blossoms had once congregated as a flower, a hairy green stone brazenly jutted out. These stones would, in months, grow and soften and finally glow, becoming the fragrantly teasing golden quinces whose preciousness could still only be unlocked after a day's stewing in a cauldron of syrup; but now the orchard was not worth guarding from anyone, man or bird or cook with a cauldron in waiting. It was a lonely and quiet place.

Or it would have been if the racket of Çimçims didn't disturb the peace.

Faldarolo settled on the blanket of blossoms, his back against a trunk.

His stomach cried out. It had become spoilt.

He unwrapped the bladder-pipe and pretended she was well, that these nightmare times had not befallen the two of them.

The day was still. No wind played in the trees. Not a blade of grass sighed nor a cricket chirped. Somewhere bees droned, birds chattered, screams and laughter reverberated against rocks, and mirrors aplenty shattered—yet in that orchard, from the time that the sun watched from overhead to the time when it reluctantly or not, had to illuminate another scene, all looked destined to be forever verdant peace.

Faldarolo's ears had adjusted to the background din of çimçims, and he took no more notice of them than he had learned to—as a musician—of respected yet out-of-tune singers.

His eyes dimmed with tears as he gazed at his Beloved.

Tenderly, he took her in his hands and lifted her.

"Not that again," yelled Nick. "No more of this finger on the orifices stuff. And *don't* wet your lips in front of me. I'm *sick* of your bloody lips. Get a move on, you artyfarty arsehole." *If you'd ever been a cook, you'd know what work is. You'd know about sore feet, varicose veins...*

On and on Nick whinged, and his heckles might as well have been silence. Faldarolo heard not a word, let alone a single uplifting bit of advice.

However, Nick was not alone. The bladder-pipe was in harmony, *and some!*

Faldarolo put his lips to her mouth, and she *bit* him.

Not only that but when he, in unthoughtful reaction, jerked her away, she hung on tighter than the twist in two rough twisted cords holding a heavy laundered cloth.

By the time he pried his lip from the crack in the bladder-pipe that had remorselessly sucked it in, he had grown a large, succulent, and infinitely tender blood blister.

High above, a swarm of bees travelled past in a sky so clear and still, you could have heard the sound of each of their golden droppings hitting leaf and stone; bird and wasp and ladybug; and crashing on the tile on an earthworm's roof ... if not for the çimçims.

A reason to dance

IF BURHANETTIN'S DESPAIR were set to music, only the plaintive cries wrung from a stringed instrument played with a catgut bow would do, accompanied by a dolorous Tom stuck behind a window that has views of an alleyway. As there was no instrument to accompany Burhanettin and soothe his savaged breast, and no frustrated beast whose protests could make Burhanettin feel the joy of shared agony, he kicked Ekmel and kept kicking him all the way from the Çimçim cemetery, out of the town gates, up the valley and down the unfamiliar rocky road that needed no additional aid to trip Ekmel, as Burhanettin had not removed the humiliating hobble. They proceeded agonisingly slowly till an orchard came within sight. A place of peace and beauty and shade, where Burhanettin yanked on Ekmel's lead just before they reached it, a boon to anyone who might be looking from above.

Ekmel fell upon the careless stones.

Burhanettin sat on one.

The donkey stopped behind Burhanettin, who sighed almightily.

"I should murder you for tricking me," said Burhanettin. He took out a knife and, with the speed of the master *helvassi* that he was, used to having to pull a pot off a fire just before it boiled over, he cut Ekmel's hobble before the honey merchant had opened his mouth to scream.

"Go," said Burhanettin. He walked away shaking his head, his grief so great that as the donkey followed, she wished he would see the sympathy in her eyes.

Ekmel followed them with his eyes, till he was ready to explode. Instead, he ran after them.

Sadness, love and rage are always funny when they're so far away, they're played out in miniature.

* * *

"Take your donkey," bellowed Burhanettin.

He turned away and the donkey followed.

Ekmel grabbed her lead, and the donkey laughed, in her own way. But it wasn't her laugh that made her so impossible for Ekmel to catch and hold. It was her grief. She was a whirlwind of hooves and teeth with Ekmel in the centre, and then she was off, following Burhanettin.

Ekmel's palm was sticky and hot from rope-burn, but this was no time for self-pity.

"Effendi," he pleaded as he ran. "Wait for me!"

Darkness would fall soon. And though the wiry, unkempt Ekmel looked a brigand from his sandpapery cheeks to his calloused brown bare feet, he was as frightened of being alone on a dark road as the most lovely young maiden should be. And the richest gentleman.

"Wolves!" he blubbered. "Please, Burhanettin, don't leave me to be eaten."

Burhanettin walked faster.

The donkey followed faster.

"I beg of you," said Ekmel weakly. This was his old honey-merchant "Can't you see I am making a loss, but for you, dear friend, I'll give up eating" voice.

Oddly enough, it worked. Burhanettin stopped. Not only that, but he walked back to Ekmel and took his arm, leading him to a thick-trunked cedar, where he gently lowered the man and asked Ekmel if he were comfortable.

"Yes," said Ekmel suspiciously.

Burhanettin picked up a rock and crushed it in one hand. Its sand poured from his fingers. He whirled away, took out two sticks of nougat. One he tossed on the ground in front of the donkey. One, in Ekmel's lap.

Gingerly, Ekmel picked his up. He was so hungry that his mouth filled with drool.

"Why?" asked Burhanettin sadly. "Why did you trick me?"

Ekmel tied the nougat in a fold of his robe.

When a man has been pushed to the edge of a cliff, it is better to dance than to pray.

"Who tricked whom?" he smiled, opening his hands. "I didn't roll you in a carpet."

"You never had anyone in mind."

"You gave me no choice," said Ekmel reasonably. "In my place, what would you—"

"I trusted you."

"Hah!" laughed Ekmel, putting as much irony as he could into the 'H'. "You always insulted me."

"That's beside the point."

Ekmel restrained himself from sighing, but he wondered when this would pass. He desperately needed to eat, and if that donkey wasn't going to eat its, he was. His fingers inched out.

"Leave it."

The donkey looked at Burhanettin in surprise. He had finally glanced in her direction.

"Eat it," he ordered.

She took it in her lips, all joy forgotten. As quickly as she could, she crushed it between her teeth and swallowed.

"The Kirand-luhun," said Burhanettin. "I suppose as big a lie as that primula honey from the forests of Xo Man."

"That honey was sold to you below cost," insisted Ekmel. "You were my only client for it, so strange it tasted." (a confession he never would have uttered but for the fact that he despaired of ever being a honey-merchant again)."I swear it came from Xo Man or this nose isn't a nose on my face."

"So," said Burhanettin, who had no dispute about that. "The Kirand-luhun," he said, hating himself for his naivety. "It's just as real."

Ekmel unknotted the cloth around his stick of nougat. He had to think. And besides, the sound of the other stick being crunched had been unbearable. He had to eat. He put the stick in his mouth, but his teeth were not as strong as the donkey's and he would have to suck it, so he reluctantly took it out—

"The Kirand-luhun!" bellowed Burhanettin, causing Ekmel to drop the sticky nougat in the dust. "It's real as that."

"There's no saying it's not."

Burhanettin's heart thumped. He knelt before Ekmel and took Ekmel's nose between his finger and thumb.

* * *

The tale of the appearance of the mysterious red in Ekmel's ordinariest honey was so unbelievable, it had to be true.

Burhanettin's hopes leapt.

"We must think," he said. "I don't know why you didn't pick a better spot to stop."

He strode out, the donkey and Ekmel following, till they reached the orchard and passed it; and a cave, and passed it; and still, Burhanettin walked. He seemed to be in a great rush, so quick and purposeful were his strides, but his legs were being pushed by his mind. He had so many questions, so many thoughts. So much to consider and weigh.

Life is a recipe from someone else's guild. He'd always considered that a stupid saying.

He stopped when the sun set.

Suspension

"FORTY LITRES OF RED NUMBER TWO," said Savva to the worker in the Paint shop, "and your biggest paintbrush."

* * *

November nights fall early in L—— where streetlights are no match for the moon (who has not yet thrown the covers from her bed) so all citizens are indoors unless it's their job to be otherwise or they're insensible. Yet *up there!* suspended like a spider from an almost invisible line, Savva drops down the face of that building across the street.

His feet, washed till they hurt and bearing new, clean socks, patter lightly across the damp-as-freshly-barbered President's huge, two-dimensional face. To the mass of eyes working every day for the benefit of their respective citizens, the man on the end of the thin line high over the pavement is a painter, for that is what he must be, since he's painting, isn't he? And since it's night, he must be late fulfilling some sort of a plan. If, however, the eyes of a real painter are employed, they will tell him to hold his breath, classifying the man up there either a hero or simply insane. A real painter wouldn't think to drop with the rigging Savva made, but what equipment does love hand out?

Savva has never painted before, but he wields the brush with unerring mastery. In this light, Red 2 looks black.

* * *

The passengers in the train that's sat here for nigh upon 24 hours, curse or snore. Those who travel prepared, burrow deeper into their coats as they sleep. The snugly blanketed Galina cries monotonously, dreaming.

The eyes of the dawn sun have yet to plumb the depths of the train, but they have reached the town's rooftops ... then, as a gaze upon a beauty drops downwards, so does—What's this?

A little man stands in front of the train station, his face lifted towards the President. And that mark! It is nothing less than The Mark on Galina.

* * *

Savva's feet were killing him. Some distant part of him announced, responsibly, that his toes might have a touch of frostbite, but he ignored it.

His eyes were bleary, but that was not why they misted now.

As he turned to fetch Galina, he sighed with the pleasure that only a Revelation can confer:

Truth IS Beautiful.

Arresting sights

AT SAVVA'S PERFECT VANTAGE POINT on the pavement in front of the
train station, first one pedestrian paused, and then another—to
pull up a collar against the cold; to drop the earflaps on a cap and
tie them under a chin; to blow a nose; to sell, and to buy, and eat:
a gherkin ... till—in a discretely rowdy way—all these individuals
became quite a collective.

Savva had not only performed a heroic act, but had painted
with great accuracy the Mark on the Leader's face. In the glorious
light of the New Day, all forty litres of Red 2 shone. Truth was
impossible to ignore, at this size. But size isn't everything. The
building was Party Headquarters.

He twiddled his cold toes in their thin Railway-issue boots,
rubbed his bleary eyes, and sighed with exhausted satisfaction.
"You'll see, my love," he vowed, *if I have to pull you out with a
rope.* Then his jaw clenched, his hands bunched, his eyes narrowed
and blued to steel, and he snapped into action.

"Comrade citizen," said a smiling man.

Savva, who had only quarter-turned towards the station's door,
choked. The back of his collar was caught in the grip of an unseen
hand. His feet dragged as that hand lifted him free of the pavement.
A button popped off his jacket.

Quicker than snow on a hotplate, the collective melted.

* * *

With only minutes left before the train was to leave, Galina, her

185

face buried in her upturned collar, burst through the train station's doors.

"Saaah-vaaa!" Her timbre fell the length of the street—and with that figure of hers—enough to satisfy two men at the same time—it was natural that she attracted the attention of one of the two men on a plank being hand cranked down the face of the building across the street.

"Hey cabbage roll," he called.

She concentrated her gaze down the street. "Savva!" she cried. She was so angry at him, she could have spat. Had he run away, too cowardly to face her after not finding any Girl Cover? Why hadn't he asked Valentin to get it? Had he gone on a drinking spree? She'd never seen him drunk, but... *And maybe he is fleeing me, sick of my face.*

"I'm coming," yelled the wit on the plank.

She jerked her head upwards.

"I love 'em sweet and sour," he chuckled. "She'll say something juicy. You just wait."

She stood still as a post. Her mouth opened and out came a long white cloud.

When the plank stopped, the chuckler spat in disgust.

Slowly, Galina turned her collar down. But not for them.

The unbearable perpetuity
of remembrance

As GALINA STARED across the street, so did Nick. He saw that huge face there in another perspective: Time.

How could I have forgotten?

Nick remembered his dad, who should have stayed in the upper echelons of Australian public service, but success there and international fame amongst economists had turned his head. Nick remembered his dad's attempts to make it in the real world of business, as opposed to the real world of government law.

Goggling at that painted face the size of a nightmare, Nick remembered laughing at his father who'd judged worth by the price tag. Nick remembered his mum's choice words. She, a corporate liquidator who delighted handing out a business card touting Rebirthing Services Inc., had lambasted his dad for wasting megabucks to spend a weekend away to see the "boofhead" up there and other famous has-beens "who couldn't run a school fete" as his mum said, in some "quote conference, unquote" called Business Leaders of the World. That weekend turned into one of his mum's grounds for divorce. *She'd been particularly scathing of Mr Larger than Life up there.*

"Losing profits can be bad luck," she'd laughed in a line she probably wrote first, "and any leader can be couped against, but if you pay a guy who lost his country for the secrets of success, then red is the new black." She was so verbal that Nick decided because of her, to go into something that couldn't talk back—stuff you put in your mouth, stuff you shit instead of it shitting on you. It would have been that weekend while his dad was away that the livid red blotch (*How could I have forgotten?*) on his father's face appeared in that big, framed wedding photo in the lounge—a fact in the grounds of his dad's counter-claim, and another subject in the back-and-forth of his "home life", in both their houses.

This was more creepy than he thought possible. The actual strawberry mark on whats-is-name's face, if he remembered correctly, and he was sure he did, was the shape of the Americas including Central America, and extended up from his forehead to the top of his shiny dome, but Nick's father had hair down to his eyebrows in the wedding photo, so the mark that Nick's mom had painted was right on the kisser, and sliding off it drunkenly and up, exactly as Galina's.

But that was history. Here and now, at the sight before him, there was still enough humanity in this shred of Nick that he felt nausea.

"It's coincidence!"

But no one heard, here.

A centre of gravity, unbalanced

THE PAINTERS dipped their brushes (into Pink Flesh 01) and began their work: to paint It out.

At the first stroke, Galina bellowed

"Stop, you—"

just as the train tooted the one toot that it was wont to utter before departure

and just as Galina's elbow was touched by the Woman in Red.

"Come," said that woman, pulling Galina gently but with sisterly insistence, towards the train station.

Galina pulled away from the Other's grip, but the woman had surprising tenacity.

Galina was two of her! With a violent jerk, she snatched her arm back as if those hands on her were flames. But this act unbalanced Galina's centre of gravity.

She slipped in the slush, tripped and almost fell into the road, caught herself just in time, but her left heel stepped heavily on something round as a hazelnut, but with a screechy metal scrunch.

It stuck in her sole.

She bent and pried it out.

Filthy gilt stamped with the face of Motherland Locomotive #1 "New Dawn", and smeared with sticky red: a button.

With a cry, the Muse grabbed for it, but Galina had it first.

"He's mine!"

Spies

THE OMNISCIENT watched them both.

So did the chief train driver.

So did Valentin.

Spying had become an epidemic.

The Omniscient watched them because he had run to see where the Muse had run to.

The chief train driver watched them because he was in love with Galina and was going nowhere without her, little did she know his love. He was so shy, he had never so much as given her a warm bucket of coals.

Valentin watched them because he'd decided that the old man as a pimp was ridiculous (how could he pimp when all he did was sit in 3C reading science fiction?) but that maddening beauty in red! She was hard to keep up with. He almost resented her incursion into his life. Such was the strain she put on him, he no longer had time to steal from the people in the carriage under his care, let alone roam the train finding opportunities. On their first encounter she had pushed aside his charm as if he were a stray crumb, so he had been forced to use a sweetener: a whole bar of Red October chocolate.

"What do you want from me?" she'd demanded, so blatantly that he was speechless. "Give it to the cook," she'd said.

His domain was carriage #1, not 3, and Savva had every right to fiercely defend his own right to whatever #3, including the mysterious and alluring 3C, had to offer.

Only in the smoking section did Valentin have a chance to get close to her. So, because of *her*, Valentin had been forced to spend time pretending to clean the smoking section (no one's responsibility), rather terrifying, what with the shaking of the couplings and the wind gusts blasting through that doorless space between the carriages where many a man had solved the futility of life by falling out. That nauseating gap in the plates. *Feel the speed shake your legs, and those sharp rocks poking through the snow, pointed at your crotch.* The endless crunch crunch crunch. And so undignified. As far as cleaning went, Valentin had always made Savva look conscientious.

Times in the carriage under his care were extremely depressing, too. The nine tourists in 1A-C were the type that are so distrustful of foreigners that they travel poor. Their coats looked like dead cats. They spent all their time complaining, not that he could understand the words exactly, but who needed to? They lurked in the hallway and pounced on him, loudly and with eloquent body language—about the toilet, carpet, samovar, the slowness and unscheduled stops. And once, though they could see he wasn't a waiter, they shouted *borscht borscht borscht!* It was a madhouse. They asked for the name of his supervisor and were not satisfied when he gave them a name. They'd been on the train forever, it seemed, and their destination was unknown, but they looked like they'd burrowed in. He couldn't even persuade the conductor to check their tickets, declare them forged, and kick the tourists out because the conductor had fallen off the train, drunk, two years ago and the collective had voted for more worker flexibility by taking collective responsibility for the incident and therefore closing the matter, except for the monthly divvying up of his pay.

Only extreme self-interest kept Valentin's spirits afloat. The woman smoked hungrily in the smoking section, flicking whatever it was in her pocket in that maddening manner of hers, and left. She didn't complain, didn't talk to anyone in fact, but often mumbled some word, "Gorgonna." Valentin hated not being able to use his charm, to treat her like a woman should be treated—so that he could be treated with the respect a man of his looks deserves. He hated having to look busy and he especially hated that there was an added danger. He had to be especially careful about what he picked up off the shuddering, gaping steel plates that constituted the 'floor'. Many a visitor came there looking for butts, and the old men were the worst. One old hero, thinking Valentin wanted what was rightly his, kicked Valentin in the ribs with a die-cast metal foot. If Valentin had fallen out, it would have been murder, not that Valentin would have had any satisfaction dead.

But the woman in red presented so much incentive. That hidden pocket of hers and the way she reached into it like a tourist who touches his chest where his passport pouch hangs secretly, or adjusts his hidden moneybelt. They might as well wear a sign: $. Not that *she* did anything blatant. *She is subtle. But that tenseness, the way she uses her eyes, the habit of charm. Like me, she is a master. A mistress!*

* * *

So far Valentin's attentions had come to nothing.

When they arrived at L——, he hadn't run off the train with the other workers but loitered till Savva had gone. Then he rushed to casually stroll past the open door of 3C. There she sat. Docile as a milk cow in her stall.

He left to see what the town had to offer, but the only trades he could make were for felt galoshes. Heartsick, he could only board the train and hope that the maddening woman delivered for him before the next town. He was getting mighty sick of working the trains.

So much for the past.

With minutes to go before the train left, Chance took over.

As he stepped into Carriage 1, a flash of red caught his eye. *Her!* Running from the train. Of course. In moments, she'd do her business and be gone. *What's she trading? Who's her contact?*

His heart pounded as he followed.

She burst through the train station doors and rushed up to—
Galina!

He watched the touching scene with disgust and some surprise. But not curiosity. He'd heard about that ridiculous compliment: "You have beautiful eyes." Galina's eyes were as attractive as the rest of her. And he'd heard about those three bowls of soup so disgusting that Galina tossed the rest of the soup, pot and all, out the restaurant window. You can never tell taste.

But taste was beside the point. That woman wafted a smell of contraband stronger than rotted caviar. She had wasted her business opportunity, or eluded him.

Whatever your taste, my beauty, you're a professional. And now it's a contest between pro's.

He didn't stay to see the denouement of the scene between the women, which must anyhow end immediately, as the train was ready to take off. Stiff-legged with anger, sputtering spite, he boarded Carriage 1. Beware, passengers. Hang on to your sodden old felt galoshes, your dead cat coats.

I've never been a hand-man like Grandpapa, but she's forced me to it.

The lurch of the Amfesh-bena

FALDAROLO THOUGHT OF taking off his shirt and binding his feet to help him walk, but as he might need to sell his shirt to afford her care, he decided that the best way to toughen his feet was to be cruel to them. And so he got to his feet and put one in front of another, barefoot.

Onwards he walked, thinking of love—out of the orchard, down the road; past a cave that he should have stopped in for the night; and on and on. When sun set, he paused till the moonrise, and walked on further.

His soles had rubbed through their blisters, and his lip was swollen and throbbing from the bladder-pipe's bite. The bodily pains were mere annoyances compared to the agonies he suffered thinking of the muted bladder-pipe, of that desperate pinching measure she had been forced to take, to focus his attention on her needs.

* * *

"Listen!" whispers Ekmel.

He hadn't slept a wink since they stopped in this exposed, haphazard place. And now, it isn't the baying of running wolves, or the demands of a group of brigands that causes him to shake.

"Can you hear it?" he hisses.

A shuffling, coming closer, and closer. It doesn't sound like any man, or any normal beast. It has to be that which he feared so much he hadn't dared to mention it. The *Amfesh-bena*, the serpent with a head at each end, coming to take them—approaching, one slither at a time.

The Amfesh-bena wouldn't eat now: it would bite with a poison that keeps you awake but unable to move. It carries you to its larder where it hangs you like a sausage till one night, it opens its jaws till they crack, and pulls you off the hook and into its mouth. But as it has two mouths they fight over you, and since it is a slow beast, the fight takes a very long while. And when the fight is over, your head faces your feet inside its serpent body where if there were light inside you could watch yourself be crushed by the ripple of its muscles. That is said to take one hundred days till there is not one solid bone in you, except your skull.

The shuffle is painfully slow.

"What a night, I wish it would last," mumbles Burhanettin, who turns over.

"Shhhh!"

Burhanettin sighs. "How far is it," he cries out, "from you to your heart?"

The beast must be almost upon them. The moon hides behind a cloud. Ekmel is so terrified, he cannot make a sound. He can barely move to place his hands over his eyes, but he manages that.

Burhanettin begins to blubber. "Your dear face I miss," he sings in his sleep.

The moon peeks out, throwing light that slips past Ekmel's fingers into his eyes.

There! The shadow approaches with a convulsive jerk.

That does it.

Ekmel jumps up, kicks Burhanettin, and leaps behind him. He is too frightened to run, but maybe the Amfesh-bena will consider Burhanettin enough. *You should,* Ekmel importunes. *Burhanettin is a big and meaty man, whereas I...*

Burhanettin sways woozily, woken from the first decent sleep he has had since travelling with this abomination of a man whose snores could cause an avalanche. He doesn't know what has awakened him, luckily for Ekmel. He *deserves* his sleep after such an exhausting day. He *needs* his sleep. A tear slips down his cheek. He was just in the middle of such tenderness.

He shifts his hips to settle down again, but something is stopping him. Digging into his shoulders. He sniffs.

Ekmel! Suddenly he's wide awake. That's Ekmel's filthy fingers, and the man is both clutching him and shoving him forward.

"Get away from me," snarls Burhanettin. "What are you playing at?"

"Look," whispers Ekmel, unfortunately close to Burhanettin's ear, which is far too close to Burhanettin's outraged nose.

"May you drown in your own breath."

Burhanettin, reaches behind and takes hold of a handful of Ekmel, flinging the man over in an arc whose point hits the earth on the path ahead.

The shadow lurches, and then falls upon Ekmel.

And then, the thing that followed the shadow falls upon Ekmel.

Ekmel's face smashes into the rocky path. He feels nothing. Blood trickles from his lips, but he tastes nothing.

He has fainted at the touch of the shadow.

A watched cook can definitely boil

"OF COURSE HE'S YOURS, DEAR," said the Muse to Galina.

That little train man with the turned up nose—he, the giver and maker of the greatest and *only* true-love declaration that she'd ever witnessed, as opposed to told about.

This was no time for a lot of explanation, but for Action.

But the fact is: ever since that day early in the train trip when the Muse had been peremptorily fetched by and then ordered by this cook to eat her cooking, the Muse had been drawn to the woman—not romantically, but not un-romantically either. That mark—irresistibly appealing. But the cook hated it. *Is it the destiny of everyone, to be unhappy?*

One day when served the borscht, the Muse said, "You have lovely skin." But that only made the woman even *more* unhappy.

Soon enough, they were both more unhappy, for if the cook wanted to observe the Muse, that made it all the easier for the Muse to watch *her*.

The Muse witnessed the torture of the chief train driver, a man who ate quickly and never said a word but was so in love with the cook that the Muse could *feel* his love. No one else noticed a thing.

And the Omniscient's friend, that little train attendant. He was so openly in love with the cook that one day, the Muse heard them arguing in the train attendant's compartment. "Can't you get it into your thick skull?" he shouted. "I love you."

The day after that, he, with comical evasiveness, asked the

Muse whether he could buy a magic potion from her that would banish a birthmark on his niece's arm. He was so distraught with the Muse's negative reply that they had a chat about beauty and the false lure of cosmetics. He hadn't meant 'magic potion' literally, you see, and harboured scepticism about the power of cosmetics, and "didn't give a damn" about the mark. "It doesn't make her less beautiful to me," he had, "but she thinks it ruins her."

The Muse almost wished ill to the cook. The Muse would have settled for half that love—*one is enough for me. Just one. For me!* The contrast between the cook's life and her own made her ever more frustrated, habitual, jumpy, *romance*-sodden, till:

The stop at the town of L——

The Muse was the only passenger who overheard one train unit employee say to another, "Twenty-four hours," and watched them leave the train. She knew, therefore, how long the train would be sitting here, knew that they'd been abandoned, as this was the second time this had happened since she and the Omniscient had boarded, but that didn't matter to her. "The destiny is joy. The joy is the journey," she'd once dictated.

She watched the workers leave the train, some rushing, some strolling. The Carriage 3 train attendant ran out as preoccupied and worried as any lover should be. What would he seek for his own true love? The Muse didn't let herself guess. She didn't see the cook emerge, deducing that the silly woman was, if not locked in her kitchen, locked in her compartment weeping to her heart's content as usual, too ashamed of her face to enjoy the town, let alone love.

When five hours had passed, the Omniscient said that he missed his tea; and later, he was surprised when the Muse said there would be no meals at the restaurant car that day.

"And why would that be?"

"Because there never are when we are stopped," she said. "Tea? I'll make it for you."

"I couldn't put you to the trouble," he said, "Stopped? Where?"

"If you weren't so immersed in that paper, you'd notice."

When 24 hours were almost up, the Muse was at her post at the window, keenly watching the platform. The train's workers had drifted back one by one till they all must have boarded. The chief train driver took leave of the stationmaster. The Muse chided herself for missing the return of the attendant.

She yawned. having been awake all night, and reached for a cigarette. Pushing up the window so her smoke didn't disturb the Omniscient, she leaned her head out, and *the cook! There she is. She's running like a smuggler,* from *the train.*

* * *

The Muse ran after her, as you know. And most likely, you also deduced that she didn't just *follow.* She drew discretely alongside and watched where the woman cast her eyes. The Muse ignored the crude calls of the oaf across the street, but when she saw the woman's eyes fill with tears of joy and what could only be secret pride, and saw the woman fold down the collar of her jacket and lift her face to the world, the Muse threw a glance to what had caused this extraordinarity.

The Muse had not had the adventures in history that gave the Omniscient all those memories that he forgot, so she had never seen a picture of the President to notice it as such. But here and now, she read the cook's expression. And ... it took a few seconds, but it *did happen.*

The wave hit her, tumbling her helpless, and floating, and exhilarated, and confused and breathless. She was swamped by Intuition, and almost unbearable jealousy, and then the wave subsided, beaching her on the sands of, of course—a higher selflessness. For the first time in her existence, the Muse was Woman.

To be loved like that.

"Savva," breathed Galina. "Gulag or not, I'll get you out." A gust of wind tore at her hair and blew it out behind her in a golden blaze. With her squared shoulders, her fist of steel, and her many jutted out parts, she was the image of that statue at the State Art Institute, "At the Ramparts" by Olya Shulpin, not that either of them knew it.

"You need me," said the Muse.

Galina narrowed her eyes. "He told me he loves *me.*"

"He does," said the Muse. "I can help."

She didn't know what she could do nor where he was, but she had to soak up this romance. She hadn't a clue what help she could give. This wasn't paper love, but the real stuff—red as roses, red as blood, red as hot, furiously beating hearts. The cook standing in front of her and the painting across the street and the hot, sticky button in the woman's fist were: Love. *I stand in its midst.* She couldn't walk away. *This is the closest I've ever been to love.* She corrected herself: *Both-sides love.* Inside her heaving breast, she felt everything that she'd ever dictated, and much much more. She shoved her jealousy as far down her gullet as it would go.

She smiled at Galina in a friendly way, but the other woman demanded: "Why?"

The Muse was at a loss. How could words explain? Besides, there is possibly *No time to waste.* "My Russian soul," she guessed.

"Ahhhh." That revealed all. *It's a poor citizen the Motherland doesn't invest with* that. *Still* ... Galina looked the Muse over from head to toe. "You could be useful," she said, taking the Muse's arm.

"Excuse me, ladies." The Omniscient startled them. They had forgotten all about the train. "We noticed." He motioned to his companion, the chief train driver, who was blushing redder than a Stop button.

"You seem to have a problem," said the Omniscient.

"Your friend—" said the Muse.

"They've arrested Savva!" said Galina.

The blushing man felt the dagger of love stab him in the heart. "I'll make a statement saying I did it," he said stoutly, hoping Savva hadn't murdered anyone.

"Savva, is it? I'm sure that won't be necessary," the Omniscient said confidently, wondering who could possibly have found fault with such a model worker and informed citizen. They must be making a mistake. "Is he not on the train?"

"He's been carted off, I tell you, for painting *this* on *that*." Galina's gestures might have been confusing if the painters across the street had finished their job of making the mark not exist, but they'd only just begun.

The chief train driver groaned. *If only I had done that.* Even now, the driver could not talk directly to the only woman he'd ever loved (besides his mother).

"Tell her," he asked the Omniscient, though he'd never spoken to the man before, didn't know him from any passenger, "that the train will not leave without her."

The distracted smile Galina gave him twisted the dagger.

Two hearts

BURHANETTIN RUSHED FORWARD.

"Good sir," he began, but the man lay there, face down on Ekmel, like a sack of mud.

Burhanettin rolled the man off onto his back and was going to open a water bladder to revive him, when he saw the hideously mangled lip. He looked more carefully and saw the man's bare, bleeding feet.

Burhanettin swore. Whoever did this should pay, painfully. And he was sure payment *would* be made. The man had obviously been attacked, but he was richly attired, was a man of substance, like himself. Travellers both, men of the world who had to help each other.

"Up, Ekmel."

"Is . . is it you?"

"No, it's the wolf." Burhanettin gave him a rousing kick.

Ekmel sat up, spat out a tooth, looked around, and laughed. Burhanettin might as well have tickled him, for all the good his boot had done.

Burhanettin had no time for Ekmel's crazes. "Get out the ... no, just hold his head up. *Carefully.*"

Ekmel slid over in the dust, and held up the young man's head.

Without that monster grape on his lip, the man would have been good looking. Strange, elaborate clothing, but it reminded Ekmel of ... *of course.* One of the reasons his father had left Ekmel with so little is that the man of discernment spent so much on clothing, carpets, wine and food, and women—all as permanent as his life. *The bigger the pot, the bigger the leak.*

Burhanettin, as a guild member of the shop *helvassis*, specifically, the *helvassian-i-dukkan*, specialists in honey-based confections, was also a non-qualified but nonetheless amateur expert in healing medicaments. He took from his travelling kit a mortar and pestle, and pounded a certain nougat, adding mastic and water and—luckily, dawn lit his hunt, and luckier still, his prey was close—certain growing things. He compounded two batches: a poultice that made your eyes sting, for the feet: and a sweet-smelling but powerfully drawing salve for the lip.

Using Ekmel as the only helper he could get, he dressed the man's injuries, muttering all the while about assistants, though Ekmel was an excellent nurse.

By now, the first rays of warming morning sun were striking the man's eyelids. His head was in Ekmel's lap, and Ekmel was not only eager to be on their way to somewhere, anywhere, but was getting a sore back. The nuisance's breath was annoyingly slow and steady.

Ekmel bent over his burden. "Shouldn't we wake him?" he whispered, wiry hairs from his beard teasing the man's left ear, whose nose twitched as Ekmel's breath invaded sleep.

Then the eyelashes fluttered, and finally, the eyes of Ekmel's burden opened. They were beautiful as a cow's. The sky above was blue as a hyacinth, but the sky was blocked to those eyes by Ekmel's face, specifically Ekmel's nostrils.

"Awgh!" said the man, upright like a corpse in a grandmother's tale.

His eyes were wild.

"Where?"

Burhanettin was prepared.

"Calm yourself, good sir." He handed over the velvet bag that had tumbled from the man's hands.

Burhanettin had not allowed himself the vulgarity of opening it, though he was very curious about the man.

"I see you have been attacked."

"Not really," said Faldarolo. He felt the bag surreptitiously, but not surreptitiously enough.

"Is that your knot?" asked Burhanettin.

Faldarolo pretended to examine the knot, all the while doing more surreptitious probing through the cloth.

"It is," he said. "Thank you, sir, for rescuing it." Burhanettin had never seen such perfect teeth. But this only made the injustice done to the man all the more outrageous.

The traveller happened to notice his feet, and blinked. They were swaddled in fine white cloth and felt curiously cool, as though he had just stepped on a patch of snow.

"They stole your shoes," said Burhanettin.

"No. They just didn't give them back."

Burhanettin's peaked cap wobbled, he was so surprised. "You are a generous man, not to accuse."

"There is no one to accuse."

Burhanettin was stunned. He gazed in awe at this traveller who had shown him what a man of the world can be. *Imagine being so high up in the way of thoughts that revenge has no place in your heart.* Only—dare he bring up the subject?

"Are you on a Quest?" he asked, as it would have been crude to be direct.

"How did you know?" smiled Faldarolo. "Are you?"

"It shows?" Burhanettin was so delighted, he stroked the horns of his moustache into the shape of a smile.

In seven more circuitous questions, Burhanettin reached the point:

"For love?"

Faldarolo nodded, astounded. *This great man has not just doctored my hands and feet while I lay dead. He has opened up my breast and felt my heart.*

It was a natural consequence that they decided, these two men of the world—travelling, each for a Great Love—to succour each other in his Quest.

And since they were not competing, to go forth together.

Party of four

THE PARTY was composed of Galina, the Muse, the Omniscient, and the chief train driver. But first the chief train driver went through the carriages informing the work unit that the State did not demand their services for a week, and possibly longer. Report to me in seven days.

A conscientious leader, he spoke quietly to each worker personally. Each left the train with a different step—bouncy, racing, shamelessly holiday-spirited. Only Valentin remained—he had locked himself in his compartment and replied to the news with a curse so rude that the chief train driver broke into smiles. He could have been a detective, so accurately did he assess the foul-mouthed shirker—only one reason could keep Valentin in. Valentin, who escaped the train at every opportunity—Valentin, the train's legendary swindler, must have been swindled himself!

The chief train driver had never liked the man and had spent endless stretches of track tortured by the question: *What value Galina can possibly see in the slimy eel? (oh yes, I have eyes in my head.).* But Valentin's presence in the work unit was something he had borne *as another pain in the May Day Parade of pains in this thing called life, a tragedy that only ends with Death.*

The meeting convened in the town's park. The chief train driver, introduced formally by Galina as "Comrade Shurov," sat literally in the background after announcing again that he was ready to confess.

"No need for that, young man," said the Omniscient ("Please call me Comrade Dangulov").

"Heroes," Galina ("Comrade Boldyrev") snorted. She looked at the comrade to the left of her, that woman in red (who had introduced herself after the Omniscient, as "just call me Valeria, Comrades," causing the Omniscient to wish he had been bold enough to be so informal).

Galina remembered vividly: "Millions." She considered their options. Breaking into the town's jail was impossible. And what if they considered him so politically dangerous that they put him in an asylum? She, a mere train cook, had nothing to use as a bribe that was better than what anyone in power would already have—except ... "Valeria?"

* * *

The meeting was in disarray. The Omniscient and chief train driver were reduced to watching, and they had no idea what was happening. They had been left out of the conversation that stirred, from scratchy whispers, to a storm.

Galina's feet were planted wide, her hands on her hips. She looked like she could carry a city's powerlines, and you could almost see sparks coming off her. "After your millions," she said at the Muse, "what would ten or so matter to you?"

The Muse, who was sitting, blinked. "Millions?"

"You'd think I was asking you to sacrifice yourself."

"I don't care a snap for me," the Muse so quietly, it might have been to herself. "But to think *you* think *I!*." A red patch appeared on each cheekbone. "What about you?"

"I doubt that their taste is that particular."

"Ladies," the Omniscient crooned. "Comrades?"

They ignored him. "I would cook you cherry dumplings," Galina lied. "Veal cutlets," she added desperately. "Pashka with candied orange peel! Fresh mushrooms!" In the old days before there was someone to live and die for, she would have killed for these delicacies.

"So you think that's the way to my heart?"

"You don't have a heart."

The Muse stood. "Our bodies are sacred temples."

"Of course they are, miss, uh, Comrade Valeria," said the Omniscient.

The ladies regarded him as they would, an extraterrestrial. One who'd butted into their conversation. He didn't warrant a reply.

Galina glared at the temptress. "You don't care."

"Yes I do!"

"Ch'm," interrupted the Omniscient, yet again.

"Yes?" the Muse asked dismissively. Her hair had begun to twitch, the first sign of a full writhe.

"I said that the *Truth* shall set him free, and I declare it will."

"As I was saying," said the Muse, directing all her attention to *this extraordinary woman, she who has hurt me so. Such an unfair assertion—that I spend my life in a daily mockery of love.*

"If the *Truth* won't set him free," interrupted the Omniscient, yet *again*, "What about my experience at the Bar?"

Trouble brews in Carriage 1

THIS TIME, when the word was given to the workers in our train of interest, a passenger managed to overhear, and in moments the rest of the passengers had been informed through the verbal samizdat—all except the 9 tourists in Carriage 1. So a few minutes after that, the only people on the train were Valentin, and they.

About 1p.m., William "Toots" Riley polished off the last of the Velveeta slices that he had packed in the pockets of his travelling coat. "If this is a Great Railway Journey of the World," he announced, "then I'm a horse's ass."

"Innit," agreed Calum Boldridge.

Riley had been astounded to learn that the English don't talk English, but the man was a head nodder, and always agreed with Riley.

"Tut, tut, gentleman," smiled Mr Sandeep Guruprasad from his top bunk. "You make a delay into a disaster. When my father inspected that disaster of nineteen fifty-six, when the Madras-Tuticorin express plunged into river because the bridge at Ariyalur had been washed away in floods, one hundred fifty-six people were killed, of which full twenty-five were railway employees. Railway Minister Lal Bahadur Shastri accepted moral responsibility and resigned. Now that was a disaster."

"I remember when—" began Toots.

But Mr Guruprasad's eyes were closed and he was in flow, not that he was a rude man. He would have been most upset to have done something rude, yet, "We must remember," he continued, "that none of us has come on this journey to reach a destination. This *is* the destination."

"Innit," said Mr Boldridge, but Mr Guruprasad missed the irony.

"It is true, gentlemen," he said, "that the service could be improved, and that the ministry of this railways has not come to the conclusion that ours did many years ago, and I quote: 'To make every effort to make the train journey as pleasant and blissful as the joy of reaching the destination.' But just think, gentleman, what an adventure we are having!"

He opened his eyes and leaned down to the bottom bunk to look fondly at his wife. "And at no pain to us."

Mrs Guruprasad looked up from her book. "I could not agree more, Sandeep." She was delighted with this delay, and as far as she was concerned, it could go on forever. An avid reader of Russian literature, she had lived and breathed its atmosphere for years, in her imagination. This trip had been her husband's silver wedding anniversary present. "Just think," he had said, "no coconut grating, no tiffin making, no cleaning up after me for two weeks."

"It's always a pleasure," Mrs Guruprasad had indignantly replied, but now after being on this train for weeks, she had experienced such a powerful spiritual rebirth that she knew, absolutely, that this life's journey had been destined; that otherwise a part of her would never have been revealed — never, but for this blissful state of enforced leisure.

Oblomov. She rolled the name on her tongue. She'd never considered herself as having been a man in some previous life, but the knowledge didn't repulse her. She'd never realized the connection between so-called fiction and reputed reality. And but for this experience, she never would have. She fully relaxed her eyelids while she thanked the stars for this wonderful life and her slightly selfish husband. After all, she had never been interested in trains as much as he, but she had never been born to serve them.

Then her fingers and eyes went back to their pleasant work, backtracking to the front page of the book so that her mind could be dazzled yet again, by this revelation:

With Oblomov, lying in bed was neither a necessity (as in the case of an invalid or of a man who stands badly in need of sleep) nor an accident (as in the case of a man who is feeling worn out) nor a gratification (as in the case of a man who is purely lazy). Rather, it represented his normal condition.

* * *

1:34 p.m. in Compartment 1A—

Faint sounds emitted from the Guruprasads' bunks: scratching, cracking and scrunching. Mr Guruprasad writing in his log, Mrs Guruprasad reading. Both eating sunflower seeds, depositing shells in plastic bags.

Mr Boldridge snoring.

Mr Riley drinking from a silver flask.

* * *

1:37—

"For goddsake!"

William "Toots" Riley slammed his fist against the wall. "You there, pardner?"

"No, Toots," came the reply from 1B. "I'm busy holdin' up this train."

"Now you're talkin'."

Riley grunted, the first sign of him moving his bulk from his bunk. He grabbed the bar of his walker and pulled himself up. "I'm comin' in," he yelled.

Mrs Guruprasad turned a page.

Mr Guruprasad repressed an emotion at the outrageous behaviour of some passengers. Imagine striking a carriage's wall! "How can it defend itself?" he wrote.

* * *

1:52—

The Guruprasads pursed their lips and Mr Boldridge sat up as:

Five passengers burst into 1A, Toots Riley at their head.

"You're either with us or against us," he announced. "What's it to be?"

"I'm widya," said Mr Boldridge, but Riley wasn't looking at him. He was challenging Mr Guruprasad, the only train enthusiast with actual work experience. Riley clomped over, instantly seeming to expand to fill every bit of space between bunk and ceiling that wasn't occupied by the tidy Mr Guruprasad.

"What's it to be, Sandy?" Toots Riley demanded.

Mr Guruprasad resented this coarse man, recoiled from the familiarity and physical closeness. But where would you berth a man who is proud of being called Toots, sounds one takes care to expel only in deepest privacy? Mr Guruprasad, the retired-after-25-years-with-not-a-day-off-sick, exemplar veteran of the Indian Railways treated his challenger as he would a man who had boarded an a/c carriage with only a 3rd class ticket.

"Please move," he said, making a swishing movement with the tips of his fingers.

But Riley's long years as a broom salesman had made him tough.

"I'm not goin' anywhere till you swear to get us out of this mess."

"Sandeep, dear," sighed Mrs Guruprasad, "I think he means business."

"If he don't, we do!" said Calum Boldridge, the longest sentence he'd uttered since boarding the train. He was what his late wife had called 'a long fuse', but once lit, he was a pretty lively sputterer.

Sandeep Guruprasad sheathed his pencil in its sleeve in his logbook, closed his logbook, put his logbook in its appropriate pocket in his coat and buttoned that pocket, wrapped a rubber band around the plastic bag holding the sunflower seed shells and put that in another pocket in his coat, and buttoned that; and buttoned the pocket that he had been pulling the sunflower seeds from. Then

211

he sat up. "Please allow me, Mr Riley."

Riley stepped back and the 67-year-old leapt lightly from his bunk, not because he was such a lightweight (he was a middleweight) but because *your body and your mind are one and to be healthy, must be flexible*, a philosophy that the other 8 tourists would have done well to embrace, including, it must be said, Mrs Guruprasad, who religiously practiced laugh exercises but could not touch her knees due to the health-giving *Badam ka halwa* that she dosed herself with daily. Though it was made only of pure ghee, *badam* (almonds), sugar, milk, and cardamom, her husband said it upset his constitution. He preferred carrot juice with cumin after his morning stretches.

He smoothed his jacket with a graceful flick of his palm. "What do you propose, Mr Riley?"

"Sandy, you gotta—"

"My husband," interrupted Mrs Guruprasad, closing her book and standing up, "is, if you please, 'Mister Guruprasad', but you may call him 'Conductor'."

The ex-broom-salesman had met thousands of women in his day. "Yes ma'am," he said.

He turned to her husband.

"And may I remind you," she continued, "that this might be the wild west to you, but we come from civil society?"

"Yes ma'am." He bent and touched his striped railroad conductor cap. "No offence meant."

She smiled graciously. "Then there is none taken."

He turned to her husband again. "Conductor Guru ... uh ... Mister Conductor. Would you please hijack this train?"

* * *

Of course the very idea of Mr Sandeep Guruprasad hijacking a train was repugnant to that model citizen, but 7 members of the group were adamant. They wanted to continue their trip, and they didn't care where they went. Indeed, "Anywhere!" several said at once, while one said "Anywheres!"

212

John Cooper, the group leader, had left them weeks ago, deserting them on that last unscheduled stop, not that they knew any more whether a stop was scheduled or not. Mr Cooper, a man for whom Sandeep Guruprasad had immense respect (Cooper had memorised the entire *1985 Indian Railways Timetable*), had said that, to his knowledge, this town first appeared on maps five years ago. And that line, *See it? The one to the south. That line hasn't been used for at least twelve years.*

The 7 passengers wanted, of course, to take the line that hadn't been used for at least twelve years, a crazy idea that only train enthusiasts like them would warm to.

Guruprasad tried reason.

Then, "This isn't like your model railways," he said. "If this ends with us plunging off a bridge that someone forgot to fix..." He rolled his eyes, calling upon their imaginations.

Guruprasad couldn't budge them, though he wondered briefly if they were deficient in imagination or were just stubborn as a rusted lock. Whatever the reason, their collective mind was completely inflexible. *We want to take that line on that map, south.*

Mrs Guruprasad, as the model wife she was, took no part in the conversation. In this subject he was the authority. She was ready, of course, to impose his authority, so she kept an ear out but otherwise exercised an aura of gentle passivity as she read.

* * *

"I must consult," announced Guruprasad. "Please wait outside."

The 7 others filed out and he closed the door.

Priyanka Guruprasad put down her book and rose. She put her hands on her husband's head and massaged his scalp.

"Such bliss," he said, allowing his neck to become floppy as a baby's.

"There is a school of thought that bliss cannot last," she said.

He tsked. "Western romanticism! This is what comes from being unbalanced."

"What are you going to decide, Sooey?"

"I only wish I knew." This was the sign that she must do her wifely work.

"There are seven votes to one," she said.

"My little Badam!" He pinched her waist lovingly. *She is not as supple here as she once was, but she has a most flexacious mind.*

She didn't need to say another word. Their mutual love for democracy decided it.

Mutiny!

But before action, a detail: He whispered, "Are we packed?"

Three seconds later, she nodded *Yes*.

The time, by Mr Sandeep Guruprasad's watch, was 2:00 and thirty seconds.

The jail is filled

THE PROCESSION OF FOUR that roamed the centre of the town of L—— attracted some attention, and more admiration. The group was obviously visitors, the two uniformed workers obviously belonging to a train and thus not warranting any notice, but the man and woman leading this group were notable. That she walked the streets in that flimsy patriotically red outfit and he wore the most inappropriate garb for this weather and seemed to relish his light costume, was evidence enough for all who saw them to conclude that here were members of the famous Moscovian Icebergs, on national tour—being escorted, as was proper, so that they didn't stray into places that weren't suitable for them. The railway unit team would have an itinerary, and one passerby expressed a wish that the itinerary would include the female Iceberg standing in front of Party Headquarters in a naturalist pose.

As was expected of visitors, the procession soon entered the police station, not the best place for onlookers to watch, so no one noticed the exact time they entered, but at the noon siren, they were still inside.

* * *

They found Savva in the police station, sitting on a wooden seat by the door. As soon as she saw him, Galina gasped in delight. He hadn't been carted off to an asylum. He wasn't even in jail.

"Galina!" he whispered. But he did not leap to embrace her.

They were lucky that the jail was full and that he had been

placed in the only location that Vladimir Shukov, acting police chief, could use for incarceration.

Although the Omniscient had been confident of his ability to find Savva and get him released, the chief train driver had been bold enough to speak to the distinguished but misguided tourist (the Omniscient) (as train employee to passenger), pointing out that Savva, as a member of Railway Work Unit 675645, was his, the chief train driver's responsibility.

His decent soul rejoiced that he didn't have to subject the old man to humiliation. He was no exhibitionist, neither with words nor his rock-hard muscles—and he cringed when he had to restrain anyone, even obnoxious drunks. So he only had generous thoughts when the old man followed but did not interfere. First they looked in the hidey holes that Galina thought Savva might have fled to. When they were Savva-less, he followed his hunch, and that's when they found Savva slouching on that bench in the police station.

The chief train driver stepped forward, leader of this delegation.

"He is a model unit worker," he swore, and since the chief train driver was himself a model worker with a badge to show it, that should have done the trick. Five minutes later Savva should have been happily flipping the carpet in 3C, the train should have been happily singing, and (the chief train driver's heart bled to think it) the happy lovers would have been united.

But this was not the case.

The acting chief of police said that the chief train driver was completely correct as to responsibility. He agreed that on the train, this "model worker" (he sneered) "is your responsibility, but as this is not a train, *the last time I looked"* —now he looked around him as if magic could have occurred, but hadn't—"I'm sorry to inform you. This is still a police station. The prisoner is *mine.*"

Galina shoved the head of her work unit aside. "The next time you are a passenger," she said to the man who had smiled at the chief train driver's badge. "I hope to serve you with pleasure." She smiled as he had smiled. She hadn't actually *said* "poison" instead of "pleasure", so there was no crime to charge her with, *but*. And she had only just begun.

At first the acting chief of police Vladimir Shukov was startled, but his lips twitched. After all, he was famous for his sense of humour. He was one of those men whose nose tells how much he appreciates a joke, by its colour. Galina's insults were rich with innuendo, though she wasn't speaking with any deliberation. Pure passion was spewing from her lips, and her armaments, head and breasts pushed to the fore—fully loaded. At first, Shukov's nose flamed red in combined amusement and sensual appreciation— such an audacious mouthful! She'd be like living with an unguided torpedo—a dangerous thrill. But there are limits. As his rational parts pushed aside his sensuality and his famous sense of humour, his brain took over.

The tip of his nose had just turned white when his mouth opened and "Perhaps..." someone interrupted, in a voice as rich and comforting as cream.

The Omniscient stepped to the fore.

Spirit of adventure

"GO, GIRL!" Nick cheered, but no one heard him.

Nick could hardly tear his eyes from Savva. Who could think *that* could be so capable, so romantic, so bloody *creative*?

Nick stood out proudly on Galina's face, his colour blazing, as she defended her love.

* * *

She did all she could do, and as fearlessly as a lobster leaping into a pot.

Now it was in the old boy's hands, *whoever he is.*

Nick wished him luck. "No", he corrected. "I wish *us* luck."

The scent of onions

"DEFACING THE PRESIDENT is a criminal offence," said acting chief of police Vladimir Shukov, feeling that he must sound like an amateur actor. He was so rattled, he wasn't sure he could say, "I am not a pickled cucumber" convincingly.

"I should think so, Comrade," agreed his interrogator, known to us as the Omniscient.

"So there we have it," Shukov laughed, infinitely relieved. In his famous style, he announced, "Case closed," and banged a stapler on the counter. But he didn't let the citizen off without playfully wagging a finger in his face. "And here I thought we were playing chess."

He and this confusing citizen had been discussing the prisoner for several minutes, but had seemed to have difficulties understanding one another's position. As Shukov turned away, he burped in anticipation of a long, well-deserved lunch.

"I'm afraid not. No criminal offence has occurred."

"And who might you be?" he blustered. He wished his superior wasn't holding a private lunch with the Governor that day, and wished even more that his superior hadn't filled the jail with those tins, and that crate. It was a habit that was getting on Shukov's nerves. He needed the jail for criminals, but that was an old-fashioned concept to his comrade superiors. Now that he had a criminal on his hands whose case had, it seems, already attracted attention, where could he be put? Shukov felt hard done by, and

219

instead of glaring at the audacious criminal who should not have been seen nor heard, he had to be on his guard.

"Remember the Tsukochevsky Affair?" the man who had stated that ridiculous denial said leadingly. Shukov didn't, but this man surely did.

"I have been on holiday," frowned the mystery citizen. "He was my attendant."

He *sounded* like a prosecutor. And that fancy waistcoat, almost as fine as the shirt that the police chief gave to the Governor, the one hundred per cent silk with the tropical flowers. *And he doesn't wear a coat.*

A woman pushed up beside the man who must be a Moscow prosecutor, and this woman was breathtakingly intimidating. The final intimidating factor hit Shukov like a club. *They aren't wearing coats.* His terrible circulation had always been a secret shame.

"What do you mean 'no criminal offence' when a criminal offence has clearly occurred?" he said. The more ashamed he felt, the more pugnacious he became.

"Please quote the offence," said the Omniscient.

"This isn't a court."

"I demand that you detail the charges." The Omniscient's voice was quiet with authority.

Shukov frisked the room with his eyes. The place was stuffed with police, all at lunch. Two of them were cutting onions. He was on his own.

"You should be able to quote it yourself, comrade," he smiled, "when a citizen defaces a leader, especially the president."

"And what was the nature of this defacement?"

"You don't know?" Shukov asked, narrowing his eyes to a look that screamed "Watch out or I'll arrest you, too."

"Please tell me the nature of this defacement," said his interrogator.

Only someone very sure of himself would willingly enter a police station. And Shukov had never been treated like this by a person on the other side of the counter.

"Tell me exactly," said the man who had made Shukov sweat. "Code, section. And I'm onto you. Cease your diversionary tactics, or..."

Shukov wasn't sweating any more. It was obvious that this old man hadn't actually been witness to any act. How could he have, being a passenger in the train? The mural must have already been refaced when this man emerged, angry at the samovar going cold or something, or at not having his private stock of caviar served on ice.

Shukov pointed to the prisoner. "Your model citizen there painted a birthmark on the President's face." That should have done it. He turned away to have his lunch.

"Doesn't the President have a birthmark?"

Shukov gasped. *No one talks of such things in such a place.*

"Come now," said the man. "Does or does not the President have a birthmark on his face?"

Shukov's lips formed a thin hard line.

"I shall return," said the daring senior citizen, raising a finger in the policeman's face, "with the *truth*."

The terrible bush

SO MUNIFER THE MAKER of the Great Tīmūrsaçi's saçiness, travelled home to his workshop with the bag of virgin hair that he had been forced, through no fault of his own, to purchase—in a Quarter of Ill Repute, no less.

He set to making the great moustache, though there were new steps he had to take this year, in crafting this anomalous hersutity. The bag was as mixed a bag as a cat catcher's. He sniffed as he pulled out the contents—no silken flow of lustrous black, such as he was used to from that special secret village-of-no-name (designated by the Great's mother) where this year all the virgins had inconsiderately died and everyone else had fled or died except one old woman with hair like peed-on cotton.

These flaming red and gold and mousy brown hairs couldn't be used without being treated. Munifer hunted till he found the perfect tincture. He bought the recipe for the powerful stuff from a blind dyer in the town of G————. When Munifer found him, the man was curled like a dried prawn, lying in filth in a hole of the wall surrounding the dyer's quarter. The dyer's lips were black with oncoming death. Munifer paid him by promising to pay for a funeral, complete with professional mourners, and a singer named Honeylips. As Luck would have it, the dyer was a man of high morality, if not business sense. The recipe was a complex and surprising one, and the dyer was a perfectionist. His last breath lasted long enough for him to say, "And don't get it in your eyes."

As for the silken flow of hair that Munifer was used to, this lot was puffed out with kinked, curly, and wavy locks. So he tamed it, using a recipe that was so harsh that no hair could last longer than a year, but no hair needed to.

Finally, he applied his special stiffening polish of waxes and gums to shape and shine the moustache out to its Great span. His hands moulded hair as expertly as a potter works clay. Moulding and stretching, thickening and thinning down to authoritative points, he employed a last sure-fingered flourish as his arms stretched the twin horns to their furthest span.

He stepped away, then walked closer. He inspected the moustache from the left side, then the right, then at the angle of a petitioner, gazing up at it from the floor. Only then could he smile grimly. *Magnificent!* he allowed himself to think. That damned village couldn't stop him from producing, yet again, a masterwork that would fool those who knew no better—and who knew better than he?

No one, he hummed, *will be the wiser.*

Night had dyed the sky black, and bright stars glowed upon it like a net of diamonds—but he was in no mood for poetic similes, let alone solitude. He locked his secret workshop and strode, tapping out a lively rhythm with his stick, to the nearest Quarter of Ill Repute where he lived for a week, his arms festooned with girls. His wealth was a source of hope (and speculation as to its origins).

But his Greatness's appointment loomed, so Munifer cut his pleasure short.

He set out as an unlucky man, the sort of man you want to keep far from, lest the evil eye stray from him, to *you*. Munifer had packed the moustache in its crafty old travelling case, one of those hideous eelskin things that itinerant long-horn players tote, *and what long-horn player isn't an unlucky itinerant?*

As he walked, he murmured praises to Providence, the dropper of the Curse upon that inconvenient village for the luck of him. No longer would he have to take that exhausting trip, climb up any rugged mountains, or go anywhere at all. He could send for a hag from the closest Quarter of Ill Repute and buy a bag of virgin hair from her—and she would not even be curious *why*.

And furthermore—this thought came to him as he reached the last hill on the night before he reached the Great City where, in seven days, he was dated by the calendar first set by the Great Tīmūrsaçi's mother, to present and fit Tīmūrsaçi's great moustache, known by only the Great's mother, Tīmūrsaçi', and Munifer himself to be not grown in the soil of the Greatness' face. As he stopped and put down his case, the thought exploded in his head with such power that he reeled. *Why use virgin hair at all?*

He had to sit, and not being a philosopher, he almost fell over with the effort of making his unexercised brain work at thinking this out. *I, a master wigmaker, which was why I was chosen in the first place, could make the moustache from anything. Horsehair. Wheat stalks. Mouse spit!*

He almost cried, such was the sadness he felt over all those wasted years of going to that cursed village, coming back, going, coming. *Aghhh.* And what made him think that anyone but him would be able to recognise virtuous fine virgin hair from any other? It was only Fortune that led him to Desperation, that led him to the Quarter of Ill Repute, where he was only too aware that the virgin hair would be like anything that you can buy—of lesser worth. But then he was a master of disguise. *Why haven't I matched my wits to my skills?*

He looked forward on the path, and back—and saw no one. So, in a transport of thankfulness, he threw himself in the dust and gave thanks. He did not ask *Why?* That just tempts the Evil One. And then he hid behind the nearest cedar, and slept.

He was just slapping a servant girl for splashing a drop of wine on his face as she poured it into his mouth, when he woke. Cold, stinging drops continued to hit his face. A spring shower.

"Cursed rain." The night was black. He pulled his cloak over his head.

He half-woke to the call of, he supposed, swallows, the drone of bees or other small winged things, and the *crick crick crick* of something else. Nature's music put him to sleep again as the sun came out above and dried the tears of invisible nymphs from their leaf seats in the trees, as stories say.

Even the air was fragrant with promise.

He lay on his back listening. The swallows seemed to have flocked off. The drone of the winged things was so distant that he wasn't sure if his ears were droning just to please him, and the *crick crick* was nowhere to be heard.

It was time to get on his way, but the sky was so pretty. He watched a cloud float aimlessly for a while, but he had to get on his way, so as he watched the cloud to see if it would do anything dramatic, he reached for the old eelskin case because a man with a case in the hand can't lie on his back and watch clouds float all day.

He must have thrashed in his sleep because his fingers didn't feel the smooth, sewn case, but instead, touched some rough thornbush. *Why are clouds like cotton?* He made a resolution that moment that from this year forward, he would devote all the spare time he would have, to thinking revelating thoughts.

But for the moment, he had to get on his way.

He rolled away from the bush. Lucky he hadn't rolled into the bush in the dark. He didn't want to get a splinter in his delicate fingers so he rolled away from it and stood up, as he might have to reach under it to find where that case had been kicked to.

He saw the bush and it was like no other that he had ever set his eyes upon—curly and scraggly and pointy and tangled red and gold and mousy brown, lying on a path that was stained, as if a flock of birds had eaten blackberries above it. An end of tattered eelskin protruded from the mass, thin and worthless as the shed skin of a viper, caught on a thornbush. The hair bush was still growing, breaking out of its beeswax stays. Each hair was reverting to what it had been when he bought it.

A lesson

THE OMNISCIENT WAS CRESTFALLEN. The local office of the *Truth* hadn't been hard to find, but once inside the hallowed doors, truth had been elusive.

The others in the Omniscient's group looked on. They hadn't known that the mark was real. Galina and the chief train driver had only heard rumours, and the Muse was ignorant. But the mark had triggered juices to flow in the Omniscient's memory glands. He had thought that he might need to go to the press when he had first vowed that the truth would set Savva free, but he had not wanted to have to resort to law.

As it was, *Truth* was a revelation of the worst order.

They knew of Savva's exploit but far from wanting to feature him as a hero who had acted in solidarity with their banner, they wanted to consider the action he had taken as non-existent. They did not want to cover it. They had not taken a single photograph of the President with the mark that nature had bestowed upon him. They *condoned* the falsification of his image, the covering of the mark.

The Omniscient was not only crestfallen. He was disgusted. And very very sad.

He wouldn't have the heart to tell that sweet little man who read their rag so assiduously, but now the Omniscient knew that the attendant's favourite section was some sort of journalistic joke, fostered on the simple people.

"Is this disappearance of the mark one of your anomalous phenomena?" he was brought so low that he sneered.

"As a matter of fact, it is," said the editor.

The Omniscient laughed bitterly. "Like the psychotronic weapon that turns humans into zombies?"

"Bekhtereva's machine isn't laughable, unless you think General Ratnikov is a clown," said the editor dryly. "The General approved it. But you act educated, so I shouldn't have to tell you that the disappearance of the mark cannot be attributed to anything bearing an ON/OFF button. The disappearance is pure physics."

"Physics!" exploded the Omniscient. "Don't decry the sacred role physics—"

"My time is valuable, Comrade citizen." The editor took out a red pencil and began to mark some papers.

The Omniscient was not defeated. "Physics is a force of nature."

"A natural rule of law."

"Yes indeed." The Omniscient was glad they could agree upon one point.

The editor looked at him with disappointment. "I would have thought that anyone who knew physics..."

The Omniscient dropped his eyes.

"Perhaps you are not aware," said the editor, "of the Law of Negative Effects, a subsection of the Law of Special Rules."

"I thought I knew law," said the Omniscient humbly. "Please."

The editor's eyes took on the glazed look of those who need to disassociate themselves from the temporal world in order to remember.

"For certain purposes and in diverse circumstances," he recited, "an Effect can occur that

(a) treats a particular event that actually happened as not having happened; and

(b) treats a particular event that did not actually happen as having happened and, if appropriate, treats the event as:

227

(i) having happened at a particular time; and as

(ii) having involved particular action by a particular entity; and

(c) treats a particular event that actually happened as:

(i) having happened at a time different from the time it actually happened; or

(ii) having involved particular action by a particular entity (whether or not the event actually involved any action by that entity)."

"I beg your pardon," said the Omniscient. "I never knew."

The editor smiled. "We can't all know everything all the time."

The little group left the newspaper office looking like a bedraggled comet. It fell to earth in the park, where the Omniscient sat heavily on a bench.

"I have failed," he announced. "If only I had remembered."

"Remembered what," asked the Muse. Listening to that rubbish in the newspaper office, it was all she could do to keep herself straight-faced. The idea that anyone could take it seriously chilled her to the core.

"You should dress warmly," she said to the Omniscient.

He didn't hear her, so busy was he, remembering. "You make your own history, remember?"

The Muse groaned.

"You see, miss, uh ... Comrade Valeria? It's the perfect confluence of Nature and Law."

The Omniscient's face lit with the unearthly joy and terrible sadness of revelation. "It's Natural Law, though that policeman couldn't quote the chapter."

"Gorgonna!"

Old puns don't die

"GORGONNA," Nick shouted, and it felt so *gooood*. None of this group would hear and he didn't know what the hell gorgonna meant, but screaming the word that this rather wacko woman used to release her inner self allowed Nick to bask in the warm clean illusion of camaraderie—instead of feeling frustrated, lonely, frozen out, and muddy as a gutter in this town—muddy with guilt.

Yes, guilt.

Are the sins of the fathers visited upon their sons? Nick had never been into philosophy but he didn't have much choice now. He felt that they must be. *Could something in my genes have caused this to happen?*

Of course not, yet he felt both guilt and an acne outbreak of memories.

The Providential Truth-Building Society.

That had been his dad's name for the Australian Tax Office. When Geoff Kippax's life as a Captain of Industry had hit the rocks, he had crawled back to his old department, the Tax Office, but it had changed. No more could he get a cushy public service post. Privatisation had become the norm. So he was forced to become a consultant. The pay was astronomical, but he didn't have the security he'd had before. He also had the bitterness Jill Kippax had left him with, the unfairness of alimony. He couldn't get any, though she was accruing company directorships faster than frequent-flier points.

Geoff Kippax, therefore, devoted his life to really *working* for those high consultancy fees, and in doing so delighted the Office and his mates there in particular. Nick knew all this because his father kept him informed, whether Nick wanted to know or not. Geoff Kippax's expertise was in Tax Law, and the brief was always the same: Maximise tax (and, his mates added, screw our exes). For a few years, he produced modest successes that were only incrementally nasty. Then he achieved greatness. His masterpiece, which he sent to his son, framed, was Chapter 4 - Special Rules, Part 4-7, Division 165 - Anti-avoidance, Subdivision 165-B - Commissioner may negate effects... For the purposes of making a declaration under this Subdivision, the Commissioner may: (a) treat a particular event that actually happened as not having happened; and *dot dot dot, exactly as quoted minutes ago.*

That nickname his dad used for his beloved department. Nick as a child tried to ignore his parents' wit, but they were pests. As an adult, he first tried to drown out their attentions and more so, their bitter influence: by creating food, and when that had proved too easy; wine judging; and when that had turned, inevitably, into a bitter joke, he had sought adventures in, first: extreme comestibles; and when that had become tame, he had sought the ultimate.

He'd had a while to tell his little joke to himself, *It's what made me what I am today*, but he wasn't into reviewing his life at the moment. He needed to think back to earlier times.

He hadn't tried to drown out The Providential Truth-Building Society. The wit had completely missed him. It was just part of his dad, like any pun repeated till it doesn't annoy you any more.

Nick's mind turned to the present, to that newspaper the old guy here put so much store in. Nick had never been a linguist but was getting pretty good now, with nothing else to do but listen— but *Pravda*. He'd known of it before, but he'd never known it *meant* anything, always thought it a brand, like Kraft, Beluga, Prada.

And the old guy's embarrassingly naïve, irritatingly evangelistic

The truth will set him free bullshit. Nick had understood it enough to want to gag, but he hadn't *understood*.

NOW I understand.

Pravda = truth. Sick!

But there was another revelation that made him even sicker. *That bloke, the President with the birthmark. He was president here, when?*

Nick had to think back, and for someone who had always considered politics distasteful, it was a hard slog, but he had a good memory for what counts. *Got it! Date this as Pre- Vodka Granita. This could be that infamous year of the sticky puddings.* which brought Nick to a conclusion that he reluctantly had to reach. *Not only is Dad a bitter old fart, but he can't even create anything original.*

Gorgonna!

Nick pulled himself out of this spiral of self-interest. *What does Dad matter? What do I matter?*

Galina had been sobbing quietly since they left the *Pravda* office. Now she lifted her face and blew her nose.

Nick wanted more than anything in the world, to hold her in his arms. *No,* he corrected. *To hold you both in my arms.*

All I've ever sought, he said, not that anyone heard, here—*is to see true love. I would make you one helluva wedding cake.*

Natural conclusions

"So you see," said the Omniscient. "Your nice young man (for it had reached his consciousness that the cook was in love with the prisoner) has broken the law and must serve his term of incarceration. We are powerless to change the way the law is administered, I am terribly sorry to say."

Galina jumped up. "Then I'll go to prison with him!"

The Muse put her hand out, but drew it back without touching Galina. "I'll go."

Galina's eyebrows rose to twin peaks, but her eyes were unnaturally shiny.

"You?" the Omniscient broke in, staring at the Muse.

Galina smiled at her.

"Out of the question," declared the Omniscient. "Outrageous." He mumbled something to himself. "I'll go. And I'll brook no argument."

He squared his shoulders and glared at the women. *I just hope they don't hang me from the ceiling like that one in—*

"No one's going to prison," said the Muse.

Galina looked her up and down. "That's right," she said, more in hope than faith. But in solidarity, she turned on her heel so that she and the Muse stood side by side.

The Omniscient turned to the chief train driver, "Comrade, er…" He wanted to remember the man's name but couldn't. "Do you know what they're planning?"

Yuri Shurov had been too shy to shout "No!" to Galina's idea of going to prison, and too sane to think that her going to prison would mean that Savva would be released. It would only add one more prisoner.

But the beautiful woman in red had volunteered and then said that no one would go to prison. He believed her, whatever she was planning. She looked tough.

He turned to give the old man reassurance. "Comrade," he began, and as the chief train driver was not only shy but an unusually polite man, he tried to remember the name of this well-meaning senior citizen. "Comrade..." *Dugov? Gogol? Dobrov?*

His memory was cleaner than a washed bottle, but all of a sudden he remembered: the time!

He ran away. There was no time to explain.

Close call

2:07 P.M., CARRIAGE 1A

Mr Sandeep Guruprasad had never been what you could call 'an impatient man', but he was beginning to lose his temper.

"Please listen, Mr Riley, for I will yet again state to you as clearly as a schedule, that to shunt to the other track, the switching apparati must be employed. And for that, someone must leave the train bodily, as only a person's physical presence can effect to throw the switches. As you must have seen when you looked out the window, these switches in full view of the railway station. In summation, if you assume that, should I be observed, I would be contemplated as an employee of this Railway, you are a more credulous man than I would deem worthy of the title 'a person of intelligence'. Therefore—"

He raised a finger. "That was not constructive. As I was about to say, there is another way. One of you gentlemen must venture from this train and perform the task, if you insist on taking this fateful measure. And you, furthermore, must perform it in the proper uniform, which perforce you have much experience of, having painted employees of this railway in one-to-one hundred scale, I believe you said, upon more than one occasion?"

Mr Guruprasad cast his eyes upon a heretofore unmentioned member of the majority of 7, who looked away.

Riley spoke up. "You're some team player."

"Damn uncooperative," said another committed tourist from

the mass blocking the doorway.

Guruprasad looked at them with the imperturbability of a public servant with 25 years service under his belt. In his unasked-for position as commander of the mutiny and thus, this speech outlining duties, he had not reached the subject of train *driving*. They assumed the unassumable. But why cross that bridge till they came to it?

Riley stomped forward on his walker till his breath was close enough to revolt the tea-totalling Guruprasad.

"Tell you what I'm gonna do. I'll give you to three and, hey!" He jerked his walker upwards, sideways, both walker and he standing on one leg, hovering.

Was that a lurch of the train? Yes! and another. The doorway unclogged instantly as 5 men scuttled to the windows along the passage. Riley toppled. His walker clattering to a prone position, and he, like an elephant seal on a pup as his arm hit the compartment's little window table and tore it from its attachment.

The train was on the move.

Not only that, but the train was now running on that other track.

"Innit abow time," said Calum Boldridge, stretching out on his top bunk.

Riley filled the compartment's floor and spread onto both bottom bunks, creating an emotional wash in the expression of Mrs Guruprasad, who hastened to move wallward, body and book.

However, decades of healthy habits had forged muscles of iron in Sandeep Guruprasad. His legs now moved with the grace and strength of pistons as he used his arms like levers. After he had balanced the bag of blubber upright and secured its grip upon the walker, he couldn't help turning to his wife, sending her a smile that said nine words: See how rewarding a bit of exercise could be?

"Thanks," said Riley grudgingly.

"I'll see to that," he heard, and suddenly Mrs Guruprasad (a woman he had never seen in any position other than lying full-length) had risen to a height that almost reached his elbow, taken his left arm in her hands, examined it with more care than he'd known humanly possible—and as he watched, she left the compartment only long enough to visit the samovar in the passage. She bustled back and cleaned his arm with hot water and a spotless washcloth, tweezed out an invisible splinter. He was pretty boggled by all that, but now she applied a bright yellow salve, and a pink plastic bandage to the cut that he would have ignored until it filled with pus, then squeezed, repeating as needed till it crusted over in a final scab that formed a scar.

In the meantime, Mr Guruprasad had unwrapped a roll of tools and in some ingenious way, firmly reattached the table to the wall. It now looked as it had before—a bit weary but not hard-done by.

The Guruprasads then exchanged guarded glances, and smiled at Riley.

Mrs Guruprasad had never been a train employee, but being married to Sandeep Guruprasad had given her as much education as she needed to know that, far from being on the move, this train had just been shunted to a disused track so that other trains that were on the move, could move through.

"Do you require assistance?" Sandeep Guruprasad asked in his most professional Railway voice.

"Thanks," said Riley. He let Guruprasad arrange him on the bottom bunk.

Mrs. Guruprasad held out Riley's rather flattened flask. It must have dropped out of his pocket. "I think a little tot would be in order," she said to her husband.

Sandeep's lip curled before he caught on. He turned to offer it to Riley, but he was already dead to the world.

The Guruprasads' eyes were big, their ears straining to hear every sound.

William "Toots" Riley was typical. He was snoring—in the same state of nervous exhaustion as the other 6 fanatically committed tourists. None of them felt the need to look out a window. They were sick of the place. Now the intolerable delay they had just endured would become another Amazing Travel Adventure, another anecdote in that fat book each was writing in his head and each assailed all others with excerpts from at every waking opportunity: The Pain of Travelling.

Snores of many resonances, breaths of many ranknesses (including stale imitation-cheese snacks) came from their mouths as each dreamt—of home.

The Guruprasads turned to each other. He motioned with his eyes.

She hardly moved, yet that roll of the eyes and wriggle added up to one hundred and ten percent agreement.

47 seconds later, Mr and Mrs Sandeep Guruprasad of 135 Station Road, Lucknow, Uttar Pradesh, India, jumped off the train. She hadn't actually jumped. He had needed to gather her in his arms, as the long jump down to the gravel of an unkempt track is not for the inexperienced—though he was proud that he could jump with ease and still thrill his wife, whose eyes flashed as they landed. As she unwrapped her fragrant arms from his neck, he almost wished that the situation had been more dangerous. He would have loved to have leapt from a moving train. *Some time in the future.* In their current adventure, this leap had been from a train that was, yet again, as unmoving as an inflexible mind.

The time was 2:14

The 2:07 arrived at 2:16, luckily late, as it was no one's job in the train station to remember such things as a train that should have been gone over 24 hours ago, being in the way of an express.

The chief train driver wiped the sweat from his brow. *If the 2:07 had been on time.*

He could hardly forgive himself for this almost accident. *Look what love does.* He didn't think it good enough that no one here noticed. It was as if they were all somewhere else.

Mr and Mrs Guruprasad boarded the 7-minute-late train with no remark at its lateness, nor a look back in sadness at the train

237

they'd just left. Certainly not that! Mr Guruprasad would have liked to know the timetable, but in that regard, this country was the wild west. He was not a superstitious man, nor a spiritual one. But no doubt about it, *this* train had arrived as a stroke of luck. He had heavily disapproved of that mutiny, and wished to get as far away from the mutineers as one small world made possible.

The train took off as if it were in a hurry to make up time, or to get somewhere.

As he and his wife settled in their higher-and-lower bunks, they both tingled with pleasure. Their new companions were not only cracking sunflower seeds already, but holding out bags of friendship.

Oblomov. Mrs Guruprasad rolled the sounds on her tongue. *Imagine lying in bed being your natural condition. Such bliss.*

"Kulak..." sang the rushing train, and soon Mrs Guruprasad was sung to sleep.

Not so for Mr Guruprasad. Far into the snowy evening, he scratched away. He could not deny his logbook. "Don't stop now," it begged. "How absolutely riveting. How revolting! How brave. How almost *unbelievable*. Tell me more."

Flags of inconvenience

THE SUPERSTITIOUS will draw their own conclusions, but rational observers will cite Luck that the last few hours had been free of track irregularities in the responsibility zone of Railway Work Unit 894685 (the station master for the town of L—— and his staff of five). The unit had been in the station master's office since just before 2:00 p.m. and had entirely forgotten about any damned trains.

The staff were in revolt, and threats by their chief to report them for insubordination had only made the instigator laugh.

"We'll go above you," threatened the assistant station master.

His superior was waiting for that. "Do, Igor Igorovich. Be my guest."

The signalman was resigned to his lot. "That's life. They've cheated us."

"To each, what he can get his hands on," said the chief. "What do you think I get?"

"Plenty," said the assistant.

"Nothing of value," said the chief.

"A tin of caviar here. A little diamond there? Don't deny it. We know. You call that nothing?"

The chief re-assessed the assistant. "Have you not been taught, 'Nothing can have value without being an object of utility,' or do I have to assign you Remedial Political Consciousness?"

"C'mon, Igor," said the signalman. "Some are born to carry,

and some to get." He had never wanted to be a mover of smuggled goods, but he had even less wanted to be a rebel.

"I'm a signalman," he said. And at the utterance, he started violently, as the Signalman's Nightmare hit him at 200kmh. *That train on the track that's been there since yesterday.* No one had moved it even though he had repeatedly said that it needed to be moved for today's 2:07, but the other members of his work unit said it wasn't their job and that it would be done in good time by whosever job it was; and no one had come, and it had been there solid as Party Headquarters when the assistant chief had forced the meeting in the chief's office at 1:45; and it was now 2:11 and the 2:07 must have been overdue; for if it had been on time, they'd have heard the crash all the way to Moscow.

There was still time to hear it.

Two EMERGENCY STOP flags rested behind the chief's chair. The chief thought them dashing. The signalman vaulted the desk, knocking the chief to the ground, grabbed the flags, and flung the door open so fast that it hit the assistant in the back.

The chief hit his head on the side of his desk, but it jolted his memory into working condition. He looked at the clock on the wall, and felt sick. He hoped against hope that Signalman First Class Zhora Bychok would be able to stop that train—if need be, with Comrade Bychok's body.

His assistant helped him to his feet. He hastily reminded the assistant of the time; and then, its importance.

The assistant, being the Assistant, said: "Uh."

Then the Chief Train Station Master and the Assistant, and the other two members of Railway Work Unit 894685 rushed to the platform, knowing of course, that there was nothing they could do this late in the inaction, but watch.

Snow and tears

THE CHIEF OF POLICE rolled into the police station, roaring happy. It had been a good lunch with the Governor. The trade in caviar was going splendidly. The case of sprats in rock salt was due to go out to the Governor's special friend on the 2:07, compliments of the Governor.

"When life is smooth, life is smooth," sang the Police Chief. "So how's everything been here, Shukov?" he asked the ex-acting police chief, now once again, merely his assistant.

"All normal," said Shukov.

The chief winked. "The shipment go off swimmingly?"

Craftily, at an unnaturally early hour this morning, he'd caught up to Shukov walking to work. Taking his inferior's arm, he gave Shukov a special job, involving "a crate that contains"—not only informing him of the contents, but adding, "I hope you appreciate the responsibility of this State secret."

Shukov pleased the chief by replying that he'd assign the big black van to transfer the "fishy prisoner" (the police chief's sense of humour was more famous by a rank, than the assistant police chief's). Their business concluded before 8:00 a.m., the chief released the younger officer whose pace increased till it was almost a trot. Shukov was, after all, acting chief of police till the chief arrived at work.

"Swimmingly," said Shukov, sweating. The time was now 2:07 and three seconds.

He'd had to spend too much time policing today to take care of the important stuff. Only with minutes to go had he remembered that blasted crate. He winced at the tone he'd used to the men he detailed to take the thing to the station. Two quiet chess players, innocently eating onions and enjoying their well-earned break. He'd shouted at them, something about "lazy bones". He hoped they would take a little time with the van, go find a loiterer to beat up or something, before they came back. As it was, there were ten men in the room who had witnessed his lack of good command, and they were still here, all writing reports. The day could not end soon enough for the man who despaired, at the moment, of ever being Chief of Police.

"Who's that?" asked the chief. He was in that stage of happiness that he wanted to cause trouble.

Shukov glared at Savva from behind the man's enormous back. The chief had been out of the office for two days, so hadn't known of the Case of the Painted President. The acting police chief had thought the chief would be *happy* to find that his second in command had so smoothly directed that cover-up operation, and now had the perp in custody.

Now that the chief was less than a truncheon away, and reeking of competitive drinking and unexercised aggression, Shukov realised that having a political incident *happen* was an incident, all right, *in the record of a police chief.*

"He's just leaving," said Shukov in as offhand a manner as he could summon. "Was waiting for a paper to be signed."

The chief looked around at the ten men and his second in command. *Bang* went his hamlike fist on the counter. "Eleven men," he roared, "and a citizen has to wait?"

"He was just leaving," said Shukov, sounding hurt and begging Savva with his eyes.

"Comrade Commander," said Savva, to the police chief. "They have been most helpful. I was just sitting for a moment." He patted his belly. "Ulcer, you know."

"Well, then," said the chief amiably. "May the force be with you."

Savva heard laughter above the call of duty as he pushed open the door and walked down the police station steps as if he were strolling in a museum. It wouldn't do to look hurried.

He didn't know which way to go, where they would be, but just then he saw the woman in red coming towards him. She looked surprised to see him, but he was surprised to see her, too. Not that he wanted to see *her*.

"Are they finished with you?" she said.

He nodded.

"Wonderful," she said, her eyes shining.

It made him uncomfortable. "Where's everybody?"

"In the park."

"Let's go."

"Let's," said she.

Galina saw them first. She didn't say anything out loud but the way she looked at Savva was plain.

But then, confusingly, she turned to the woman in red, the one who'd just stood passively behind the others in the police station. "From the bottom of my heart—" Galina said, reaching out to the woman, who turned away.

"I didn't do anything," said the woman. She wasn't looking beautiful at the moment. Savva compared them—Galina, upright and proud in her uniform, and the woman in red, rumpled and oddly, now dull-eyed.

"Let's go," said the woman.

"Let's," said Savva. The sooner the better.

"Are you released?" asked the old man.

"Yes," said Savva, already walking.

"I'm delighted to see you, young man," said the old man. "I look forward to your tale of adventure."

"On the train," said Savva. "Where's—"

"There he is," said Galina. And indeed, after moving the train to that out-of-the-way track, Comrade Shurov had returned. He could see that Savva was safe and well, and that Savva and Galina were eager to get home.

The group made their way in a purposefully casual stroll, as fast as they could. Galina looked out of the side of her eyes at Savva, but he was preoccupied. He seemed to be looking out for something, or someone.

Galina pulled out a hairpin and stuck it somewhere else in her piled up mass. *We'll never leave the train again.*

A block before the station, he saw something.

"Wait here, please," he said, and ducked around the corner.

Of course they waited, but for Galina, it was torture. Each second took an hour to come and go; and still, no Savva.

It was all of 92 seconds when Savva appeared again, strolling like any family-man citizen on a winter day, carrying ice creams for everyone. What better time to eat ice cream than when it's snowing, as it had just begun, lightly, to do? He handed the ice creams out one by one, till he got to Galina. His eyes travelled down her jacket to the buttons straining on her belly, and then up to her eyes. "From me, according to my ability,"—he held out the last two ice creams—"to you, according to your needs."

"Znnnnnh." The chief train driver had burst into tears.

The woman in red wiped her eyes.

Nick would have bawled his eyes out if he had had eyes.

"Is something wrong?" asked the Omniscient, who had been very involved trying to solve the mystery of the guilty man's release.

"Let's go home," said Yuri Shurov, a great train driver.

Git 'im up

RILEY WAS TORN FROM A DREAM of sitting in a fast highway-side Bob's Big Boy, polishing off one of their Super Big Boy Combos, a plate of Chili Spaghetti waiting on the side. He was just dipping a fry into ketchup when he woke to a screech of brakes.

It was the sound of that late 2:07, which, in the manner of late trains, took off almost as fast as it had arrived. Riley knew diddlysquat about the 2:07, but he was no fool about trains.

"Wouldn't you just *know* it," he bellowed. "We're stuck in this place tighter'n a dog turd under a shoe."

In moments, he'd rousted the mutineers from their trusting slumber, and they met at his bunk—easier than him moving.

Two tidy bunks met the outraged stares of the members of the group.

"No good cowards. Musta cleared out under our noses," said Riley's pardner.

"Musta," said Riley. They'd even taken their plastic bags of garbage.

"Shoot!" said the member of the group whose house was built to accommodate, at scale, the length and twists of the Atchison, Topeka & Santa Fe Railway as it was upon completion in 1901. The spectacular part was where it ended at the Grand Canyon. He'd had the canyon excavated, too, and it was not only quite a sight, but impressively dangerous, seeing as how he hadn't covered it over, but just flanked it with big ol' sofas and a wetbar. By rights, he should have been Riley's pardner, but Riley, whose wife banned trains from the house, ignored anyone who had better than a K-Mart Christmas special.

Riley's pardner scrunched his mouth up and tossed his head. A gob of spit hit the top empty bunk, and though there was no *ping* like there is with a spittoon in the movies, it was *something*. The pardner was an actuary from Vermont, but the best part of a holiday is the chance to be anyone you want to be. "What we gonna do?" he asked Riley.

"Well..." said Riley.

They waited while he thought.

"You've roamed the train?"

No one had thought to do that.

"Go huntin" he said, "and if you find anyone, bring him here."

"Yes, boss," someone actually said.

There wasn't room enough for six men to make it through 1A's door at once, but once out the door, the posse broke into a stampede.

They might never have found anyone if it weren't for the noise Valentin made as he closed the door to his compartment.

The actuary saw him. Not only that, but 4 men burst the door open, and the actuary caught him red-handed. "Why, you little weasel," said the actuary, who was himself the very model of a model little weasel. "Lookee here, boys!"

"Hey!" said one man, grabbing the plastic bag that Valentin had in his hand. It said Marlboro. He looked in the bag, and shook it at Valentin. "Whadya do with my stuff?"

"Nothing, sir," insisted Valentin. "I clean. You like clean, no?"

"I stored my dirty underwear here," the man whose bag was stolen said to the others. "Where is it, you little turd?"

"I do the same thing," said someone.

"Only way to travel," said someone else.

The actuary narrowed his eyes at Valentin. Though the actuary had never been a leader before, he pulled out his L.L. Bean

Collectors Knife, the one with the serrated blade.

Valentin's eyes bugged out of his head.

"What else you got here?" said the actuary, who in one swoop, fell upon Valentin's bunk and slit it open, wide as a hog's belly.

That bed was packed tighter than a hog's guts. The insides came out, first, as a swelling multicoloured mass ... and then that just expanded and expanded. Marlboro, Courvoisier, Payless, Red October and Los Angeles Duty Free. The names kept coming. There were names from everywhere. Dozens of names. And there was silver and gold, red and blue and pink and green, and lots and lots of white. That mattress must have had more plastic bags and wrappers than a day's pickup in the city of Denver.

The posse kept their prisoner at bay while they tore open the rest of the compartment. They found nothing else that could have been stolen except, possibly, one pair of felt boots. They left the compartment only after the ones who'd had their laundry bags stolen were satisfied that each bag had been retrieved and was now in its owner's keeping, safe and sound.

As to the prisoner, he was a grizzling mess, especially after the one with the knife had made strips of the red leatherette, and directed the others in wrestling the thief's hands till they were tied tighter than a—

"Hold on," said the actuary. "He's gotta be searched."

So they untied him and tore his jacket off.

"Here boss," said the man who had a thing about bosses. He handed the actuary something from the jacket's inside breast pocket. It was a book, and it was damp.

"Whew," said the actuary, making a face at Valentin. "You sweat more'n you clean. And ... lessee. You read better, too!"

"Lessee," said his acolyte.

The men gathered around. "That dirty little," said someone.

"They act like they don't know English—"

"And then they read porn."

"Just what you'd expect."

"Innit."

"Think I got all day?" The voice of the former leader of the gang broke, like a plate glass window, all over them. He loomed in the doorway, not being able to get himself and his walker through without some heavy manoeuvring. "Whadaya got?"

"A thief, boss."

"You *idiot*," yelled Riley, "and call me Toots. We want a driver, and I couldn't give a cotton pickin' if he stole the teeth outa your mouth."

In his response to the admirably succinct report, Riley made an enemy to the end of days, but that is another story.

"You're gonna drive this train," he said to the almost naked Valentin.

"I *can't*," said Valentin, who truly, scout's honour, couldn't even drive a car.

"I don't care if you can't," said the ex-top brush salesman of the state of Nevada, "You WILL." And he lurched one leg of his walker, forward.

Roundup

THE TWO MEN detailed to take the crate of salted sprats onto the 2:07 express threw the crate into the back of the big black wagon with a degree of viciousness. They got in the van and drove around the town for a while, to cool off.

"The way we're treated," said one.

"Pawns."

"Exactly."

They were good and steamed up by the time they remembered that they had to get this crate on the train. The time was 2:07 and they were somewhere on the outskirts of town.

The siren helped clear the way till it broke, so the driver put his hand on the horn and drove faster, all over the road.

"It's probably too late," said the other one, but they were young enough that neither truly believed that.

"Salted fish!"

"What do they take us for?"

"Do you think the rumour's right?"

"Diamonds?"

"Yes."

"Pawns," said the one who'd already said that.

Pedestrians scattered. The van almost overturned on a curve, but as the policeman turned the last corner, they knew they weren't too late. That crowd of people clutched belongings in the way people do when each is ready to push his way into something that doesn't care who gets in and is in a hurry to leave though it's only just come. The train was late, but it could come any second.

The driver hit the brake and two policemen jumped out, threw open the back doors and manhandled the heavy, sharp-edged wooden crate of salted fish out, till they held it balanced between them.

Just as each policeman had loosened his grip because he thought the other guy held the weight, the kvass barrel across the street sprang an explosive leak. The sweet, golden, irrepressible ferment shot out everywhere, on screaming pedestrians and on the street itself, slippery with freshly falling snow.

Then, whether it was one policeman or two will never be determined, but one or both dropped the case, which smashed open. In seconds, a helpful crowd had gathered. Helpful as in the posters of the people Working for a Common Cause, only in this case it looked like that for the first moments, but quickly the scene turned into a case of Rampant Capitalism as each person kneeling in the road sorting fish from salt began to want to be more helpful than the others.

In the midst of this the late train came and went with no one, including the two policemen, being close enough to hear.

The citizens were throwing fish at the feet of the policemen in their enthusiastic sorting of excess salt, from fish, a model scene of cooperation, even if there was individual initiative.

The work went so fast that within two minutes, there was not a single fish lost under a foot or wheel. The policemen put the crate together, threw the fish back in and sealed it up.

"Think we missed the train?" said one.

"What does it matter?" said the other with a grin. "They're not passengers. They're fish."

They picked up the crate and walked into the station. It was empty, but something was wrong.

"Hear that?"

"What is it?"

"You think it's a train?"

It was a curiously thin, high, steam-engine scream.

"Drop it!" yelled the stationmaster, running towards them. "Get them!"

* * *

Valentin hung out of the engine car, screaming for all he was worth. He was so terrified that he could do barely more than in those nightmares when you open your mouth and nothing comes out. A dozen hands were clutching at him from inside.

"Pull him in! Pull him in, you idiots," shouted someone with a deep voice. "Pull him iiiiin!"

Inside the office of the train station, the Railway Work Unit 894685 and the station master were still lustily arguing—about what, they couldn't say—but when one of them opened the door to spit, he heard "iiiiin!"—and that call to arms inadvertently saved Valentin.

The whole work unit raced to the train, whooping and blowing whistles. In moments, two policeman also jumped on the train.

To the cheers of the station master and his staff of five, and the tearful relief of Valentin, the policemen arrested 7 tourists who were to become the principles in a celebrated International Incident (but that is another story).

The policemen were not only delighted with the diversion. They also delegated work, assigning the train station staff to hose down and sweep up the mess of slush mixed with muddy trampled fish guts. That left the policemen free to load the 7 prisoners in the back of the big black van. They took off, siren singing.

The members of the Railway Work Unit had had a busy day. They took off en masse to discuss its events for an hour or two, just as our other group of interest sidled in.

It was only a matter of moments before the train they had arrived in, was on its way, not on the regular, shiny track, as there was no time to waste, but on a rust-red track—a Track to the Unknown.

The time? Nobody noticed.

Brothers in love

"AND SO I think that the nature of love..."

Burhanettin and Faldarolo never stopped talking while they walked, these two men of the world—each accompanying the other on his lover's Quest.

The donkey followed at Burhanettin's heels.

Far enough behind the donkey not to be kicked, Ekmel followed, a picture of disconsolation. Only his stubborn attachment to life kept him trudging onwards—where to? He suspected that the noisy twosome were travelling for the sake of it, but as long as he possessed his attachment to Life (*or*, he sometimes wondered, *is my reason, fear of Death?*), he had no choice but to travel with them.

First of all, these were strange and frightening lands. He was penniless and he didn't know the way home. If he ran away, he could be eaten by wild beasts or, if set upon by brigands, beaten up for sport.

Secondly, it had been many months since that night when Burhanettin had stolen him, Ekmel pined for his honey stores. Without him to protect and love them, the place would now be a scene of horror, as plundered as a pharaoh's tomb—prey to mice, rats, ants, bees, and his wife's male relations. As for his customer list, by now it wouldn't be worth a memory.

So Ekmel plodded behind, slumped when they stopped, bore the disinterest both men bestowed upon him, and Burhanettin's casual cruelty. Ekmel couldn't puff himself up in self-importance, or spout advice about love. Indeed, he considered himself well worth despising—*Ekmel: now an ex- honey merchant who owns only one thing—a donkey who snaps at me when it doesn't turn its back on me and kick.*

She didn't actively dislike him. Her viciousness was a side-effect of over-protectiveness, for she was a fanatical follower of a religion of her own invention. You could see it in her eyes, the pain of love, the passion. She was devoted, helplessly, to Burhanettin.

"Burhanettin," Ekmel mumbled. "The Evil One himself, in a hard sweetmaker's shell."

The donkey followed Burhanettin like a dog, stopping when he did, walking when he walked on. Shading him from the rain. All her attentions, he ignored. Sure, he tossed her *helva* nougats, but he *tossed* them. He didn't hold them in his hand for her to nuzzle and eat while pulling into her nostrils the scent of his personal, sweet perfume.

Burhanettin no longer dropped his head for her to take a horn of his moustache between her teeth and pull, in gentle playfulness—her lover's kiss. She couldn't complain of bad treatment. He didn't yell at her like he did at Ekmel. He never, of course, kicked her as was his wont with Ekmel. Still...

Yea, she followed him. She looked after him, though he did not notice her. She listened to him, though his "dear friend" to her was now nought but a bittersweet memory. And every day her ears drooped lower till they stuck out on two sides in such a sign of sadness that anyone who *cared*—alas!

Ahead,

"My patience is unmeltable as frozen fat," sang Burhanettin, "I will not give up to the unknown. I will never go home without you."

"I have no home without you," said the other man, who never sang.

"Your eyes are like coals," sang Burhanettin.

And on and *on*.

To be truthful, the other man mostly nodded, and Burhanettin talked and sang. The donkey had no eyes for the other man, and Ekmel didn't notice this fine point. He was too miserable. And by now, sick of the taste of *helva*.

* * *

Faldarolo had never had a companion, either as a musician or as a friend. But this man had acted as a friend does, restoring Faldarolo to such health that he was in no time able to walk with fervour.

And so they did, keeping each other company on each other's Quest.

As love was the cause, it was natural, Faldarolo realised, for Burhanettin to speak of love.

Faldarolo protected his love with the greatest zeal. He never spoke of her specifically, considering that vulgar. And to him, it would be a great injustice to expose her to a man who blithely spoke all day of love, sang openly of it!

Faldarolo had always been a man of the highest sensitivities, which allowed, or possibly forced upon him, his fine attunement to the delicate needs and wants of his Beloved.

He distrusted the crude way that Burhanettin, master confectioner though he might be, sang of his love. And furthermore, Faldarolo was sickened by the way Burhanettin turned love into something to be talked about abstractly, like men in a café talk about singers. The more the sweetmaker talked—and he talked all the time that he didn't sing (and his singing voice was not a joy to hear)—the more Faldarolo thought that 'love' as the sweetmaker knew it, was a drum that you hit, and you call that music. Sometimes Faldarolo burned to say, "Love! if you only knew it. You haven't suffered!"

But Burhanettin was a master of something, and Faldarolo respected professionalism. As for that frightening brigand—all wiry muscles and dark mutterings, Faldarolo thought him an odd servant for any master. The man had the look of a filthy cutthroat, and he didn't deign to treat his master with deference, even after he was kicked into work. It was a wonder that Burhanettin hadn't abandoned him. But this Burhanettin was kindness itself.

Kind, but crude and repetitive. Sometimes Faldarolo envied the brigand, for the man didn't have to pretend to listen to Burhanettin's ceaseless chatter. The sweetmaker was a bore, and not just a bore, but a boring bore. The kind of bore you can't drown out. The kind that after an hour, makes you feel that his words are drills, into your teeth, into your ears and skull. Yet even in the head-ringing agony of a Burhanettin-induced headache, the musician maintained an appearance of interest and alertness and brotherhood, all the while keeping his ears and eyes open to find what he was looking for but never spoke of in any way—the Master who could restore the bladder-pipe to health.

Burhanettin was certainly chatty, though hiding behind loquaciousness was caution. He didn't know how much he should trust this travelling suitor. What if, when Burhanettin found Her, this man would want her, too? Burhanettin noticed that this gentleman was very secretive—a mistake. For by the stars, it is folly to think you can hide anything from a master of 117 secret recipes!

Burhanettin slid his eyes over to his companion's face and figure. *He is handsome as the day is long.* The day he realised this was the longest day in summer.

In this thought, Burhanettin wasn't quite objective. Faldarolo was so handsome that women who had seen him through a filigree wall had been known to faint. But then Burhanettin would have been able to achieve that, too. Burhanettin, Master of 117 varieties of sweets for every taste, was a fool to forget the variety of tastes that make a swoon, but his thoughts of potential reasons for jealousy made him unobjective.

* * *

So you know now the secret thoughts of these four travellers, but not their secret actions.

Their actions were curious if anyone had watched, and it just so happened that two brothers did.

The two brothers travelled as pilgrims. They were dressed in the garb that pilgrims wear who seek answers from the Sand Dragon in the Desert of the Cinnamologus. They sighed so much when anyone was within earshot, that even the most sighing pilgrim didn't want to hear *them* sigh, and they were quickly deserted on the road—the better to trail those two elegantly garbed gentlemen and the one they feared—that frightening serving man. What a companion! His looks made each of the brothers quail, but each thought that if they watched for long enough, they might slip in while he was sleeping, or then again, he might murder the two gentlemen himself, when they could swoop down and take what he could not carry, for he'd have to carry it on his back, that much they saw.

The brothers noted a chink in the armour of the serving man's protection for the two otherwise well-guarded gentlemen. Every night when the big man in the front called a halt and the group stopped for the night, he walked a bit to the side and the donkey followed. The other gentleman walked to another side and sat down. The first man took something out of a basket on the donkey's side—two pots. He opened them and peered into them and, even at long distance using their hands as tubes, the brothers could see that he secretly gloated. They argued about many things, but they agreed about that. It was the most blatant secret gloat that they'd ever seen, and possibly the greatest gloat in the land—a pot of gold at the end of the rainbow gloat. And there were two pots! And every night the second gentleman, the one dressed in magnificent, if very old-fashioned clothes, took something out of a large blue velvet bag that he carried slung around his neck. At first the older brother said that it was a preserved duck, but the younger brother said that no gentleman would carry a preserved duck slung from his neck.

"Then it's a goose."

"You're a goose."

The older brother glared at the younger. "Then *you* say!"

"It's not a goose," the younger blustered, though goose looked a pretty good guess. But who would carry a plucked, dead, bloody goose?

"It's a wand with rubies. See that shine?"

"I'll give you rubies."

They grappled silently in the dust for a while, and when they were winded, they sat up and watched companionably.

"It's precious."

"That's for sure."

"We'll find out soon enough, young one," said the wiser one. "Water the steeds."

If you had been watching the two brothers, you might have laughed at him saying that, for the two beasts that carried the youths were dusty, shaggy, mangy bags of bones that you wouldn't have wanted to saddle yourself with, for even their skins were bound to be worthless.

But beneath those unprepossessing bodies beat—when the youths let them—the fastest, most daredevilishly adventure-loving donkey hooves in the land.

Munifer's bequest

As UNNOTICED as any unfortunate, Munifer tottered through the Great City's gates.

Sure, he could go to the city's Quarter of Ill Repute, rent a room and make a new moustache. But that revelation of the hair that turned into an uncontrollable bush had been a shocking, unforgettable lesson: he'd been sold a bag of fakes!

At another time, he would have been furious at the money he'd spent in his pleasure jaunts. Sometimes he'd wondered from one visit to another, how much the girls look alike, but—but this was not the time to be furious about that.

Instead, he began to imagine, really *feel*, a crocodile's jaws clasping closed around him. You might think that he would think to hide himself somewhere, but he was no hermit, and couldn't imagine where. *I have not even been a good man.* When this thought burst upon him, he began to think of the Life that Comes After the Last Breath.

And *that* gave him an idea.

* * *

"Sign here, Effendi," said the notary.

Munifer duly signed.

The notary clapped his hands, and tea and water was brought.

Munifer drank his scalding hot.

The notary blew on his, all the easier to rest his eyes on this unusual public servant.

"You are a man in full vigour," he fished.

The man in full vigour, though dressed in clothes that had

never been well, sighed.

"How generous to give away everything you possess," said the notary.

"To be generous is to be." Munifer was sure there was something more to the saying, but he had always hated sayings, and all the pretence that is necessary in these meetings that pretend civility.

"Loved. How true," smiled the Notary. He prided himself on being an expert of the human soul, but this one was a puzzle he would have loved to take apart. *Is this man a sinner of the Past, or of the Imminence?* The notary licked his lips. *Is this man before me planning a murder that might be famous tomorrow?* He could also have asked himself *How did this man come by his fortune?* but he'd always loved murder more.

Two sighs broke the thoughtful silence—Munifer's, for somesuch reason; and the notary's, for the regrets he bore. He'd always wanted to be a policeman, one who didn't note, but *caught*.

With more briskness than is normal in a notary, he got back to work.

"The disbursement will commence immediately."

Munifer uncrossed his legs.

The notary did not uncross his.

Munifer had forgotten the notary, such was his grief. He had already handed the notary all his gold coins as part of the generosity (and for the bulk of the rest, he had told the notary where the rest of his fortune was, including the hoards—one thing about being Munifer. He had been paid so well that he had a problem thinking what to do with his wealth, so he had buried it like a squirrel).

All Munifer possessed now was a few coins, a sum that any public servant would consider an insulting pittance. He touched his beard apologetically. "You'll have to adjust the disbursement amounts."

The notary clicked his tongue. "I will have to rewrite the whole document."

"Then," said Munifer, "you must adjust accordingly." He stood, and with a cursory "Peace be with you" on both sides, he left the office.

Though you throw a bridle over the ass's head, he does not become a horse; though you dress a captured girl in a robe, she does not become a lady.

Beyond rubies

Mulliana sings while she works. Over a fire hangs a cauldron of water. She unhooks it and tips it in dribbles all over the mat till the pot is empty and the white cloud of fluffy carded wool, flattened and grey as any waterlogged cloud. She kneels again and rolls the mat tightly, binding it with cords that she has also made, this of her own strong hair.

And now she steps on the steaming roll, and stamps on it in a rhythm that she first felt in her mother's womb.

The water runs into a drain and escapes laughing into the face of the sky.

Yes, yes, you say. *I remember.*

Do you remember her father?

One day, well after that particular day that you remember, but which was like every other day since her father locked her in the tower—

"Dearest daughter," cried Mulliana's mother as she climbed the inside ladder, Mulliana's breakfast in the basket on her back. "Today I bring you joy."

"What more joy can I have, my darling mother?" said Mulliana. "Oooh, new figs."

Her mother spat in the fire. "Your father's dead."

Mulliana's teeth tore into the steamy bread. She poured her mother's tea into its little sparkling glass, and poured the rest of the jugful down her own throat as if she hadn't had a drink since *ever.* She cut into a fig with her teeth, gazed into its red, red heart; and ate it, and all the rest of the figs, one by one, till they were all eaten up.

And still she kept her silence. Her mother was ready to burst, to tell Mulliana (bragging, it would have been, so she had to lock it safe within her breast) how she had finally done what she had wanted to do ever since her husband had taken her beloved daughter Mulliana and imprisoned her here for his pleasure and his profit for however long he lived (and he came from a line so longlived that he had loved to speak warningly to his wife of an ancestor who had lived for 969 years—and therefore it was an act of Providence that her husband was an only son of an only son).

Mulliana's mother sat, as patient as she had almost always been, watching her daughter eat. It was unbearable.

"Has he broken you?" she said.

"I live for your eyes," Mulliana trilled. Then she cocked her head, perhaps listening for wisps of her trill in the air. "Do you think my voice sounds broken?"

Tears sprang into her mother's eyes. *I live for your eyes.* Mulliana sang this painfully tragic lovesong every day for their secret joy—there were no lovers for Mulliana.

Mulliana's mother reached into her robe and drew out the giant key. It swung on its chain. "Why haven't you asked me if it's safe to escape?"

"Escape?"

"The key is yours now. Your father now sits in the afterworld. And your brother is fighting in distant lands, may his soul—"

"Mother?"

"Pomegranate seed?"

"Haven't you always told me what a bane marriage is, and how blessed I am to be free?"

"Have I said that?" Mulliana's mother clapped her hands over her mouth. Her eyebrows leapt in fear. "I'm sure I said it to make you accept your fate. I must have."

Mulliana's eyes crinkled. She slid over to her mother on her knees.

"Sing with me," she cried, making sure she sounded happy.

Her mother sang, and didn't stop when Mulliana, still singing, stood up and climbed down the inside ladder made of Mulliana's hair, and climbed up carrying sticks which she fed to the fire; and climbed down and came up with a bucketful of fresh water hung from her neck, which she poured into the cauldron that she hung over the fire; and then took from her mountains of wool piled against the walls, pieces of coloured wool which she shaped just so, and began to place them on a mat so that they took the shape of wonderful creatures and plants; and so on, just like every other day.

They sang together for two songs, but halfway through the third, they stopped.

The sounds outside had grown from the normal whispering hush around the tower at Mulliana's first songs of a morning, to a raucous crowd.

Mother and daughter peered out through the slit in the wall. The men's raiment was so colourful and strange, and not one man stood still. So from the tower looking down, the town seemed planted with precious, exotic, heavy-headed flowers, each fingered by its own unseen breeze.

"I'll wager you a horse!" someone said. "Too much," yelled another, to much laughter. "Come out and show yourself, Bird of the Day." "Let me climb your locks, Geunivere!"

"Enough," a man growled. Ostrich feathers trembled high over his cap, and his hose was dotted with pearls large as carbuncles, which unfortunately emphasised how like his legs were to an aged rooster's.

"Don't tempt me to skewer you," quipped a young man from the top of a skittery white charger, and the peaceful collection of flowers began to push and shove.

Mulliana's mother sighed and pulled back from the window. Her daughter had already turned away and was laying out a mat near the drain hole.

"I'll keep it safe," said Mulliana's mother, hanging the key from her neck.

Mulliana looked up from her work. "May you live forever in peace now, Mama."

The woman who had grown old before she might have become beautiful, choked back tears and smiled brightly.

"More figs when I come tonight?" she asked as she climbed down the ladder. *What will become of her with no man as her protector?*

"Yes, dear oil of my light," Mulliana called down, pulling the ladder up.

She had already turned toward the hearth so she didn't hear her mother's uncharacteristically sharp "What can you expect?" as she once more secured her daughter with a turn of the key.

The crowd made way for the old woman, but they paid her no mind, their attention on the tower. Still, it was fortunate for her that she had to keep her face lowered in modesty. No one could see the illicit triumph in her eyes, the glow of joy on her withered cheeks, from a murder well done.

Later at the river, her voice was strident. "He strokes the ruby," she sang, "and turns it into a donkey."

The chorus shouted the refrain: "Marry your donkey!" as they lustily beat their laundry.

Almost every woman at the river sang the refrain as mightily as the others, but there were some who secretly hated it, and thought as they beat — of their own loves, and the feel of their strokes.

Indeed, a small voice hardly more than a trickle, sang lispingly, "My love is sweet as honey..." But the walnut-faced old thing was deaf.

Approach of the tongue

KLASHICKY-LAKISH-KHHU went the train on the track to the Unknown. Yuri Shurov, being the great train driver he was, listened and drove and got out and shovelled when he needed to, without disturbing anyone on the train.

They might have thought this an unfair distribution of duties if they had been thinking of him at all. Instead, like evolution speeding backwards, each reverted to the mindset of a passenger.

Valentin had scurried to his compartment two and a half carriages away, where he barricaded himself in—with what looks like piles of garbage. Come! Listen in the passage but *don't* let him see you. Hear him making incoherent noises like something that is black and grey, and has horrible bent posture and long fingernails and the breath of the crypt—and your health at heart? Let us leave Carriage 1 to its demon!

Now let us make our way to the restaurant car. Ooh la—don't look.

* * *

Galina had cooked for Savva the most delicious meal, but not just for him. She had made a gala feast for everyone, including Valentin. And she had made everything without help, though Savva had wanted to help. At least he had said he wanted to help, not that he was any help at all, so passionately did he hang around her and cover her neck with kisses.

She had a feast's-worth of food, too, since the town of L——

was a normal re-stocking point for food and fuel, and the workers of that unit had done their job.

When the meal was ready, Galina went to get Yuri Shurov because, as she said to Savva, "There's no schedule to follow. He might as well stop."

Savva agreed wholeheartedly. He'd never been able to say a word to Shurov because he was so shy in the great train driver's presence. And why this hero should have defended *him*, Savva couldn't fathom. He followed Galina to the engine. And there, like the hero in the mural "Through the night", stood Shurov, peering through the window into the beams that led the train like reins on a horse and sled (not that anyone has ever been interested in that mural except, briefly, the committee that wrote its specifications). Indeed (where were we?), the train was slowing and beginning to make the shhhhuhing sound of a sled getting clogged in insufficiently icy snow.

Shurov braked, and picked up a shovel. He had not noticed that he had visitors.

"Comrade," called Galina gaily, stopping him with her hand on his arm. "Come have a bite."

Shurov turned beet red. Muttering something about having to get something moved or they'd be stuck, or somesuch nonsense, he jumped out and got to such energetic work that in the beams of light he looked like that hero in the mural—you are not interested?

Then let's follow the kissing couple as they make their way awkwardly, with many stumbles and giggles, to the carriage under Savva's care, specifically the compartment of such fascination, 3C.

The door was open, so there was no need to knock. Instead, Savva leaned in and wittily said, "Knock knock."

"Yes," said the Omniscient, who was on his upper bunk, slumped as a pile of old pillows.

"A feast for your eyes and tongue awaits," announced Savva, more poetically than he'd ever thought possible. Galina regarded the chapped back of his neck with shining eyes. She'd never known him like this. She didn't see, because she felt shy and a bit embarrassed for the woman, the way the old man in the compartment looked at that woman in red, nor did she see that strange woman not look back at the old man, nor look anywhere, nor even pretend that she noticed any invitation.

"Upset stomachs," apologised the old man. He rubbed his own stomach to prove it, though Savva was not convinced. For a moment, Savva felt bad for Galina, but then he shrugged. *Passengers! Who can understand them?*

Savva turned to Galina, whispered something about crazy tourists, and politely took his leave of the old man. He had barely gone a step out of sight of 3C when Galina pulled him into 3B, where she gave him a kiss that made Savva forget all about getting Valentin.

So they made their way to the restaurant car by themselves, where because there was no one to hide from, Galina didn't tape any cardboard over the windows. And where, because Galina had done all the cooking, she didn't want to eat now, and where because of the kiss, Savva's insides were too turmoiled for even a slice of pickle; here they swept the feast off the restaurant table and Galina unbuttoned Savva's jacket (which was missing one button) and unbuttoned his shirt, and tore it off.

She ran her fingers over his sunken chest, and laughed.

Instinctively, he reached out for his shirt.

"Leave it!" she ordered.

"I'm sorry I'm no hero," he said. "I'm cold."

"You!" she laughed. "You can't fool me. Besides, you can take your heroes, and stick them where Stalin lies."

"Shh!"

"Speak to the wall," she laughed. "Who wants an old-fashioned hero? I'm a modern woman. And you—" She ran her fingers over his standout collarbones. "You look like a rock star."

"Rock..." Savva gulped. "Mick Jakhar?"

"No, stupid."

He looked down, wanting to put his shirt back on but afraid to. Tears welled in his eyes. She was playing with him, cruelly. And he had thought it love.

"I must go to my duties," he said.

"Your duties are here." Galina pointed a finger at him—*Stay!*

She ran behind the counter, felt behind some pots, and emerged with a magazine.

Flip, flip, she made the pages turn, until she found what she was looking for.

"Mick Jagkhar," she said prissily. "He's an old man. See?"

So that's what he looks like. Savva hoped he never aged like that, but Savva didn't have time to examine all the wrinkles, because Galina was off again, flipping the pages without mercy, till she found what she was looking for. "Look!"

"You don't want me to wear eye makeup, do you?"

"Only look at his chest."

The resemblance was remarkable. And from the crowd, the man looked to be adored.

Galina closed the magazine and kissed Savva on the tip of his nose. "If he had your nose, I might think of him and not you when we make love."

"My nose is my best point," giggled Savva.

"This is not a time for critical analysis," said Galina.

Soon after, in a flight of creative fancy, Savva smeared caviar on Galina's upper lip. He had never liked its taste but this was no time for a thought like that, when Galina was spread like a tablecloth under him and he was poised above, tongue out.

Stop yelled Nick, and for a moment, Savva paused. Nick pulled as delicately as he could (pulling with all his might) but he was powerless. Savva's tongue drew closer, and closer, and finally, just as the pink tip of Savva's tongue touched Galina who was shaking like a train with all diesel engines fired up—just at the moment of touch, with one almighty pull, a greater effort than he had made in his whole life, Nick popped off Galina's face and flew out of the restaurant car so that the loving couple could consummate the beginning of their ever after in the privacy they deserved.

It all happened in an instant, yet Nick was out of earshot when Galina reacted.

"Yo!"

Savva fell to the floor. "What's wrong? Am I too heavy?"

"You bit me," she giggled. Her eyes opened. "What are you doing there?"

"I didn't bite you."

"Yes you did."

"No I didn't."

Galina's hand flew to her face. She wiped the caviar off as if it were a fly, and felt her upper lip. "Help me stand up."

And of course, a very confused Savva did.

He stood shivering as Galina rummaged in the mess of clothing on the floor.

She plucked out her mirror and shoved it in front of her face.

"My mark! It's gone."

"No."

"Does a mirror lie?" She spun round, and it was true.

"It must have been a rash." *Rash, no rash. What does it matter at a time like this?*

Galina threw herself into his arms.

"Oh Savva!"

"Galina!" *This is more like it.*

"Can you ever love me again?" she wailed.

"Oh no," he groaned.

"I thought not!" she shrieked, tearing out her hair.

"I didn't mean that! My love!"

. . .

and it comes out excellently, so understand that.

—the end of many recipes,
Kitāb waṣf al- aṭ'ima al-Mu'tāda

The time on the hill

MUNIFER WOULD HAVE LIKED to have strangled the notary for the interruption in a scene that Munifer had planned as his life's heroic act—his selfless generosity destined for immortality in poetry and song. Instead, in a mood of mixed temperance and superstition, Munifer restrained himself, prescribing himself a walk out of the City.

By the time he reached the City Gates, he was admirably stoic. *What does it matter if he steals it all? I did what I could.*

He tossed the rest of his coins behind his left shoulder, and continued walking. His goal was the top of the hill. He would camp up there by the bush of revelation for the next few days. And then when it was time, he would bravely walk to the Palace, where he would present himself to the Great Tīmūrsaçi as expected.

And so he walked to the top of the hill, where he saw, not the 'bush', but two crows fighting over a hank of kinky yellow hair. Still, this place was as good as any to spend his last days, so he sat under a stunted fig and thought about his life and what a waste it had been and how happy he would be when it was over and he was in that Paradise that only men lucky enough to have found revelation can earn entry to.

Only some wizened figs passed his lips. And each day passed till he lost track of days and had to go running after a traveller, who cuffed him cruelly.

Munifer broke into tears. He had been spending far too much

time than is healthy, grizzling like a sentimental drinker. "I only wanted to ask the day."

"A fool where one least expects it," laughed the traveller. He tossed a coin into Munifer's face, and walked on.

"What *day* is it?" Munifer cried out, but his voice was weak.

The cuffing did him good, though. It focussed his mind. He soon came to the conclusion that *Tomorrow is the Day*.

Therefore, he planned the rest of this day contemplating.

He contemplated till his eyes were so puffy that they were painful. He needed to stretch his limbs, too.

As he stood, a gust of wind shook the leaves in the stunted fig so much that they sounded like midnight in a gambler's den. That thought brought a smile to his face. *Life had been good.*

He stretched out his arms to the sky, and the good fresh air restored him. His eyes rose to look at the wonders of nature—not the ugly stunted fig but those swallows swooping, those clouds scudding, and the beauty of genuine virgins' hair, just like that ribbon of it floating by. Floating by???

Munifer jumped. He missed, but it caught in the highest branch of the stunted fig.

The tree was too wizened for him to climb, so he broke it down.

The hair that he pulled from its top branch was long, black, lustrous as eyes in love, *and* (he breathed in deeply) possessed the incomparable fragrance of virginity.

Underneath the skin you see,
is the skin you want. Have it now.

—Estée Lauder, Inc.

Siren in the wilderness

"PSST," hissed the bladder-pipe.

"Not now," said Faldarolo.

"Dare you speak to me like that?"

"Can't you see?" muttered Faldarolo. "We are not alone."

"Could *you* see, if I shoved *you* in this shroud?"

Burhanettin paused in his stride. "Troubled stomach?"

"Nothing a sleep won't cure," said Faldarolo, stroking the velvet bag.

"I beg of you," he mumbled to the bladder-pipe. "Wait till we stop for the night."

Faldarolo was not in any hurry to stop for the night. He dreaded it.

"I tell you," he said later, when the naked bladder-pipe lay on his lap and the stars shone down on them. "I *asked* for its butter, for the third night in a row (as if she didn't know) but he said it could not give. Not tonight. Not any night."

And he *had*, though tonight he had felt ridiculous. He had asked Burhanettin for butter from the donkey, and Burhanettin had looked at Faldarolo in an odd way, and then he had asked Faldarolo with a pathetic slyness, if maidens like the scent of ass's butter on a man's hair, and Faldarolo had had to say he didn't know and that he wanted it for a ticklish throat, at which time the sweetmaker had lost interest other than to point to his servant and say, *ask him if you want butter*; and the servant had said the donkey couldn't give milk because she was—and the murderous-looking servant had blushed oddly and Faldarolo didn't know why. When Faldarolo had said that it wasn't milk he wanted but *butter*, the man laughed in a way that filled Faldarolo with awe, it was so disrespectful. He expected Burhanettin to teach the man flying with his kicks. Yet nothing of the sort happened.

Faldarolo was surprised that Ekmel was allowed to be so insolent to a man Burhanettin called "brother", till he saw that Burhanettin wasn't even listening with half an ear. He was doing what he furtively rushed to do every night—unpacking two jars (obviously honeypots) from the donkey's back. *Now he's going to look into them for a while and sigh secretively, and then pack them away again looking around as if we might want them for ourselves.* Faldarolo couldn't help sneering. *As if we would think that precious.* The jars had never earned a glance from the servant. Besides, Burhanettin could have been a puppetmaster, so completely did he seem to rule his man. And if the servant had stolen them, who would deal with him? *He couldn't sell someone a clod of mud and not earn suspicion that it's a fake.*

Yet Burhanettin, in his attitude to the honeypots, reminded Faldarolo of some of the hosts Faldarolo had played for. A man could talk all evening of a pear that he remembered eating forty years ago. Another would spend a fortune on a bottle of liquid, talk of it as if it were his love, and keep it under guard, and all the other men would nod as if this were expected.

"Why do you forget me?" said the bladder-pipe.

"I'm a musician, not a magician."

"That's no explanation."

And it wasn't.

So the bladder-pipe was very discontented, as she had decided that she had to have fresh ass's butter and here was an ass, and no one was making it give up its butter. And no! she didn't want milk, so why had anyone talked about milk. She didn't care that the ass didn't want to give up its milk. "Did I ask for milk?"

"No," muttered Faldarolo, massaging her with ass's butter—the sweet, clean ass's butter he had carried with him, so that she would be treated as royally as she deserved. It was still sweet and clean, but—

"Is a bit of fresh butter too much to ask? ..."

She gave Faldarolo no peace till he promised that *tonight* he would sneak up on the ass and squeeze some out of it. For the bladder-pipe said that a squeeze was all it takes to get butter from an ass. And if that didn't work, Faldarolo had been forced to promise what the bladder-pipe said was the other way, though he'd have to be sure to clean the butter.

"I'll slit the beast's stomach open," Faldarolo promised, "and scoop it out."

What would happen after that, he didn't have the peace to contemplate. If he didn't satisfy this need that he privately thought might merely be a whim, she would certainly drive him mad before he reached the man who could restore her to health. For her blotch had not only not faded. It positively glowed. And although she made noises, she could no longer, with all those holes burnt in her bladder, make any sort of music—making him a worthless traveller in the clothing of a gentleman, soon enough to be a worthless man in rags.

* * *

Ekmel had had his eye on the scoundrel for the past couple of days. You can't be as lonely and soul-lost and tricked by life as Ekmel without noticing that a man who talks to a velvet bag and glances furtively at a donkey has evil in his soul.

Ekmel was certain that the man had no intention of stealing the donkey. What would he steal her for? He hardly knew one end from the other, and called her 'it'.

And there he is, looking at her again.

Ekmel walked over to her and put his hand on her neck. She started, she was so surprised. But she hadn't been touched for so long that she forgot how Ekmel had, in the old days (just the previous year but it seemed like the old days) beaten her when she didn't want to take his route; and now she bent her neck and pressed her forehead against his stomach, breathing his rank, familiar reek.

Awkwardly but carefully, he folded his hands so they were in the shape of feet, and slipped them down her long sensitive ears— down and partly up, and down as he had seen Burhanettin do in the old days when Burhanettin had called the donkey "my friend". She folded her ears back and the long hairs on the inside of her ears tickled Ekmel's wrists, but her ears were as warm as his wife's thighs were once, and comforting.

"Is this the right way?" he asked, but it was plain to see. Her eyelashes lowered and her bottom lip fell away from her teeth, and wobbled. Ekmel had never had a fine bull-horn moustache like Burhanettin, but he had once been proud of his brush moustache. Burhanettin hadn't packed Ekmel's razor and he had never given Ekmel so much as a few piastres for a barber, so Ekmel now bore a thick curly rug on his face, with a hole for his mouth. He lowered his face as he had seen Burhanettin do, and the donkey put her nose to his, and he smelled her donkey breath—sweet, not from that revolting nougat (she had stopped enjoying hers, too), but the bark of some broken-down stunted tree they'd passed this afternoon.

One of his curly hairs must have tickled her nose, for she stepped away, yawned, sneezed three times, and wagged her head till her ears sounded like slippers flapping. She lifted up her head again, paused ... and it was as if she waited—Ekmel galloped through the Blessing of the Three Sneezes—at the last word, she exploded.

Ekmel laughed so hard, you'd think she was a storyteller.

She leaned up against his side.

He pulled away and narrowed his eyes at her. "You don't have a name, do you?"

A plethora of almostnesses

"Go!" yelled the older brother, and the younger would have liked to kick his heels into his steed's side, but he didn't get a chance, because the steed's long ears had been turned towards the older brother in anticipation for so long that the o! was lost in the sound of its pounding heels. Not for these steeds that frippery of the neighing, rearing horse, all *look at me get ready to get going.* At the first half of a two-letter word, these steeds were off—and though they galloped so fast that their heels didn't need to touch the ground, each steed made sure they did, for the excitement of 8 heels striking flames from flint, smashing uplifted roots to smithereens, crushing wild melons into slush, slithering through choking sand, and in the case of the younger brother's steed's right front hoof, coming down with the force of a mountain falling to earth, a toenail away from a tortoise that looked like a stone and causing it to cry out—but the boys and their steeds were long past by then.

So the younger brother would have liked to kick his heels into warm flesh and say Hi ho or suchlike, but then if he'd been able to do that, it wouldn't have been half the ride. Onwards, the donkeys raced, and he had to wrap his arms around the neck of his while his heels flopped limp as rags.

Eventually the older brother ordered: "Whoah."

When the donkeys stopped, the younger slid to the ground. He could hardly walk, he was so bruised, but he pointed to his older brother's eye and laughed.

"You look like a suitor."

The older brother grinned. "It's already black?"

"People will think I don't love you."

"Come. Let's see if you can punch the other."

While the two boys rolled in the dirt, the donkeys wrapped their necks around each other, companionably biting to each other's skin for fleas.

Soon enough, however, "Now we must travel back to the road," said the older brother.

"For how much longer?" The younger could not disguise the whine in his voice.

"Patience."

* * *

By the time the older brother called a halt, the steeds were ready to munch leaves and the impatient one was fast asleep on his faithful friend's back.

While the younger ate, the older brother crept forward till the group they had tracked for so many days was in view. They had stopped for the evening and they were separated as he thought they'd be. He'd decided that tonight must be the night because there had grown a disturbing increase in traffic on the road—well-dressed, and very well armed men from what looked like all corners of the earth were flowing forward as if they were worried they'd miss the call to Heaven. If the little group below linked up with them...

This was to be the first raid in the boys' career, and as the Commander, he could not let it fail. He had chosen this little group, first, because of its weakness, and then, because of the wealth that they gloated over—those two men down there.

Overhead, in the velvet of the sky, beauteous stars appeared, lighting the scene below with wonderful approval.

And what is that? He motioned to his brother to come.

"Hey hoh!" cried the boy, and got a fistful of dust in his eyes to calm his spirits.

"Look at that," whispered the older.

When he'd finished grizzling, the younger looked. "What?"

But the older had already mounted. "Follow," he commanded.

For what he had seen had convinced him that fortune itself was lighting his way.

* * *

Burhanettin was huddled over on the other side of an unruly pile of sticks that might have once been a nest, for all the fluff stirring from its splintered ends. As usual, he was crooning to his jars. "We approach, dearest. It must be only a few days more, and then I shall arrive. And Then!"

He gazed across the flat plain towards the hill, and lifted one jar to it.

"Take too little, my sweetness, and madness seizes you. Take too much, my star in the heavens, and Death would swoop you up. Take just the right amount, which must be as expertly judged as the amount of powdered pearl to stir into a batch of helva-i-golub, which is why I am the one for you ... and this Kirand-luhun, my darling, gives the unearthly sweetness that is love."

He sighed mightily. "I wonder what she'll be like."

For to be honest, he had been travelling aimlessly, loving just anyone without having a name to put to them, till he'd heard of a woman named Mulliana. And when he heard of her he was willing to chance his love at first sight, to her. He had carefully weighed, furthermore, the dosage that each of them would need, and felt content with his decision *One for you, and one for me. If it kills us, what is better than to die for love?*

"When you speak to me in that tone of velvet, my heart grows soft as pounded meat," he sang, as he stroked the horns of his moustache.

Over near the sloughed skin of a sand dragon sat Faldarolo, pretending to be interested in its scales. The bladder-pipe was securely bagged and hanging from his neck, which only just muffled her insistent "What are you waiting for? Butter Butter Butter!"

Over near a pile of desiccated droppings colourful with feathers, Ekmel snored, every inch the useless surly servant who had fallen into a sleep so deep that a master's kick would be a tickle.

"Now!" whispered the older boy.

And to the younger boy's surprise and the steeds' utter disgust, the older one said, "Now—leave them!"

And he led his brother as they crept down to the plain, and then crawled along, and darted from bush to bush.

By the time they reached our little group, the big man with the pointed hat and the two jars he gloated over was lying down where he had sat, but the two jars were packed back in that basket on the donkey. And the man with the velvet bag was lying down and snoring just as loudly as the—now that the older boy was close enough to see—utterly bloodcurdling servant.

Home! wished the older brother. *To be home with a stomach warmed by Mama's soup, even if her slaps make my ears burn.* From afar, these three men had looked like dolls, and the raid was to be only the best game the boys had ever played, a life of play that could make you rich instead of work that made you sore.

He just wanted to run away, but he had to accomplish something, so he said to his brother, "Greediness will call the Evil Eye upon us. Let's leave the one with the bag." Formerly he had decided that it would be a doddle to slip it off the man's neck while they slept.

"Let's just get the jars," he said.

His little brother nodded. He had taken a look at the murderer, for that was what he had to be, and was so frightened he was swallowing hiccups, which only made him more terrified. And as for the velvet bag, it looked from here, not like it held anything fat like riches or a goose, but something bony—the ghost hand that clutches you when you relieve yourself at night.

Onwards the two boys crawled. They were now on the far side of the donkey from those men.

The older boy opened the basket. *Creak*, it said. He stopped.

His heart pounded louder than the snoring, but the snoring did not stop.

In went his two hands, and like magic! Out they came, each clutching a jar.

He smiled at his brother and crouched again. They took one step, and then as fast as they could while still crouching and being very quiet, they took another half—and then the snorer with the blue bag rose, still snoring. His eyes were open and they gleamed. And he crept towards: the donkey. The older boy put a hand on the younger, perhaps to stop his brother from moving, or maybe because the older boy was shaking like grandfather's hand.

Onward, the snoring man with the wide-open eyes crept, nearer, towards the donkey, till he was al ... most *here*.

He reached inside his robe and his hand came out, with a knife.

And at that very moment, the murderous-looking one leapt forward and grappled him, and the two boys ran screaming into the night that enfolded them like a mother in its arms. And in the murk, the two men separated with many yells, and the man who loved his jars leapt up and rushed to the donkey, only to find the basket opened and no jars there, and he stumbled about till he almost fell on a jar and crying out, reached for it, and the donkey dropped her head so her nose was beside his, and he yelled at her, "The Kirandluhun is for me, not you," —and he punched her—"beast!"

And she jerked her head up, with one horn of his moustache hanging from between her teeth.

And the murderous-looking man ran up to her and shoved the big man away and he stood in front of the donkey and said, "On my life!" glaring murderously at the man of the jars and the man of the bag alike—by this time, the two boys had made their breathless way back to their two unimpressed but faithful steeds, who, without having to be told anything, waited till their charges had boarded, and headed, at a swift but careful pace, home.

Dear friends

IT WAS ONLY SELF-PRESERVATION that caused Ekmel to stop himself from killing two fellow travellers.

No one could sleep, so the little group set out again (Burhanettin, followed by Faldarolo followed by Ekmel, and the donkey, last) and made their way through the scrubby, rock-strewn plain, though they had reached that point in a trip where, between some travellers, antipathy grows rampant.

The two men Burhanettin had once called "brothers in love" strode with long steps and hunched shoulders, Burhanettin clutching the two jars in a fold of his striped cloak, and Faldarolo holding that velvet bag and mumbling into his chest.

Ekmel was close enough to leap on him, should the fool get any new ideas, for it was no use talking. *You can squeeze blood into a stone easier than talking sense into a fool.*

Another man with less responsibility might have considered the crazy man funny, but *a funny fool only hurts himself.*

"Imagine, splitting you open!" Ekmel turned around for a moment to smile at she who was soaking up every drop of emotion towards her that flowed from him. She laid her ears forward.

But Burhanettin had once called her "dear friend". As a donkey, she could not quote the proverb, *A forsaken friend is never as great as a forsaken love*, but Ekmel felt that she had learnt it. Furthermore, he felt that he finally understood the proverb of a wiser man than he: *Though an ass carry your burden, you can never look into both of her eyes at once.*

But there is also the proverb, *A hungry lion never waits for the proverb's end.*

So let's go further up this caravan and listen to Faldarolo's troubles.

"So now you don't want its butter," he mumbled.

"Whatever made you think that I wanted its butter?"

Faldarolo held his temper. He had learnt the hard way never to remind the bladder-pipe of something she had said.

"You are almost there," she said now.

"Yes," said Faldarolo, knowing what she meant because in some ways they still had perfect harmony.

"Then you will show your true feelings," said the bladder-pipe.

"As if I haven't?"

"Only then will I know if you really love me, rather than just swearing it."

Faldarolo had never been a talker, so he just repeated what he'd said when he set out from Çimçim: "I'll travel to the ends of the earth to find the best bladder-maker in the world to fix your delicate skin. And," he added, "from what I understand this town to be, this trip has been worth the walk. The master we seek should be here, though he might be rather busy, so you might have to be—"

"Tell me again about this town," she commanded.

"Well, that sweet master wants to go there because he thinks he's got something to offer some famous beauty that will make her want him, though why she should want the bore I don't know."

"I did not ask about him!"

"No. Of course," he rushed to say, stroking the bag. "There are many who have settled in the town for a sight of her, and there are more who hope to win her, and rush there as we do. They must have their entertainment, so the town has a festive air to it, and is famous, also for its airs. Where there are musicians, there must be instrument makers, and since any place that is famous for something becomes more famous because of that, this place must have instrument makers who are masters, and since the bladder-pipe is, above all, an instrument who needs a master—"

"Yes, yes," yawned the bladder-pipe. "I'm sorry I asked. "

"This is why I go there," he said, embarrassed at his wordiness.

And, he most certainly did not say nor dare to think, *because I have no other idea of a place to go.* On their long trip they had not been to a single place that had been of good cheer, or of good taste.

"Tell me about her," said the bladder-pipe.

"Who?"

"The one all seek to win."

"Not I."

"I didn't ask that. Tell me about her."

"She is more beautiful than a summer's day, they say."

"Which kind of summer's day?"

"How do I know? The beautiful ones, of course."

Faldarolo strode on, making his feet ring against the stones.

"Don't pretend that you don't hear me," said the bladder-pipe.

"What is it?" sighed Faldarolo.

"What does she look like?"

"I told you."

"You told me 'beautiful'. Ask *him*."

Faldarolo wouldn't have dared ask Burhanettin, for fear that the big man would take Faldarolo for a sneaky rival. "Her breath is like honey, he says. The look from her eyes would turn you to a pool of melted butter."

"If you continue in this vein, you'll choke on your own spit."

"That's what he says."

"If I told you that, could you play it?"

"No," he admitted.

"Well?"

"No one has seen her," said Faldarolo. "So I can tell you no details, except for the fact that she was shut in the tower as a young girl, and she has never been touched by anyone including the sunshine since."

"That, Faldarolo, is what I was asking for."

Faldarolo gulped. She had never called him by his name. "It is?"

"It is."

"My dearest," she said...

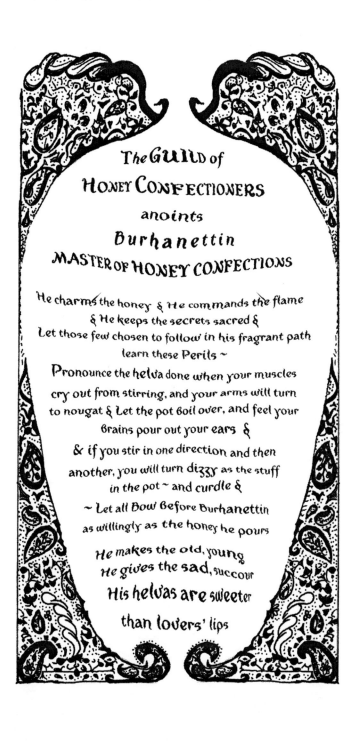

The GUILD of
HONEY CONFECTIONERS
anoints
Burhanettin
MASTER OF HONEY CONFECTIONS

He charms the honey & He commands the flame
& He keeps the secrets sacred &
Let those few chosen to follow in his fragrant path
learn these Perils ~
Pronounce the helva done when your muscles
cry out from stirring, and your arms will turn
to nougat & Let the pot boil over, and feel your
brains pour out your ears &
& if you stir in one direction and then
another, you will turn dizzy as the stuff
in the pot ~ and curdle &
~ Let all bow before Burhanettin
as willingly as the honey he pours

He makes the old, young
He gives the sad, succour
His helvas are sweeter

than lovers' lips

Light pink as the dawn

"WHAT SHOULD I DO?" asked Mulliana of the creature that only now appeared on the hearth.

"Let me look," it said, scritching towards the window in its horridly lopsided way.

"I'll pick you up," said Mulliana, and though the crandolin did not need to be picked up, and furthermore, had very sharp claws, Mulliana swept the crandolin into her arms and they looked out together while the crandolin hummed quietly, and hmmmed now and then.

"You may put me down," s/he said at last.

It was once-upon-common-knowledge that crandolins were light pink as the dawn they imitated as they probed cracks in the shutters protecting pink virgins in their beds. Mulliana had never had shutters in the tower—only slats and cracks, but that was no barrier to a determined crandolin, especially the last crandolin in the world. And though it might not be true that the crandolin who lived with Mulliana was the last, this crandolin had never seen nor heard of another living crandolin.

So—insofar as *this* crandolin and Mulliana were concerned, this crandolin *was* the last, and meant to last as forever as a crandolin is meant to, as *A Crandolin* (the crandolin had taught Mulliana) *is Not Meant to be Perishable.*

Mulliana, of course, would never have told the crandolin, because the crandolin could be sentimentally stubborn, but

Mulliana felt herself the happiest woman in the world, as she was protecting the most worthy protector—someone who also knew pain and suffering and loneliness, and had been horribly damaged, yet never talked of it.

For the colour of this crandolin was indeed light pink, and anemia in crandolins is not natural any more than the loss of several limbs. Both states in this crandolin were due to incidents earlier in life—terriblenesses the crandolin had only ever alluded to darkly with the odd proverb.

"Fear not," said the crandolin. "I will continue to be your protector," not saying *until that Fateful day, when I must disappear from your life (and*, the crandolin thought dreadingly, *make my way in the world and hope to find another)*.

"But without your father," said the crandolin, "we cannot go on like this."

"What can I do?"

"Tomorrow, I think," said the crandolin.

And so—as Mulliana was used to the unspoken with her protector, she bent to her work and sang in her normal way—too softly to disturb a sleeping baby in the town, but loud enough that no one heard the thud to earth of a nightingale who died of jealousy.

Journey of self-discovery

"I'M GOING OUT," announced the Muse.

The Omniscient coughed delicately.

"Yes?" she said, and though her "Yes" sounded rather like, "Go drown yourself," he asked delicately, "Would you like me to accompany you?"

"No thank you," she said. "I'm sorry," she said, and left.

He listened to her red-booted footsteps go *crunch crush* down the carpet. He heard the heavy latch of the carriage door give way to her impetuous rough pull. He heard the door slam closed. His cheeks were touched by a little cold fresh air that had slipped in and raced down the passage and into 3C.

The train said *shussssh* as it travelled slowly but inexorably, onwards.

The Omniscient's eyes began to run—thick salty tears coursed down his saggy cheeks.

I'm just an ancient, self-indulgent windbag.

"What's the use of being eternal?" he asked the window as if his reflection were someone to ask of, someone to discuss with. *Someone ready to—yes—teach me! But with my memory, who would?*

"Why did I ever think I could be worthy of her?" he blubbered. "I can't even fly in her slipstream." And with that, he broke into great, choking sobs, till he grew so dizzy that he felt pleasantly drunk, which made him sob some more.

"Enough is..." (Never having had a childhood, he had always had to discipline himself, but being an only, he had always been late.) "ENOUGH!"

"Remember the Web?"

He did!

"It's ahead of this time, so what are you waiting for. It has Answers!"

A little part of him asked, "If I improve my mind, do you think there's hope with her?"

All he got as an answer was the memory, for some reason, of the look on a child's face the first time anyone tasted a burnt grain (though the Omniscient couldn't help but qualify that first time as a presumption on his part, based on his observation).

Then the look on its mother's face popped into his mind.

Distractions. But they focussed his mind, on now.

* * *

And so he did improve. With Her gone, possibly forever (*why should she come back? She's not a nursemaid. She's the Muse*) he worked frantically. First of all, he managed with much more ease than ever before, to get on the Web. This time he linked up with no machine in sight—just his mind. *I must be in a further future than we came from*, but there was no time for thoughts about time when he had so much work to do, so much *remedial* self-improvement.

First things first. And it was almost like a Muse story, like rubbing a lamp and *shabam!* The answer to his first wish was "The Memory Experience—A Journey of Self Discovery".

In just a few steps, he discovered his Amazing Memory.

"Why have I never gone on this journey before?" he asked himself, and smiled ruefully because the answer lay in the text. *I had to want to change and re-organise the way I think.* "Isn't it wonderful to have no choice?"

So then he careened around the Web, amazedly, non-creatively of course. He fully recognised the distinction between his skills and the Muse's, but perhaps she could like him just a bit for maybe a crumb of fact that she might need to feed her Olympian imagination—*just a crumb?* (If he could only see himself, he might have laughed, because his face had the funniest expression—Amazing Begging Walrus) but anyway—

He was so absorbed in researching and learning and *remembering* that the time flew, but it didn't fly fast enough, for all of a sudden he thought he heard a noise and looked up hopefully, but he must have imagined the thrill of her step, the flick of her tresses. She had not returned.

Will she?

And what would she come back for. *Me?*

The Omniscient began to cry, and admonished himself just before he reached the Antarctic state of what he'd only minutes ago assessed as a psychiatric disorder needing medication.

Self medicating was not an option. "You need to work again."

"Doing precisely what?" This wasn't a good time to remind himself that not a single writer had called for him since that day in the library, whereas the Muse...

"It doesn't do to compare yourself."

"But"

"Facts."

"Just facts?"

"Yes indeedy."

"Facts are cold. Why would anyone want them?"

"You've seen people eat ice cream in the snow, and you ask?"

Just then, he felt an unmistakable call, and without knowing how it happened, he was on his way to a new appointment, and possibly a new life.

Donor

BETTER LATE THAN NEVER is such a comforting cliché. It should cover all inefficiencies, but in the Omniscient's case—for this first client in his new career—lateness boded ill.

Not that Ekmel cared. To him, this old man who'd sidled up to Faldarolo was a pest of the garrulous wanderer sort. He was glad not to have to lend an ear to him.

By this time, the road had become so full of people of all garbs going in the same direction, that a worry that the Omniscient had harboured—of looking futuristic—was put to rest. Instead, the pattern of his waistcoat was strikingly in harmony with the magnificent, though road-soiled outer robe of Faldarolo.

But this Faldarolo—the Omniscient's first client—was in a state of nervous exhaustion. He had first called upon the Omniscient when he needed an answer about the ass's butter. Now he despaired of getting good advice, and was walking quite hopelessly toward his doom.

For the most recent demand of the bladder-pipe's was— Faldarolo didn't know what to think of it.

So when the Omniscient introduced himself jauntily as "The Answer System Here," it took a very confusing while for Faldarolo to get the idea that the Omniscient was sorry for arriving too late to be of service re the question of equine milk products, but had arrived to answer Faldarolo's second question.

The Omniscient felt let down that Faldarolo wasn't *exhilarated* and striding with a sense of purpose towards this new Challenge (not to mention awed by the presence of the Omniscient himself). Instead, the troubled young man trudged on as if he were not only too exhausted to care—but as if he hadn't called for help. *Yet he certainly had.*

Faldarolo thought it no wonder that the old man had heard of the ridiculous quest to get butter from that beast's stomach. He understood now how silly he'd been. Ass's butter couldn't come from an ass's stomach any more than honey came from a bee's. Probably everyone on the road had heard of the fight by now, and had a good laugh.

But no one knew of the latest. The old man was harmless but conceited, thinking himself a seer. So Faldarolo asked him bluntly: "If you take the skin from a virgin's face, does it hurt the virgin?"

Faldarolo felt stupid because *of course*, he thought, *virgins do feel pain.* And furthermore, he had no slight to right against Mulliana. She had neither harmed him, nor did he wish to cause her harm. But the bladder-pipe was done accepting compromises, experiments, fixes that didn't fix—and was now insisting upon the cure. Mulliana's face-skin was the only membrane that could do. Now, a mere sheep's bladder? Faldarolo could almost hear the bladder-pipe snort.

According to her, all Faldarolo had to do was declare himself in love with this Mulliana virgin creature, and get up to that tower and into her bed and then he could cut her face skin off and take it to the master who would fix the bladder-pipe, and then they could go wherever Faldarolo wanted and they could live happily ever after.

"So can you take the skin off a virgin's face and not hurt her?" asked Faldarolo.

"I'll have to think about that," said the Omniscient, who immediately searched his memory for this question, and didn't find it. So then he searched laterally ... and when Faldarolo had sighed in hopeless despair for only the third time in the Omniscient's presence, the Omniscient said:

"Yes! Though I should perhaps, qualify that." He turned to Faldarolo. "You're not taking her from her natural environment, are you?"

"I don't want to take her anywhere."

"Good." *Several hundred years from now,* the Omniscient refrained from saying, "taking the example of horseshoe crabs—and I quote: 'we bleed horseshoe crabs using highly controlled and monitored procedures that help to ensure that the donor crabs are returned to their natural environment unharmed.' "

He smiled broadly at his first client after re-training.

His satisfied expression met one of utter blankness.

The Omniscient was shaken, but he remembered how dull so many of the clients in his former profession had been.

"You look like a man who scorns paraphrases," he said, trying to stimulate by flattery, "so I'll quote: 'Crabs are collected daily during specific seasons and brought to a nearby bleeding facility by truck.' You plan to do it in-house, I think you said, eh?"

The client did not respond. Gamely, the Omniscient proceeded. " 'Those crabs without visible injuries are placed on a bleeding rack and bled via a heart puncture using a large gauge needle.' "

He tapped the young man on the arm. "Whereas you plan to do it on her bed. Quite the improvement, as you certainly couldn't contaminate the donor material with sedatives."

"Blood. That was about blood."

"Absolutely," said the Omniscient, whose broad smile was going limp around the edges. *Were they all like this?*

"I asked about skin."

The Omniscient slapped himself in the forehead. "I didn't complete my quote as it was, I thought, obvious. So I quote: 'On average, thirty percent of the crab's blood is removed before the wound clots naturally.' End quote. So there you have it. You're home and hosed. Go for it!"

"Skin."

"What's more important," huffed the Omniscient, "skin or blood? And what percentage of skin would be on her face? You've lost skin off the back of your hand, I see, and if it's not bigger than a healthy young woman's face, well..." He rolled his eyes, delighted that the first job was really such a simple one to answer, and itching to be off to his next, hopefully more interesting client.

Faldarolo looked at the back of his hand as if the hand belonged to someone else.

"It hurts," he said.

"Forget your stupid hand!"

The Omniscient thrust his hand in front of Faldarolo's eyes, and executed a perfect mid-20th century fingersnap.

"Young man," he said, when Faldarolo picked up his head. "If only you'd listened. Doesn't 'donor' mean *anything* to you? Donors make another well. Isn't that what you wish for?"

The client nodded fervently.

"Well?" laughed the Omniscient.

But his pun was wasted.

"What is his problem?" muttered the Omniscient. To the dullard: "How much education did you have?"

"My father taught me to play."

"Eureka," sighed the Omniscient. "All play and no work makes Jack a—"

But the client had begun to mumble. The Omniscient heard the word 'hurt', and almost lost his temper, but caught himself in the nick of time, for that would have been unprofessional. Instead, he assessed the mental age of this man who'd grown up in a deprived background...

"Ranger Rick," he cried. "Ages seven and up. Too bad you didn't grow up with Ranger Rick. Listen to what he says: 'Bet you're wondering how a horseshoe crab gives blood?' But you already know that so blah blah blah till he says: 'The crabs aren't harmed and their blood soon gets put to work!' Now, that's his exclamation, not mine, so isn't that a marvellous win-win? And you can trust him because he's from the National Wildlife Federation, though (the Omniscient chuckled) you wouldn't know the National—"

The client was not chuckling, nor smiling, nor looking relieved or the least bit thankful. His strides had increased in length.

"So is your question answered?" said the Omniscient, somewhat tersely.

"I think so," said Faldarolo, but by the time he'd said that, the old man had stomped off.

An expert is someone who always makes sure of the spelling.

—The Onuspedia

Cookies and dog tails

"RICK?" said the woman on the other side of a heavy new security door at a house with a shiny new sign out front—WEE CARE SMALL ANIMAL BOARDING. "What you want with Rick?"

"This is the residence of Richard K. Stubbs, is it not?" said the Muse uncomfortably. She didn't know if the woman recognised her, but *she* recognised *her*. And she remembered quite clearly that Stubbs' wife's regard for him matched her own.

"Not any more, lady. Now, unless you got a ferret in your bag... But I see you don't carry a bag," said the woman quite pointedly.

"What do you mean by that?"

"What work you dressed for?"

The Muse smiled. She hadn't changed her clothes for this client, but if she had, the diaphanous gown might have attracted more hostility.

"I was helping him with his manuscript," she said.

"Bungendore!"

"Yes," the Muse said simply.

"Well, do come in. And call me Melissa. I was his wife."

* * *

"I didn't think he had it in him," said the Muse.

"You can say that again! Have another cookie."

"No thank you," said the Muse. She had travelled here in a kind of exploration of self-hate, wanting to take a bath forever, but deciding instead, to visit those clients she'd resented and felt dirtied

309

from the most, just to—*I dunno, make myself hate myself more.*

"What's wrong?" The woman who had cooked, by her estimate, twelve thousand meals for her late husband, chose a frosted cream cheese brownie and picked off some hairs. "Watching your figure?"

The Muse blinked. "That hadn't occurred to me."

"I bet," said Melissa. "You must be some helluvan editor."

"Yeah," said the Muse, "to get Richard K. Stubbs."

"Hey sister," sniggered Melissa. "Gimme a hug. At least you did it for the money."

* * *

The Muse was halfway out of the front security door, her arms full of a bag of cookies, a pack of Size 1 Gourmet Peanut Flavor Chew Bones, and a pile of brochures for Wee Care, when Melissa said, "I forgot to ask..."

"Yes?"

Melissa dropped her voice to a whisper. "Do you want the manuscript?"

"What for?" whispered the Muse diplomatically.

"Don't you want to get it published?"

"Why should I want that?"

"Gawd!" Melissa tried to subtly pull the Muse back inside, but the Muse subtly resisted.

"Okay," said Melissa. "But don't blame me if the neighborhood has ears..."

But her guest was not going to go back inside, so Melissa dropped her head so that no one could lip read from across the street. "You know what it's worth."

"Why don't you finish it?" said the Muse. "You said that you changed back to your maiden name, which would look good on a cover, so?"

"I can't do that," laughed Melissa Rowe. "I'm not creative like you."

"I'm not creative," laughed the Muse.

"However, if you were to—"

"Sorry, I'm late for my next appointment," said the Muse, rushing off as if she were.

Cracking

THE WOMAN IN RED caught the train with one hand and swung on, her long hair snapping. Only a passing lark saw her board but the fact that the train had not slowed was of no interest to the bird any more than it was to Valentin, who had crouched next to the samovar in Carriage 3 for so long, waiting for her to come back from wherever it was on the train that she had—that unbearably tantalising woman of mystery—hidden herself (to do what?)—that his knees had almost locked.

She rushed past him into 3C. He'd already spied on that compartment (because the door to 3C was hanging open and, for once, her companion was absent, but Valentin had no time to waste, as wherever the old man was on the train, it couldn't be far—and whatever he was doing, it couldn't be for long, as he seemed to have no other purpose than to accompany this woman).

So Valentin crept forward extra fast and extra low, the better for him, once in 3C, to spring to his full height and lock the door and leap upon her and have his way with her, and after that he planned to rush out of 3C (he was vague about how he would incapacitate her, but thought it most likely that she would be lying in a lazy swoon, not knowing that she was missing anything at all) and then he would leap off the train into the unknown to escape so fast and so thoroughly that no one would ever find him. *Farewell, comrades who know nothing but work! Farewell, the carriage life!*

So Valentin crept forward one step, and *crunch* went his foot.

Savva, you pig! Valentin froze, but she must not have heard him. She didn't look out of 3C. In fact, he could see her now. She was staring at her companion's empty upper bunk.

"Gorgonna!" she cried, wonderfully covering the sound of Valentin's rush forward which was so fast that he almost ran into her, but she didn't notice him as she stumbled blindly out of 3C and into the smoking section between the cars.

"Fate smiles upon me," declared Valentin. A more perfect place for his raid, he could not imagine.

He watched through the window as, with a shaking hand, she reached into one of her hidden pockets and produced a box of matches and a battered packet. She extracted one bent cigarette, lit it, and drew deeply, lifting her beautiful face and closing her eyes.

"Now!" cried Valentin as he reached out to wrench open the door, but his undisciplined cry was covered by the blurt of the train's horn, and he would have been thrown backward and fallen or his head would have smashed against wall of Carriage 3 if Yuri Shurov had not been the great train driver that he was.

In no time, the train came to a complete stop in the considerate way that a train *should*, and the woman in red tossed her cigarette out onto the steps and reached for the door, and Valentin scurried off into the first place he could find, which was the toilet, where he locked himself in, and if you'd been listening at the door you would have heard a long, muffled, spluttering hiss of filthy curses, but why would you be listening to that when you've got the uplifting sight of Yuri Shurov, the great train driver, striding down the hall?

C!

Yuri Shurov might have *looked* like a model worker, but his soul had always lurked, waiting for its moment.

He had been trained to be a train driver and decorated for his skill, but driving was, to Yuri Shurov, a function of his autonomic nervous system. He didn't need to think of levers to pull, gauges to watch. He just drove. And he certainly didn't value the honours heaped upon him as a model work unit member, not when no Plan called for him to achieve what his soul cried out for. Revolution!

To make every effort to make the train journey as pleasant and blissful as the joy of reaching the destination.

And now that his soul had been handed the means, nothing was going to stop him. He was on his Way. He touched his breast pocket in thanks. This wasn't just Revolution! It was *СВОБОДА! Freedom!*

And since that way was no longer the track way (not even a track distinguished by over twelve years of neglect) he drove the train where he would, to fulfil *his* Plan, for, after all, he was the greatest train driver in (yes, it must be said though he wouldn't have because he was a modest man) the world—but that to him, was only a means to an End.

He smiled cordially at the female passenger who was loitering in the passage (and he noted that she looked unhappy, and this made him most unhappy).

"Though it might seem a featureless landscape, there are several places of interest here," he said. "It would be my pleasure to be your guide. You will be welcomed with refreshments and will be both stimulated and relaxed so that when you resume your journey with us, you will be in that state of blissful joy that is so necessary for a peaceful mind."

The female tourist regarded him with such a complicated set of expressions that he didn't quite know how to satisfy her every whim, so he turned slightly, just enough to see into 3C without being intrusive. But her companion was not there, so he could not have heard Yuri Shurov's maiden speech.

He blushed, remembering the newspaper scraps in the toilet and wondering how he would ever find whisper-soft toilet paper and soaps scented with lilac and leather; and he looked down at the carpet and *tsk*ed. But to get back to the moment, he smiled at the female in a reassuring way and waited without seeming to wait, for the old man to get out of the toilet, for he must be there and old men can take forever in the toilet; and in the silence he heard a stream of filthy curses coming from there and he blushed bright red, for probably Savva had left the hook naked of newspaper scraps.

He was ravaged by conflict. "Your companion?"

"He's indisposed."

Yuri Shurov was devastated. "I hope it's not food poisoning."

"It's only his soul," she said in a loud, strained voice, hoping that wherever he was, he'd hear her, feel her pull, *if he remembers me.*

"Let's go," she said, smiling bleakly.

The virgin guide smiled as confidently as he could. "Rest assured, if Comra, uh, your companion wishes to join this tour, I will have him brought to you at no inconvenience to yourself, and—"

"I'm sure," she said, working him up into a new frenzy of insecurity. Her eyes were dull as crushed expectations.

And so, after he ran to the restaurant car and shoved a note under the door, he helped the female tourist off the train in the manner no one had ever taught him, but that he had dreamed.

Mackerel must be perfectly fresh, or it is a very indifferent fish.
—*Inquire Within Upon Everything*

The maiden tour

THE PLACES OF INTEREST were a short walk away, just over the hill enough to be hidden as the hopes that had flourished in Yuri Shurov's soul. Yes, he had loved Galina with a fierce, protective passion, so much so that he had planned to give her his only precious possession—it had once belonged to his mother—the tin of "*СВОБОДА*" dental powder that he carried next to his heart. He still did love Galina, but he wanted her, above all, to be happy, and what was he compared to Savva?

So Yuri Shurov was happy, in a way, that he had seen Savva's superiority with his own eyes—and that his failure as a lover had led to *this*.

Their heels crunched through snow till they reached the steps of a grand pink and white building with lots of carved gingerbread around the windowsills.

"I hope that I am not assuming," he told his tour of one as he held the massive door open for her and closed it so gently it sighed, "that you value places of great cultural significance. No?"

"You are a privileged visitor," he whispered, "to gain entry to this unique polytechnic."

"What is it?" whispered the Muse, amused despite her heartsickness.

"The Philological Institute of Advanced Art."

"Sounds fascinating."

"But you've probably read all about it," said Yuri Shurov,

suddenly riveted in place by the thought, *What if she is bored?*

"I'm not well read," she said.

He beamed at this model tourist and led the way to Room 1, where they stood just inside the doorway and watched.

"It must be an advanced class," whispered Shurov.

"How do you know?"

"No professor."

Indeed, there was no standing, nor was there any chatter. The twenty students were arranged in neat rows, each with a canvas, paints and paintbrush, etc. laid out on the floor.

The Muse had only seen pictures of flounders before, so when the distraction of the visit caused their eyes to move, she had to suppress a giggle.

"They're kind of adorable, don't you think?"

Shurov couldn't answer for a moment, but then he rebounded. "They revolutionized art."

"Them?" She looked at the white canvases. "They don't seem to have produced much."

"Well, not them."

"That's good," she laughed. "Humour always arrives when one least expects it," she said at the same time as he said, "Their great grandfathers," so both drowned out the other's revelation.

He showed her into Room 2 where the stories *Hurry to Do Good* and *Dad will Come Today* and *Nothing Special* were said to have been planned, but she yawned.

Panicking, he rushed her out of the polytechnic, though he'd planned the visit to take an hour and fifteen minutes.

"You must be hungry," he said, as he led the way to what looked like a collection of long igloos.

"Welcome," he said with a flourish, "to the world's most northerly Tropical Plant Institute."

He grunted as he yanked open the door, its hinges stiff with ice. Inside, a profusion of plants tangled up and around the glass walls, and everything—grossly thick vines, leaves large as tables, gorgeously vulgar flowers—everything was frozen stiff. The Muse pulled an icicle off an orchid and tasted it. She touched a leaf, and her finger made an imprint in the rime.

"The coal must have been cut off again," said her guide. He looked angry.

"Come," he ordered.

The next greenhouse was exactly the same.

"I'm terribly sorry," he said, "I don't know what to say."

"Don't mention it," said the Muse, looking behind her despite her instinct. *Where are you?*

"Third time lucky," she said, not meaning it but trying to help this really quite sweet man out. *He's a loser of the first order, but then, what am I?*

He opened the door to the next greenhouse, already apologising. But his words froze. *You should be fired for your pessimism*, he warned himself, smiling broadly for his tour of one.

"Close the door," shouted a woman in white.

* * *

"And this, as I'm sure you know," said the white-coated Dr. Irina Platinov, the director, "is our *Monstera deliciosa*."

"Please tell me," said the Muse, suppressing a yawn.

Dr Platinov raised one eyebrow, but her passion got the best of her.

"As you can see," she said, pointing to the long curved thing that looked like a cross between a bright green crocodile and a bright green banana, "the fruit is unripe. Feel it," she ordered.

The Muse touched it obediently, but with such a lack of enthusiasm that Yuri Shurov shuffled from foot to foot, trying to think how to break into this tour and whisk this thoroughly bored tourist away.

"Hard, isn't it?" smiled the doctor. "It's exquisite torture, you know."

"Torture?" asked the Muse, and Yuri Shurov almost fell to the ground with thanks at the look on her face.

The Muse, Yuri Shurov, Dr. Irina Platinov and the four other white-coated fanatics who peopled the Institute of Tropical Plants were seated around a table.

The Muse picked up the first piece of the torture fruit that the doctor had cut from the vine just for the pleasure of giving this adventuress the taste she sought.

The skin was a plasticky green, and the inside was gold flecked with black, as if pieces of burnt paper had become caught inside the fruit when it was born.

"That black stuff is the glass," said the doctor.

"Good, said the Muse, and she popped it in her mouth.

It *was* torture. In the moment of impact, every part of her mouth felt slashed by a thousand cuts.

She took the next piece, and repeated her act.

Tears came to her eyes, and still she ate, masticating slowly so that each piece's particles sloshed around her mouth before she swallowed and they serrated her throat and she felt them pierce her insides so she hurt everywhere inside equally.

She was halfway through, her eyes now closed, when Savva opened the greenhouse door—verrrry quietly—and ushered in the Omniscient, who stood in the doorway even more quietly. They were unobserved, as all eyes were on the woman in red who was eating something that was causing her such pain that she was crying, yet eating it as if she could never get enough.

When she finished the last piece, Dr. Platinov led the cheer, and in the rush of her colleagues to jump up and surround this hero of dangerous gastronomy, Savva and the Omniscient exited as unnoticed as they had arrived.

* * *

Dr Platinov blew her nose as she stood in the snow, waving goodbye to the woman who was now no longer the visitor in red, but an honorary colleague in a starched white coat. It was a strangely humble request that the visitor had made (which only made Platinov cry more) when Platinov had impetuously offered the hero "anything" for her bravery. "Anything the Institute can award."

She stepped back into the greenhouse in her quick, practiced way.

"Tear that," she said, turning to her senior colleague, but she didn't need to, as the team was already using the red dress in the form of lagging strips to protect the precious pipes from the cold.

* * *

Yuri Shurov almost floated back to the train, so delirious was he, and *relieved*, that his first tour group had enjoyed itself so much. The group was of only one person, and that person had strange tastes. *But we must begin somewhere!*

As he handed her up to her Carriage, he was encouraged enough to ask: "Where would you like to go?"

"To drown myself," she said, giving him quite a challenge.

Best wishes

IT SO HAPPENED that Burhanettin, Faldarolo, Ekmel and the donkey reached the top of the last rise before the valley of the town of their destination, just as dawn silhouetted them magnificently against the sky. Of course they paused, and though they didn't see themselves as a stirring tableau, Ekmel said:

"Dear friends:"

He looked first to the startled Burhanettin, then to the astounded, blushing Faldarolo.

"Our journey has almost ended," Ekmel said. "We part soon, most likely never to meet again."

"What?" said Burhanettin. "You're not going home with me?"

"There is nothing left for me."

"Your honeys! Where will I get your honeys?"

Ekmel leaned back against the donkey's side, but addressed Burhanettin: "Would you have waited faithfully for me to visit your town again?"

"Of course not. How could I?" said Burhanettin before he listened to himself, but he must have heard the echo. He frowned, and pulled irritably on the one horn left of his moustache.

"And you," said Ekmel to Faldarolo.

"As She," and Ekmel laid his hand on the donkey's neck. "She forgave me. She and I forgive you. And we wish you to find the answers to the troubles in your soul."

Faldarolo hung his head.

On the bladder, Nick broke into the closest thing he could, to tears. How he wished he could *do* something!

Creeping forward with a dreadful deliberation, she arches her neck over the worm, considering it with her beady eye. Then, as it begins to take refuge beneath the shingle — for worms seem to understand that toads are no friends to them — Martha pounces and grips it by the middle. Next comes a long strain, like that of a thrush dragging at a branding in the garden, and after the strain, the struggle.

Heavens! what a fight it is! Magnify the size of the combatants by five hundred, and no man would dare to stay to look at it. The worm writhes and rolls; Martha, seated on her bulging haunches, beats its extremities with her front paws — cramming, pushing, gulping, and lo! gradually the worm seems to shorten. Shorter it grows, and shorter yet. It is vanishing into Martha's inside. And now nothing is left but a little pink tip projecting from the corner of her mouth, in appearance not unlike that of a lighted cigarette.

—H. Rider Haggard,
A Farmer's Year

The white breast

INSTEAD OF GOING DIRECTLY TO 3C, the Muse went to the smoking section, attracted to the noise and discomfort.

At the window, in Carriage 2, Valentin was waiting. He'd almost used up his patience, but had distracted himself by estimating the haul, for he had the confidence of the optimist that she would return, and *this time* when she did...!

He'd calculated that, with a wad she flicked that much, he could live for the rest of his life in some seaside resort and have a different woman every night, and two on Tuesdays.

She stuck her hand in a pocket—a different pocket than before, but it made the same irresistible sound.

She was wearing a common white coat, the type worn by lab workers and shop assistants where they sell cabbages—but what did that matter? What this woman's game was, he'd ceased to care. The only thing that mattered was that that incomparably sexy sound she made, flicking the wad, was soon going to be something he did for himself.

He opened the door casually, and the cold air tore open his jacket which had lost every one of its buttons in that skirmish with the tourists.

He ignored the cold and smiled, as the baring of his pure white chest was something that had always been another of his tricks.

The woman pretended to ignore him, and halfway turned to the door of Carriage 3.

"Not that way, my beauty!" growled Valentin, and he threw his arms around her.

She went completely still, the better for him to run his hands down her sides...

Just when he'd reached something, she clasped her hands to his, and clutched them to her.

"Ahh," he grrred.

She whirled around and faced him, her nostrils dilated and her hair gone so big and sexy, he almost lost his sense of purpose, but "patience!" he cautioned himself, and smiled into her eyes.

She smiled into his eyes and shimmied back in little tiptoed steps of those incredible red boots.

"So it's games we play, my cherry tart?" said he.

"If you say," she giggled, raising one shoulder in the cutest little gesture.

Don't play games! something in him said. *Get it now! and kick her off the train.*

She took a small step forward with her left foot, and swung her right with supernatural force, right at Valentin's heart.

He flew off the train and into the air, passing over birds both singly and in flocks, overflying experimental institutes and towns that existed on no maps. He soared through cloud banks and beyond, up through the inner and outer atmospheres of Earth, where he grabbed at a glove reported lost by some astronaut whenever, and a biodegradable plastic bag, and a robot hand that twitched, and where he passed spiders trailing gossamer lines, and he was dropped down into shattered forts where he grabbed at cornerstones and those wooden posts that stick out of towers, and tore the skin off his hand as he was whisked away and along and through, and he counted the humps of camels in caravans and sneezed on particles of early gunfire and choked on the fumes of burning towns with mouldy straw roofs and lots of decaying bodies—and he sped through forests of bluebells, just high enough from them to almost pick one, when he was whisked back up to the vastness of noplace where he was just a spec in a zillion unidentifiable flying and floating objects as he travelled in an oblique orbit—hitting and breaking through space and time continuums till he didn't know where he was at any time, nor when it was, but whenever it was and wherever, it didn't matter because there was nothing he could do about it nor was there any way he could just die.

But, he hadn't gone without a fight. When she kicked him, he grabbed at her hair, and it was one small comfort that he tore out a good handful. He dropped it of course, while his eyes were closed and he whizzed around screaming his guts out. But it was a small satisfaction.

Another small satisfaction was the bit of red on the tip of the Muse's right boot, which is where Nick ended up after he pulled himself loose from Galina's face.

Being in the best of all positions when the Muse gave the putrid Valentin, who'd been such a pig to Galina, the old what for, it was good he had no gullet or he would have choked himself laughing.

329

Flush

THE OMNISCIENT slunk away. He had watched through the window of Carriage 3, so he saw Valentin wrap the Muse in his arms. He saw Valentin's hands, saw the passion in the man's eyes. He saw the Muse clutch Valentin's hands close—and he wanted to do as he'd seen so often. Yes, he wanted to hoist Valentin on something tall—and watch him scream at first like a worm on a hook ... and then watch him ... die ... whimpering.

But love made him clutch his passions and stand as still as a watcher through a pinprick in a paper screen, for: *If She loves him, who am I to interfere?*

Her creativity allows her to find value where I do not.

He was just turning to slink off to travel into some sort of oblivion if he could find a way, *since I am cursed with useless immortality*, when he saw the denouement.

She rejected him! Maybe she never loved him. Maybe he ... that cad!

The Omniscient wanted to rush to her, but stopped himself just before this foolish act.

Yes, he slunk away. *What do you have to offer?* he asked himself.

Sentimentally, he walked back to 3C and climbed up to his bunk.

A moment later, she wandered in, her face tragic and brave and lined and, oh, so very beloved.

She didn't look up to his bunk. Indeed, she acted as if his side of the room had never existed. Instead, she sat on her bottom bunk and reached in her pocket and took out that pack of cards she was always flicking, and laid one card on the table.

Without daring to breathe, he stretched forward, and saw:

Death.

"Hah," she said.

She flicked another card on top of that.

Two Fools.

"I could have guessed," she shouted.

She tore the next card from the top of the pack, and threw it on top of the others.

A Spotted Youth.

Her forehead creased. Next she took a card from the middle of the pack. The Omniscient smiled at her cheating herself.

"An Unintended Consequence", it said.

The Omniscient had never seen a tarot deck like this, so he was all afire to see the next card.

"An Apple", it said, but it showed distinctly a medium, flushed and russeted (and the Omniscient was willing to bet: crisp, sweet and aromatic) Golden Harvey, otherwise known as Brandy Apple, first grown in England (Herts.) in the 1600s.

"Geeveston Fanny," he said, and though she dropped her cards and they fell to the table and floor, neither the Muse nor the Omniscient noted them.

"That's another nice apple," he said.

"It's a lovely name."

"Frequin Rouge."

"Go on."

"Forfar Pippin, Striped Beefing, Brabant Bellefleur, Black Taunton, Brown Snout."

"Don't stop now!"

"Golden Reinette, Hyslop Crab, Hubbarston Nonsuch, Hollow Crown, How do I love thee."

"Go on," she said.

"The last isn't an apple."

She knelt on the floor and began to pick up cards, but before she had completed, he was beside her picking up the last of them, and now he gently but firmly took them from her and rearranged them pedantically with their strangely ugly backs facing upwards.

"This is the Upset Dragon," he said, and at a wave of his left hand, his right held a stack of cards that arched its back like a dragon with indigestion.

"And this is the Somatic Stretch," he said, and the arch fell and cascaded almost to the floor.

"And the Three Card Flippant," he announced, "and the Antigravity Buckle," his eyes not on the cards, but her...

"Of course," he said as he dropped the pack lifelessly to the table before her, "they're only tricks."

"Of course," she said.

"I'm shamelessly worthless," he said, shaking his head and not bothering to hide any more, his infinite grief. He hated himself for showing it, as she might think he was begging, but he had to confess.

"I can never be worthy of your bravery," he said. "Your sense of adventure. Don't look at me like that. I'm low enough to have spied upon you! I know your creativity craves—"

"Creativity!" The Muse jumped up and threw the cards in the Omniscient's face. "*That's* my creativity!" And she burst into inexplicable tears.

"So you wind down with cards?" he said. "You'd need to with so many stories. Oh yes, I know you sneak out and work. I know you cannot stop the flow of stories coming from you any more than—"

"You lovable old fool!"

"Lovable?"

"Fool!" she said, and somehow she was in his arms and he was in hers

The beginning of the book of making an old man into a young man... It is a million times efficient.

—unknown author (Pharaonic Egypt)

First impressions

AND SO THE TOWN WHERE MULLIANA LIVES comes closer with every step.

Faldarolo's heart is in a turmoil, so he doesn't notice that the crowd gets thicker as the town's gates loom. There are many loud and coarse jests tossed which he ignores, but all of a sudden, in that coarseness gleams a needle of sound. He strains his ears to hear it, but it grows thicker and suddenly pierces through every word and guffah and gesture, till it shines above everything and the crowd pauses, and is silent.

"That is Mulliana," mouths a mounted man on a horse beside Faldarolo, and Faldarolo whispers to Burhanettin. "You didn't say anything about her voice."

"What voice?" said Burhanettin.

Faldarolo raised his hands to the sky.

"That? What's her voice matter? You can always get a musician if you like music."

Faldarolo and Ekmel exchanged glances, but did not speak. Indeed, they were both too overcome with emotion, but it must be said that Ekmel, who had never been overly affected by music, had become very soft in the heart.

First impressions count. Faldarolo had never heard any instrument as heavenly as Mulliana's voice. He had always considered himself a musician above mere musicians—that music-making for him wasn't a trade, a set of skills such as any apprentice could learn, given enough time and diligence. No. From the time when his lips were too small to properly kiss the bladder-pipe, he was attracted, a love that had matured when he met the bladder-pipe that changed his life. Faldarolo became a musician as he was destined to, but he thought of his living as letting others listen in to him make love.

Now, the sound of Mulliana's voice—rising, falling, insinuating... That voice fell upon him, entered into him, and his insides stirred in ways that made him laugh bitterly at his previous transports of love.

Faldarolo walked (actually, he was jostled this way and that) through the town gates a changed man, a man who knew that he was only a bladder-pipe blower with a bladder-pipe that needed fixing.

"Bletted medlars," cried an old woman, plucking at his sleeve. In her basket was a pile of brown fruits with skins as wrinkled and brown as she. He bought three, as he could hardly move, and the man ahead of him, Burhanettin, had stopped altogether.

"Old women's hair!" shouted Burhanettin at a little boy. "I should tan your skin for calling it Palace helva."

"Kind sir," said the boy, "I only tell what the sweet maker tells me to."

"I'm sure he does," said Ekmel, looking kindly at the boy but not having a single coin to spend to help him.

"That," said Burhanettin, pointing at what the boy was holding—five wooden skewers stuck into a base of what looked like wads of white hair—

"That abomination—get it out of my sight and smell, boy—that is *tepme helva. Backfire* helva. Old women's hair!"

He glared around him, and well he could, for there had grown a crowd that had given him the space he needed, so wild had grown his gestures—and he still had the greatest physique of anyone in almost any town. He was, however, as funny, if his hands were not touching you, as an angry bull, and some sniggers broke out of the crowd.

"You *like* that!" he shouted at them, pointing, for the boy was too frightened to move, so Ekmel had reached out for him and was holding him out of harm's way, but the offending sweets were still in sight, as big as a bouquet.

"That..." sputtered Burhanettin. "That..."

He was so angry he didn't know how to put it, so put it in the crudest terms he could, lifting his upper lip so that those who hadn't noticed, pointed to his hilarious half-moustache. "That *sugar* candy! If you like that, your town deserves to rot in hell."

Faldarolo sidled around till he reached Ekmel, and he gave Ekmel a handful of coins, and Ekmel gave them to the boy and pushed him off with soothing words, and then Ekmel walked up to Burhanettin and had some quiet words with him, which seemed to work, for Burhanettin stopped glowering, though his shoulder-muscles rippled unpredictably.

And the little group proceeded onwards, molested not, till they reached the crowd amassed under the famous tower.

At this point, Faldarolo should have bid the others goodbye and wended his way to the musicians' quarter even though, with her heavenly voice floating over the rooftops, mere musicians such as he would have been a crude joke here.

But as Burhanettin had pointed out, there is no accounting for taste, so Faldarolo was confident that there would be a musicians' quarter in this town—and furthermore, he just knew that there would be an instrument maker who could fix the bladder-pipe.

Still, he tarried with the crowd below the tower.

Burhanettin also tarried, though his soul was curdling worse than a helva that is stirred one way and then another. "Backfire helva," he muttered, wanting to kick himself. No matter that this Mulliana had no choice living in this town or being locked in that tower. *This town that's spread her fame for beauty and worth calls Old Women's Hair, Palace Helva.*

He sighed mightily, but he did not leave. Having come this

far, he had a certain amount of curiosity. The cord that he'd used to hang those two jars around his neck, chafed.

"Her father died yesterday, so it's only a matter of who steals into her chamber first," said a man beside Faldarolo. He was dressed in gold brocade and sat on a restive dark horse. The horseman beside him, dressed louder than a peacock, pulled on the reins of his snorting white. "You want to wager who holds whose horse tonight, and then we can be off?"

"A coin for a rose," said the first. "I hear there's a sweet thing in..."

Burhanettin didn't hear them, so moiled were his thoughts.

Beside him, Ekmel didn't rightly know where to go or what to do, but he didn't want to spend life aimlessly, so this is where he decided to take his leave. He was just reaching out to touch Burhanettin's shoulder in farewell, when —

"HARK!" boomed a voice, out over all the crowd assembled below the tower. The voice was so loud, and of such authority, that a flock of birds overhead paused in flight.

Hark

"CLOSER," said the crandolin.

Mulliana lifted the crandolin higher towards the slit in the wall, but the crandolin huffed, dissatisfied.

"This won't do," said the crandolin. "Put me down."

So Mulliana put the crandolin on the floor.

"Now wrap your hand in that rug there," said the crandolin.

Mulliana did as she was told.

"Now punch a hole through the wall."

"But I can't do that!"

"Delicate maiden, are you?" chuckled the crandolin.

So Mulliana punched the wall, and to her surprise, the rocks fell out in a shower of dust. They gave less resistance than that obstreperous stage in a pile of fluffy wool when it doesn't want to be beaten flat and turned into a felted rug.

The crowd below rose up in noise.

"Now hold me up again, dear."

So Mulliana did, and she gazed, from behind the crandolin's head, through the fist-sized hole.

"Did not I say HARK?" asked the crandolin of the crowd.

"Yes," said some, though they knew not whose commanding voice this was. Others just trembled, and some men reached, in show, for their swords, all the while looking behind them for the clearest path to the town's gate.

"Mulliana shall choose between three men," said the voice.

"Ahhh," said the crowd, and some sat higher in the saddle, and some preened their moustaches, and some ... but you know.

Faldarolo hoped she chose well, but he couldn't help tears dropping from his eyes, as he thought of the fate of nightingales. *If only she could be let free!* he thought, quite irrelevantly. He couldn't bear to watch, so he turned and began to push his way back away from the tower.

"Psst," said the bladder-pipe. "You're going the wrong way."

"You just wait," said Faldarolo. "Trust me," he added, to shut her up.

"This is no place for me," said Ekmel, finally taking his leave of Burhanettin.

"Wait," said Burhanettin. "I must have been mad." And he turned away from the tower, too.

"YOU!" said the voice. "Point a broom at that one," said the crandolin to Mulliana. "Before he gets away."

And as the crowd jostled with many a "Me!" and "You!" and "Not him!", a broomstick suddenly poked from the little round hole in the tower and pointed at... "Not him. NO. Not him. Yes, him!"

And hands were put upon Faldarolo's shoulders—some kind, some jealous, some merely curious, but nevertheless, all waylaying.

"That's the one," boomed the voice. "Go to the tower door."

And so Faldarolo did make his way, in front of the crowd, to the door of the tower, though it was the last place in the world he wished to be—*me, the unworthiest.*

And there, in the glare of scrutiny, he stood at the door, and though his head was bowed and his cheeks flushed red, the crowd was able to see him fully. And a sigh rose from them, and about a third of them turned their faces and horses' heads away, toward the town gates, whence they proceeded like a funeral procession. For each of these had thought himself more handsome than any other, and had dressed himself to suit. But this whoever he was in his torn and dirtied and archaic garb outshone the sun in the beauty of his visage and the graceful litheness of his form. Several men were so jealous of his beestung lip, *and those eyebrows*—that, from that day, their lives were forever blighted.

"And YOU!" said the voice.

Now the broom handle pointed to the great bull of a man with that ridiculous half moustache.

And at this choice, the second third of the crowd of men broke from the crowd and slunk toward the town gate, and away. They had thought themselves strong, but they were calves compared to this man, and any man who can travel the world with a single horn! "He can't wear the both of them," they said on the road as they rushed away, "because if he did, his strength would be too strong to caress anything but a mountain."

"And YOU," commanded the voice, and though the crowd below the tower was now a third of what it was only moments ago, there was much confusion, because no one believed that the broom could be pointing to the one it did. It waggled, and the crowd *still* could not believe.

"Stop them, you fools! Them that's gone ROUND THE CORNER!" and the crowd moaned, for they could not believe, but it was true. Only Ekmel and the donkey had just gone round the corner.

At that, the crowd drifted away, for whatever maiden would have *that* for a choice? That ragged ruffian who looked fit to murder you in your sleep, just for the joy of it.

"I'd wager you he stole that ass," one disgusted would-be suitor said to another. "Hardly worth the wager," said the other. "Where's the nearest tavern?"

Three men and an ass

AND SO, assembled below at the door to the tower were now, three bemused men and one ass.

"Open the door and come up," called the crandolin.

"How does *she* come up?" called Ekmel.

"Leave her out there."

"Then I go."

The crandolin rubbed some claws together. "Then bring *her* in, but she must stay below, for the only way up is a ladder made of hair."

"Can the door be secured below so that no one harms her? I'm not coming up unless—"

"Yes, yes," chortled the crandolin, and for the worried one's benefit, the crandolin boomed out in a voice heard as far as the other side of the horizon, "Anyone who harms *her*, pains me!"

That seemed to satisfy the one who looked like a murderer, so he entered with the donkey, and climbed the ladder first.

The other two came up after him. Firstly, the bull of a man, who sniffed the air and peered around the room as if he expected to find that the place was overrun with mice.

Next came the handsome one, who was all blushes and nervous clutching at a velvet bag that hung from his neck.

The room was dim, so the crandolin waited till their eyes had adjusted to the light, and then waited some more.

And finally, s/he stepped forward.

"Wondrous," scowled Burhanettin, though what *this* was, he couldn't say.

Ekmel had travelled widely in his hunt for the best honeys, had met many beasts such as the cinnamologus and the amphisbaena, and the ostrich and the one-humped camel. Now he considered what he had missed in having thought them beasts and gauging them merely for their usefulness or nuisance value in his procurement of the precious fluid.

He stepped forward and ducked his head. "I don't believe I've met you."

"An admirable understatement," said the crandolin, with a wink at the open-mouthed Mulliana.

"Nor have I met *you*," said the crandolin to Faldarolo, but the beautiful young man's eyes would not meet his. He only had eyes for the floor.

"Nor have I met *you*," the crandolin repeated, and scritched over in that tragic lopsided gait, to the feet of Faldarolo, where s/he gave his robe a sharp tug.

"No," moaned Faldarolo. "I dare not stay." He looked longingly at the hole in the floor where the ladder hung.

"You interest us," said the crandolin.

"Your interest is sorely misplaced. Please let me go."

"No!"

The crandolin climbed up Faldarolo's robe and touched the velvet bag. "Is this why?"

"Don't!" cried Faldarolo. "I must leave before I hurt another."

"You will not," said Ekmel, who turned to the crandolin. "He is a good man."

The crandolin climbed down and examined Ekmel.

"We all have our troubles," Ekmel said.

A harsh laugh made them both turn to the musician.

Faldarolo ripped the bag from his neck, rived its jaws open, reached in and wrenched the bladder-pipe out with such force that the torn bag fluttered to the floor and the bladder of the bag swung limp.

In the jars around Burhanettin's neck, Nick quivered with the overwhelming pain he felt for Faldarolo. On the skin of the bladder-pipe, Nick gleamed. "Tear me off," he urged, but of course, Faldarolo couldn't hear.

"Let me go," said Faldarolo to the crandolin. "But before I go, take *this*." And groaning as if he were tearing off his own arm, Faldarolo tore the bladder off the bladder-pipe and threw it—

"Throw me in the fire," screamed Nick. "It's better to die than to live with *her*."

"I'll take that," said the crandolin—and calmly plucked the skin from the air, and laid it against the wall furthest from the drain hole, the ladder hole, and the hearth itself.

"You haven't looked where a young man should," said the crandolin slyly.

Indeed, Faldarolo had not.

"I thought I was a musician," said Faldarolo, his eyes sweeping the floor at Mulliana's feet. "Till I heard your voice."

"Hmph," said the crandolin in a satisfied way.

The crandolin turned to Burhanettin. "Now," s/he said. "Do *you* have something for me?"

Burhanettin turned his gaze from Mulliana and smiled ruefully at the crandolin. "You already know." And Burhanettin handed over the two pots.

"They can never rival the ones in your dreams," said the crandolin.

"Such a wasted chase."

"If you poison it with bitterness," snapped the crandolin. "Consider it a burnt batch. That is all."

Abashed, Burhanettin nodded.

"For long enough," said the crandolin, with stern kindliness, "you have forsaken those who depend upon you."

"Oh," sighed Burhanettin. "Oh that I had—"

"Please! None of your poetry. Be off!"

"He leaves a happy man," said the crandolin.

And indeed, the others could hear Burhanettin crooning as he stepped down the ladder—"Pillows of delight. Lips of love. Pshaw! The higher the pile of pillows of delight, the lonelier the lover of my sweets. The hotter the tongue that melts my helva, the icier the bed."

He had rudely left without leave-taking, but he boxed his own ears when he'd pushed past the donkey with not so much as an "I once knew you" and opened and shut the door, leaving the tower behind; "You should suffer," he said, and his frown was so vile that a beggar scuttled out of the sweep of the big man's arm. "You have deserted the lonely, who need your succour, for a taste of what? What madness!"

* * *

Said the crandolin to Faldarolo: "Do you not have a bladder-pipe to fix?"

"Not any more," said Faldarolo, throwing the pipes into the fire. "A bladder-pipe clashes with such beauty," and his glance almost reached Mulliana, and plummeted to the floor.

"Too common an end," declared the crandolin. "Toss it here, dear."

So Mulliana reached into the fire, snatched out the smouldering pipes, and threw them to the crandolin.

"My beak needs honing," said the crandolin to no one in particular.

"I've always wished..." Mulliana said, and fell silent.

"Achem," said the crandolin, and poked a claw into Faldarolo's slipper, making Faldarolo look, finally more boldly, possibly to the toenails, of she who'd always wished.

"Now now, Mulliana," smiled the crandolin. "No one's on the floor or in the ceiling beams. Do tell us, and do look at us when you say: What ... could ... this ... wish ... be?"

"Tell, or I'll *eat* you," boomed the crandolin, and though s/he

345

certainly could, s/he stuck out a lasciviously flaming tongue, and cackled with delicious coarseness.

Always, this threat had made Mulliana burst into giggles, and rush to fulfil the beloved crandolin's any wish. And always before, the crandolin had been treated also, to a sweet and saucy song. But now?

Mulliana's mouth twitched, her hands tore at each other, her eyes shone with tears.

The crandolin held out a long curved claw. "I'll *tickle* you."

"I'vealwayswishedadrumwouldaccompany me," Mulliana said, in a voice so small, it was almost a held breath.

"She said, good sirs, in case you didn't *hear*. Such poor enunciation," tutted the crandolin, glancing up at Faldarolo, who was now looking through his eyelashes at Mulliana, now that her eyes were gazing, as if they'd been ordered to be fascinated by it, on a stray wisp of wool on the floor.

"She said," repeated the crandolin, "that she wishes a drum to accompany her."

For one half-moment, her eyes disobeyed her commands, and met Faldarolo's. His fled.

The crandolin's blue eyelids crinkled cruelly. "She doesn't mean what she says."

"Oh?" "Oh?"

All eyes were upon the crandolin, two sets most of all.

"I've always wished a drum to accompany me," the crandolin minced, a perfect imitation of Mulliana's tortured confession, though shockingly slow and loud.

"You mean," continued the crandolin crisply, unremorsefully, "not drum, but drummer."

The crandolin turned to Faldarolo: "Good day."

Faldarolo left in a swirl of robe and swish of rushing slippers— breathing such a sigh that the tears already in Mulliana's eyes were pushed out when a new sea of them pushed in.

"What's this?" chided the crandolin. S/he climbed up into

Mulliana's arms—arms in which the muscles fought, just as the expressions on Mulliana's face.

"Do you wish to throw me in the fire?" murmured the crandolin. "Good day doesn't mean goodbye."

Mulliana's breath fluttered in her windpipe.

Just as the doorlatch clacked below, out flew from between her lips a warble—a wild, shimmering, air-beating song that ended in a longtailed ululation too complex for the nightingales, too terribly, tragically beautiful to repeat. It flew out the rough window Mulliana had punched in the stones, and was gone.

For a moment in that tower, in its absence, sound was a vacuum. Mulliana's lips closed. Her eyes shut tight as jail doors, and her eyelashes sparkled like jail door nails.

A slight, muffled thud somewhere close outside was too common for her to notice. The faint of a jealous nightingale.

"But what is *that*?" she said, for fainter still, was another thud of a different timbre. And then another. *My own blood, my own heart?* pausing— little deaths, each waking to fierce-winged life.

She had asked the crandolin what *that* was, but answered now as only Mulliana could, as another impossibly-rhythmed song of songs escaped her mouth—timid and brave and wreckful. Her very heart smashed the door to its cage, and flew.

* * *

Almost at the town's wall now in his urgency to leave, to find a Master of the Drums, Faldarolo's heart stopped yet again just as it had an impossible moment ago—this time for two and almost three-quarter heartbeats ... and now, it answered yet again, louder than before, answering that wildly irregular, wholly seductive shimmering ululation with a beat as wild, seduced and yet seductive—but a heart is just a heart.

And though it's said by musicians that drumming needs a Master, and by lovers that the heart is the finest instrument—at the third of Mulliana's warbles, Faldarolo threw off every memory of all that wisdom *said*.

He stopped in a swirl of dust, took the bottomlessly deep breath of a bladder-pipe Master, tore open his robe ... and beat his chest.

Her warble trembled, caught his beat, and then they flew, high above the crowd, into realms of sound that only lovers hear...

His playing was, however, just clenched fists upon a man's bared chest in the midst of the shoving crowd where those places for travellers cluster. His eyebrows moved as tenderly as loving lovers do, but a prince from afar who'd just drunk well and was coming this way noticed not the softness in Faldarolo's face, but the fists pounding, proclaiming the obvious—an insolent handsomeness that the prince could only dream about.

"Spoiling for a fight?" he sneered, swinging before his opponent had a chance to answer.

Faldarolo missed the drunken punch. Indeed, he might as well have been deaf and blind.

But, *swack*, *thud*, the prince was swept off his feet by a brisk swipe of an olive staff, by someone in the swirl of the crowd.

And the beats went on, pitilessly, as if Faldarolo was pounding himself tender for a meal.

And Mulliana was no less kind to herself. Her long fluttering ribbons of love she ripped raw from her throat.

* * *

"Cruel love," smiled the crandolin, who clearly wanted to continue. "You must let him go."

Mulliana opened her eyes and wiped her eyelashes with her sleeve. At that gesture, at least one heart in that close room tore, thinking that 'go' meant 'go'.

"And now to you," said the crandolin, turning to Ekmel, who had not only shed a tear at Faldarolo's departure, but whose face was as mottled as a stained map now.

"Why does life have to be full of hopeless loves?" he asked the crandolin. "Why do I, unworthy worm that I am, find love when these worthies—"

348

"Silence, worm!" said the crandolin. "And wipe your nose."

Ekmel's hands waggled impotently.

Mulliana handed him a cloth, which only made the red features on his face more complex. He snorted inwards, and choked down an unmanly gulp.

"Finished?" said the crandolin.

Ekmel nodded, turning to the hole in the floor.

The crandolin grabbed for Ekmel, ending up with a clawsful of rotten threads, but that held Ekmel poised above the ladder.

Said the crandolin: "Do you snore?"

"No," said Ekmel, so surprised, he laughed.

"Do you know anything of carpets?"

Ekmel almost lost his balance and moved away from the hole, remembering painfully that middle-of-the-night act of thievous villainy—when he was woken from a sweet dream, bundled in his own carpet and stolen from his home.

His nose wrinkled. "A good carpet deserves a regular beating. That is all."

"Capital!" spat the crandolin, who rolled on the floor in an excess of delight.

Ekmel stood politely, but was only waiting for his dismissal, for he knew it was a mistake for *him* to have been called up here at all.

"No man should know too much, especially about himself," said the crandolin to Mulliana.

"Should you wish," said the crandolin to Ekmel, "here is a client list..."

A rise and fall

I⊤ was a good while before Ekmel left the tower, but as soon as his steps and that of his companion's could no longer be heard—

"Unstopper those jars, dear," said the crandolin.

Mulliana unstoppered the jars.

"Give me your paw," said the crandolin.

Mulliana put her hand in that of the crandolin's, who announced:

"Arise, Nick Kippax."

A sort of sound came from one of the jars, and then the other.

"Fear not," said the crandolin to Mulliana, and commanded in a voice of unarguable no nonsense: "ARISE!"

The stuff in one of the jars began to seethe, and the stuff in the other, to bubble, and then they boiled, and then, before Mulliana's incredulous eyes, the stuff in the jars rose till she could see it, and it rose some more till it was two ropes red as pomegranate; and one rope twined round the other and rose still further till the rope of many twists lifted free of the pots and rose till it reached the tangle of cobwebs in the ceiling where it hissed like water thrown on a fire; and the rope bent as if it weighed too much, and it fell to the floor, and kicked up stuff into Mulliana's eyes so that she had to rub them, and when she opened them, before her stood a man—or most of one.

He was rubbing his eyes, too, patting himself all over, till he fell.

"Are you?" he said, pointing.

"I expected wit," said the crandolin, "if not manners."

"You are!" said Nick.

"Still neither," said the crandolin to Mulliana. "Shall I put him back?"

"No!" said Nick, scrabbling over on his hand and knee. "Please don't condemn me."

"Condemn! Thou ungrateful wretch."

Mulliana put her hand out to Nick, who turned his eyes to her with what looked like annoyance.

"A song for your story, sir," she said prettily.

"He's got no taste for song," said the crandolin acidly. "Something got your tongue, Nick?"

"Did you do this to me?"

"Not I."

"But you know what happened."

"Not all of what happened," laughed the crandolin. "I see you've lost yourself somewhat."

"Here and there," said Nick.

"I commend the speck of humour you've retained."

"What happened?" asked Nick humbly.

"Only you can say," said the crandolin.

"You talk in riddles."

"Then let me be plain," said the crandolin, crawling in the crandolin's noisy, broken way, up to Nick, and then up Nick's lap till the crandolin's claws pierced Nick's black t-shirt.

"Not everyone is for eating."

* * *

Mulliana had never been impatient before, but the silence now, between the crandolin and this man who'd lost much but not his mouth, was making her chilblains itch.

"Does he speak?" said the crandolin finally.

"Okay," Nick said. "I get it. It's some sort of curse against meat eaters."

"It's a bit more complex than that," said the crandolin, climbing down and proceeding to the hearth.

"Remind you of anyone, mister Kippax?" said the crandolin, who turned and posed in noble profile.

"His nose!" said Mulliana.

"And my father's," said Nick, feeling his own nose.

The crandolin nodded.

"And gran's flaring nostrils," said Nick.

"And *her* father's great beak," said the crandolin, "and so on, till ... how many do you think, Nick? You got that gas chromatograph done on the blood, but tut, tut."

"Tut tut, *what?*"

"DNA."

"How do you know about DNA?"

"Oh, I don't know the details any more than you, but if you'd taken that scraping from the cookbook, and profiled it—and taken, say, one of your hairs I think would do just fine, you would have said more than 'crikey'."

"Tell me," said Nick, who somehow knew what the crandolin was going to say, almost as if he had known it all along.

"But why did you explode me into so many parts? A limb for a limb?"

"You suppose me more powerful than I am," said the crandolin. "But if you'd been stuck in that book for hundreds of years, wouldn't you be overexcited at the prospect of release?"

"So you blew me to smither—"

"I know not how you were blown, but as a cook of your renown, you must surely know the old palace saying."

"Remind me."

"Never spit into a pot of seething oil."

* * *

"So this Guy de something," said Nick, "didn't manage to bag you, but he cut some of your legs off as you sampled some of him ... a hand, was it? But he got away and gave your legs and most of your blood, which he managed to scoop up in a flask, to his cook, Theuroy."

"Yes," said the crandolin, "And Guy ate the dish all by himself, all of it except the sample that Theuroy saved ... a drop of which stained the cookbook. And so I guess you could put this in a nutshell: I live in you, and you in me."

"And it would have all stayed cold under the surface if I hadn't found that Theuroy cookbook."

"Possibly," said the crandolin.

"What happened to the rest of that sample?"

"I knowest not."

"I knowest neither," said Nick, to his surprise. "Sorry, but it takes a while to absorb all this information ... Kippax, crandolin,"

"Kirand-luhun, and many more."

"So there's no virgin blood," mused Nick. But..."

He twisted violently in some sort of spasm. "Achbejesus. Gross! Yich. God I wish I could retch. I've got it. Ech, how GROSS!"

"What's gross, Nick?" said the crandolin.

"Get that glint out of your eye. You're enjoying it."

"Could I ask what?" said Mulliana politely.

"I ate myself."

"Though he thought he'd be tucking in, as I think he'd say, to part of you, dear Mulliana."

"You did? You wanted to *eat* me?"

"Not *exactly*," said Nick.

"But," said the crandolin.

Nick hung his head. "Nothing personal."

"She's a pretty fair damsel, isn't she, Nick?"

"Beaut, I'd say," laughed Nick. "Pretty lame gourmandism, eh? But hey. I've had a great time, and though I'm not all here, I've had a good one. Do your thing."

"And what, pray tell, is my *thing*?"

"You plan to liquidize me some way so that you can pump me

back into you as type whatever crandolin blood and Bob's your uncle and though you won't have all your red blood cells back, you'll be a helluvalot healthier than you look now."

"And you're ready to be killed for that?"

"Would I die, or live in you?"

"You'd die."

Nick swallowed, thought briefly of the parts of him that were having wonderful experiences but were so small that he expected they'd die, too.

"I'm ready," he said. "But can you do it fast?"

"Why?"

A boot to the solar plexus of a stinking rat at dawn. Love painted... Nick's lips opened and his nostrils flared. *The scent of a cinnamologus.*

"Forgive me for interrupting your thoughts," said the crandolin.

"Because," Nick shrugged. These loves of tastes weren't for putting into words, like ... like a bloody *wine* review. He looked the crandolin in the eyes. "I've had the best whatever of my whatever."

"How poetic. You know, of course, that some things cannot be."

"You should have told my father that. Now, can we please get this over? I'm no hero."

"I'm sorry," said the crandolin. "We cannot. I cannot put you into me. And now that I've met you more fully, I would not, if I could.

"But," said the crandolin, "I can give you three choices."

"I should have seen that coming," said Nick, but his eyes were flooded with tears.

"I can make Mulliana love you."

Nick had already assessed her physical charms as quickly as he used to, the early morning catch at the fishmarkets. Her physique, that of a great cook—hands scarred from boiling water and livid flame, arms that could toss a cow or an omelette with equal finesse.

And to top this, as if he needed it to be topped, her face was so beautiful that... "No," he said, though he smiled at her.

"Good," said the crandolin, and Mulliana smiled at Nick.

"Or I could, with the powers that I possess, gather the rest of you and get you all together minus some superfluous matter— spleen, appendix, an ear or two. And I can set you back where you came from ... or perhaps a bit further away, safe from temptation."

"Of course no."

"Then you want the last choice?"

"Wouldn't you?"

The crandolin chuckled.

"Subside, Nick!"

And Nick, without ado, melted back into two ropes and dropped into the two jars.

And the crandolin picked up the bladder-pipe's skin and tossed it out of the hole in the wall, where it presumably fell upon the pile of rubble or perhaps didn't reach that far but no one in the tower looked to see—

but where were we?

To the two jars, which the crandolin now ordered Mulliana to pick up.

"Here! By the drain," said the crandolin, "Dash them to the floor!"

And Mulliana did as she was told—and the jars shattered to dust amongst the fluid so that the stream that came out laughing from the tower was a sort of shocking pink milkshake.

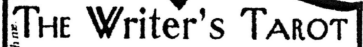

THE Writer's TAROT

"Never be blocked again"

★ ★ ★ ★ ★

EMINENTLY CONCEALABLE
Ever Effervescent
SAFE & EFFECTIVE*

Imperturbably Unpredictable
in **27** Unexpurgated
Multi-Universal editions
Every permutation *of*
Every Story Told
& Untold

"THE Source"

Only revealed by

M&O ENTERPRISES

*when taken correctly.
We bear no responsibility
if madness seizes you.

"For thou art with me."

"Next stop, unexplored."
The wine was — inscrutable.
Their deadly frauds

"Eat me if you dare."

"Forever ends at four o'clock."

"You have an honest face."

Fortune's smile

MUNIFER PEERED—with a stupid look on his face—at a long, black, lustrous as eyes in love, hunk of hair, which possessed in every hair, the incomparable fragrance of virginity. The hair had just floated down before him, and caught in the branch of a stunted fig.

And only that day, Munifer had bequeathed everything he possessed because he knew that, if he did not turn up at the palace with the Great Tīmūrsaçi's new moustache tomorrow, then he would be found and taken to the Bridge of Dispatch and Divorce where he would be tossed into the Pond of Sighs where his fate would be hotly argued, and where the Greatness's crocodiles would frolic with his form.

So now he got to work with the skill he—only he—possessed.

And in no time he made a moustache that was more magnificent than any he had ever made. Perhaps it was his time in life, or the challenge of the job, but the hairs seemed to almost leap to obey his every wish, so easily did they stretch out to their great length at each side, and so readily did they bend to make those indubitable curves that further distinguished the moustache that gave the Great Tīmūrsaçi his distinguished saçiness.

And every hair in this moustache, Munifer knew without doubt, was 100% virgin, unlike those dubious hairs from the Quarter of Ill Repute that had reverted to type.

He finished the moustache by the light of the moon, and then he threw himself to the ground and gave thanks.

Now, it is said that a man who has said farewell to life is as welcome back as a guest who fails to leave a party, so he wasn't giving thanks for saving his life. No. He was giving thanks for tossing him this one reprieve, for once he fitted the moustache on the Great Tīmūrsaçi, and his Greatness was delighted again (as Munifer knew he would be) then Munifer could drown himself in the river, which would be a much less terrifying, not to mention much less humiliating end than the one for failing his Greatness. For truly there was nothing to live for. He had no possessions, nor any hope of making any more moustaches, for he strongly doubted that he'd ever see another miracle, and didn't know what he'd ever done to deserve this one.

So,

it went as he had planned. The next morning he went to the palace... And the Great Tīmūrsaçi was more satisfied than he had ever been.

And therefore Munifer, with a relatively light heart, walked out of the town, to a slow bend in the river where he tied a stone to his feet and jumped into the brown waters which closed over his head before you could say 'moustache', and he was quite dead before he was nibbled by the resident sturgeon, a docile creature the length of the Tīmūrsaçi's barge.

Particular tastes

🌢

"But what *kind* of open-worked tarts did the lady buy?"

"Barley scented with musk, your Greatness," said the girl with the great green eyes, the newest of his storytellers.

The Great Timūrsaçi popped a "lady's thigh" pastry into his mouth and wiped his sticky fingers on the story-teller's arms. He took a pinchful of her flesh and twisted it.

"The lady didn't like musk," he said. "Nor do I."

"A thousand pardons," said the girl, smiling with her mouth. "No, she made a mistake with them, forgetting that she didn't like them but the pastrymaker took them back and—"

"After or before she ate them?"

"After ... Before!"

Her arms were patterned with blue places that his fingers had kissed, but he could not make those eyes overflow. He leaned back on his cushions. She was no fun.

"Go on," he said. But before she did, he was inspired.

"Tell me the story of the combs," he said. There *was* no story of the combs.

"The story of the combs?" she repeated.

"Are you a parrot?"

"There was a comb," she began.

"Combs!"

"There were two combs that..."

"Two combs that *what?*" exploded the Great Tīmūrsaçi, reaching for her nose. His fingers hovered there, the better to enjoy watching her eyes grow big. *There, they are beginning to grow extra bright.*

And they grew brighter, because as he reached out, the ends of his moustache reached back, and they wrapped around his neck, and around, and *around*, as each side of his moustache was of a length that was greater than the armspan of a man. The ends had much wrapping to do, but they did it quicker than a word, and they tightened so that they pinched the Great Tīmūrsaçi's neck with more vigour than he had ever pinched flesh. And his face grew thick and red and then dark and blue and black, and the storyteller's eyes grew bigger and greener and they shined like jewels and finally overflowed, as the storyteller overflowed with fear and joy.

* * *

The next Tīmūr left the Prison of Princes and Old Wives with reluctance. He had no wish to rule, having been quite happy painting pictures of ships and other impossibilities from his imagination.

The duty was his, however—so he buckled to. And though he called himself only Tīmūr the Twelfth, he is known as Tīmūr the Beloved.

Kiss the beast you cannot eat.

By the same author:

Monterra's Deliciosa & Other Tales &

Spotted Lily

蝶
夢

Chômu
Press

ALSO FROM CHÔMU PRESS

Looking for something else to read?
Want a book that will wake you up, not put you to sleep?

"Remember You're a One-Ball!"
By Quentin S. Crisp

I Wonder What Human Flesh Tastes Like
By Justin Isis

Revenants
By Daniel Mills

Lives of Notorious Cooks
By Brendan Connell

Nemonymous Night
By D.F. Lewis

For more information about these books and others, please visit:
http://chomupress.com/

Subscribe to our mailing list for updates and exclusive rarities.

"Borscht! Borscht! Borscht!"

CPSIA information can be obtained at www.ICGtesting.com
Printed in the USA
LVOW06s2107041213

363886LV00005B/747/P